DIGGING UP THE REMAINS

The three of them piled out of the car and went to the back to grab rakes and push brooms. Lilly took the broom and swept a few feet. The leaves came up and she pushed them to the side.

"The broom works, and will be faster," Lilly said. "I'll do this end. Roddy—take the middle and Delia, take the other end. We want to clear it enough that a runner won't slip, but let's not obsess."

"What, me obsess?" Delia said. She gave Lilly one of her rare smiles and went to the end of the path. Roddy walked to the middle and started to push the leaves into one of the existing piles.

Lilly started to sweep, exorcising her frustrations with Tyler Crane with each push of the broom.

"Delia, call the police," Roddy called out.

"What's the matter?" Lilly called to him, hustling over. Roddy stood up from the pile of leaves he was bent over and walked to Lilly, stopping her from getting too close.

"It's Tyler Crane," Roddy said. "He's under that pile of leaves."

"Is he—"

Roddy nodded. "He's dead . . ."

Books by Julia Henry

PRUNING THE DEAD

TILLING THE TRUTH

DIGGING UP THE REMAINS

Published by Kensington Publishing Corporation

DIGGING UP THE REMAINS

A Garden Squad Mystery

Julia Henry

KENSINGTON BOOKS
www.kensingtonbooks.com

To Courtney O'Connor
Thank you for all the support you have
given me on this journey

CHAPTER 1

"Lilly, I have bad news," Delia Greenway said quietly, leaning in toward her friend Lilly Jayne so that others couldn't overhear her.

"Oh no, what now?" Lilly asked. Between unidentified 150-year-old skeletons in Alden Park, a 400th Goosebush Anniversary Planning Committee that had more tension than a tightrope, a reporter who had moved to town to dig up the Goosebush dirt, and the preparations for the Fall Festival, Lilly was on edge. She might have snapped a bit at her housemate, Delia Greenway, something she rarely did. She stopped raking and repositioned her garden hat on the top of her head so that she could see Delia more clearly.

"Our 10K is 9.8 K," Delia said solemnly.

"Oh for heaven's sake, is that all?" Lilly asked. She went back to raking the path and looked pointedly at Delia. "That's the least of our problems. Could you go and get that tarp so we can bundle up these leaves?"

"Lilly, if we tell people it's a 10K, it should be 10K," Delia said. The younger woman dragged the tarp closer so that Lilly could rake leaves on top of it. "People count on accuracy for these things."

"I wish Nicole had never suggested making this a timed event," Lilly said. "The original idea was to have the Fall Festival be one weekend, get people to go around town on a Halloween stroll to look at our gardening projects, and to muster up support with a low-key event. But now?" Lilly dropped her rake and nodded to Delia, who picked up the other end of the tarp, folding it in half to help keep leaves inside it. The two women shuffled over to the truck parked in the middle of the path. Lilly nodded to Delia, letting her know that she was ready, and they swung the tarp up onto the back of the flatbed.

While Delia wrestled with the tarp, emptying it on the truck without releasing the leaves, Lilly continued. "Now we have a two-weekend festival. Somehow, I got talked into having a haunted house on my front lawn and I'm raking leaves on this path every day so that a hundred runners don't slip and slide on Saturday."

"More like three hundred and fifty-four runners, last I checked," Delia said.

Lilly glared at Delia and then took a breath. Being precise was one of Delia's strengths, and what made her an excellent researcher. Her preciseness was a constant refrain, and since Delia lived with Lilly in Windward, Lilly's large house, she dealt with it a lot. But Lilly tried not to show her impatience with Delia. Though they were almost forty years apart in age, Lilly considered Delia one of her dearest friends, and was grateful that Delia had decided to stay at Windward rather than move into an apartment this fall. The choice also suited Delia, or so it seemed.

"Of course, most of them aren't going to run," Delia said as she shook the last few leaves onto the truck and folded the tarp over her arm. "I think a lot of folks signed up because it is going to be a fun way to go around Goosebush. And then there's the T-shirts. Stan did a great job on the design, don't you think? I bet people are going to be wearing them for years."

"They're lovely," Lilly said.

"Anyway, I was thinking, if we don't have runners down this path and they do the whole loop, it will be closer to 10K." Delia laid the tarp down on the ground and picked up her rake again.

"But then Cole Bosworth will have gotten his way, and we can't have that," Lilly said, starting to rake. Cole had a large house that abutted the path they were raking. He and his neighbors, Fritz Stewart, Cheryl Singleton, and Scott Forrest, had begun to consider the path theirs, even though it was owned and maintained by the town. Few people had realized it wasn't a private way, and no one would have considered using it until Cole applied for a permit to extend his driveway onto the path so that he could build a bigger garage. Surveyors were sent out, property lines were established, and the use of the path came into question. When the board of selectmen denied him his permit, Cole threatened to sue, since no one had used the public egress for years. That's when the Beautification Committee, the group who was overseeing the Fall Festival plans, decided to incorporate the path into the 10K so that it would get used. Actually, it was Lilly and Tamara O'Connor, Lilly's best friend, who made the suggestion.

"Yeah, Cole winning is not an ideal outcome," Delia said. "I'm so sick of raking the leaves on this path. Where do they all come from?"

"It wouldn't surprise me if Cole weren't dumping them," Lilly said. "Notice how clean his yard is? That's why we're taking these leaves to the dump instead of putting them in the woods where he can get at them again."

"You don't like him, do you?" Delia said.

"I'm not particularly fond of him, no," Lilly said. "He's pretentious and a pain in the neck, not characteristics I admire."

"Would you like him better if he was from Goosebush?" Delia said. She continued to rake leaves, so she didn't notice that Lilly had stopped and was staring at her.

"What do you mean?" Lilly said.

"He's only lived in Goosebush for a few years," Delia said.

"Ten," Lilly said. "I remember when the Clark house went on the market."

"Ten years. But he does sort of act like, like . . ."

"Like he owns the place," Lilly said.

"Or he owns the history of it," Delia said.

Lilly started raking again. "He does take his familial history very seriously. Not that it isn't impressive, mind you. Being related to one of the people who came over on the *Mayflower*."

"I guess," Delia said. "But there are plenty of folks who have actually lived in Goosebush for a lot longer. His great-great-however-many-greats grandmother moved away from town in the 1800s. Your family has been here longer than that."

"How long we've been here really doesn't matter," Lilly said. "Stop smirking. It really doesn't. What does matter is when you act like you own the place, but you don't do anything to make it better. That's why Cole bothers me. He contributes nothing but his opinion to the town. That doesn't sit well with me. Back to your question. Would I like him better if he came from here? No, but I do have to wonder. If he'd lived here in Goosebush a bit longer, maybe he would understand about what matters and what doesn't. What doesn't matter, or shouldn't? When your relatives got here. What does matter? Trying to take over a public path."

"And so we rake," Delia said.

"Just for a few more minutes," Lilly said. "I promised I'd bring Ernie his truck back by three."

"Are you sure I can't help you with the leaves?" Delia asked Ernie. "I don't mind making a run with you to the dump."

Ernie Johnson took the keys to his truck from Delia and put them in the front pocket of his Bits, Bolts & Bulbs apron. He took two bottles of water out of another pocket of his apron and handed one to each of the women.

"The mulching and compost centers in the dump are open today, and I've roped some of the volunteers from the Beautification Committee to meet me there," Ernie said. Ernie's kind face broke into its normal state and a smile that enveloped his entire being broke out. Delia couldn't help smiling back. "They've been doing clean-ups all over town, and we've been sorting the recyclables here. I already did a couple of runs earlier this morning, and they'll meet me there. There's plenty for them to do after school."

"After school?" Lilly asked.

"Yeah, it won't surprise you to know that the volunteers for the crunching and mulching duty are all under eighteen. Woodchipper duty is particularly popular. Don't worry, I'm going to supervise. They're great kids, it will be fine. But there is great joy in group mulching. They all cheer."

Lilly laughed. She loved that Warwick O'Connor had encouraged his teams to volunteer for the Beautification Committee and they'd all taken to it, contributing a lot of work. The Girl Scout troop had also provided invaluable energy.

"Ernie, you won't believe how many more leaves there were," she said. She pulled the stool out from under one of the potting tables in the garden center of Ernie's store. She held the cold bottle of water up against her forehead and closed her eyes. "Honestly, the truck is almost full. I don't know where they're coming from, the leaves, but we can't seem to get ahead of them."

"I can imagine where they're coming from," Ernie said.

"If they're coming from Cole's yard he must be storing them off-site, because his lawn is a pristine green. He doesn't do that himself, does he?" Delia asked.

"No, he has gardeners come in once a week. The Sayer brothers. I only know that because Herb buys a lot of his supplies from me. I give him a wholesale discount."

"That's nice of you," Delia said.

"It's good business," Ernie said. "I'd rather they buy from me than a box store over in Marshton. Besides, when you order in bulk for people they tend to come back and pick up things they forgot to order. I'd rather be the supplier to folks here in Goosebush."

"Keep it local," Lilly said, nodding her head. "The Sayer brothers do a great job, but I'm not surprised. Both of their parents were wonderful gardeners. Cole's yard looks well-maintained, if impersonal. But that's just my taste. I can't stand a yard without a few garden beds strewn about."

"Yeah, the most gardening that Cole does is window boxes and he doesn't even deal with those himself. He's not what you'd call an enthusiastic outdoor person. I tried to talk him into buying some patio furniture for his backyard and he looked at me like I had three heads. 'Why would I want to sit outside?' he asked me with a concerned look, like he'd stepped in something. Honestly, I think he's more of a condo guy, but he has to keep up appearances."

"Delia, perhaps we should engage the Sayer brothers to help put the front yard together after your haunted house next Saturday. They can lime the yard and get it ready for the winter at the same time they clean up from heaven knows what."

"Lilly, it's going to be fun," Ernie said.

"Define fun," Lilly said. "Costume-clad strangers trampling all over my yard does not sound like fun."

"Speaking of Saturday, Lilly needs a costume," Delia said to Ernie, ignoring Lilly.

"I am *not* going to wear a costume," Lilly said.

Ernie roared with laughter and walked over to a rack at the side of the greenhouse. "You may as well give it up now, Lilly," he said. "We're all wearing costumes, like it or not." Lilly glared at him and Ernie laughed again. "Tell you what, I'll save you a witch's hat and you can call it a day."

"Are you casting aspersions on my character?" Lilly asked sternly, but with a smile.

"Never," he said, giving her a wink. "Delia, your plant order came in. Is this what you're looking for?"

Delia walked over to the rack of plants and took a look at each shelf. She was able to pull them out to get a better glimpse of some of the plants.

"Perfect," Delia said. "I was hoping to be able to grow these from seed, but I haven't had much luck this fall. I waited too late and I've been so busy with everything I haven't tended to them the way I should've. This is kind of cheating, I know. But I think a poison garden will be perfect as part of the second weekend of the Fall Festival and I need to deliver. These look beautiful. Thanks for helping me, Ernie. I'll go home and get the Jeep so I can pick them up today and get them in the greenhouse."

"A poison garden?" Lilly asked. She walked over to the rack and looked at all the plants. "I'd forgotten you had that on the schedule. Where are you going to set the garden?"

"PJ Frank is building me a flower box that looks like a coffin," Delia said. "I haven't decided how exactly I'll use it, but it has holes in the bottom for drainage. I'm going to set it up on some cobblestones in the front yard during the haunted house, and do some sort of display. I may put them there, or do something else with the coffin and put these on the side. Afterwards I'll put them back in the greenhouse."

"And the coffin planter?" Ernie asked.

"I'll store it. You never know when we can reuse it," Delia said.

"Always good to have a coffin on hand," Ernie said, smiling.

"Exactly," Delia said. "That's why I had PJ build it, so it would last. These plants are really lovely, aren't they? So hard to believe that they're all so deadly."

"Or medicinal, if used correctly," Ernie said.

"True," Delia said. She paused, and shook her head. People had tried to cross the line last summer. Delia felt compelled to rehabilitate the plants' reputations. "Ernie, if you're sure you don't need me to help with the leaves, I'll go home and get the car."

"I'm sure."

"Lilly, do you want to come with me?"

"No, you go ahead. I'll visit with Ernie for a bit longer and then I'll meander home."

"Don't forget, we're all having dinner at the Star tonight," Delia said.

"Of course I won't forget," Lilly said. But she had forgotten. Not that she would've forgotten completely, since she'd gotten into the habit of putting all of her appointments on her computer calendar and checking her phone before she did anything. Lilly didn't blame age for her forgetfulness. She blamed too much going on in her life. She was busier now, in retirement, then she had been while she was working. But the busyness was her choice; her decision to rejoin her friends and the citizens of Goosebush. She might complain, but she wouldn't want it any other way.

Delia left and Ernie turned to Lilly. "Would you mind helping me with a project before you leave?" he asked her.

"I'd be happy to," Lilly said.

"We got in another huge shipment of fall plants—see them back there?" Ernie and Lilly started to walk toward the back of the garden center.

"I do; I noticed them when I came in. Lovely. You know, I'm always sad when my garden starts to go fallow and I need to move back indoors, but mums help make the transition easier. What glorious colors. It's late in the season to sell these many plants, isn't it? Halloween is in a week."

"There was an order mix-up. I didn't explain well enough. Anyway, I'd rather try and sell them than have them all rot. So I need help enticing customers."

"Well, you could do a lovely display—"

"Exactly, that's why I need your help. Mary has been a godsend; really, she has. With her working in the store I don't have to worry about what's happening on the floor. She handles it all."

"I'm so glad she's working out. It was kind of you to give her a job when she moved to town," Lilly said.

"Listen, when Ray asked me to give his daughter a job I may have thought I was doing him a favor. But Ray was doing me a favor. She's a hard worker and I think she's beginning to relax a bit." Ernie and Lilly exchanged a glance and Lilly nodded.

Ray Mancini was the former chief of police of Goosebush and served on the board of selectmen. He and Lilly had gone to school together, so they'd known each other for almost sixty years. Ray and his wife, Meg, had four children. The first three had been born right after they got married, and then Mary came along ten years later. It wasn't easy being the police chief's daughter and it didn't suit Mary well at all. She left Goosebush as soon as she could and barely came back for visits. In fact, no one had seen her for years. Lilly had stopped asking after her, noticing the look of sadness that crossed her parents' faces whenever she did. Mary had married young, very young, and Ray did not hide the fact that he disliked his son-in-law. As it turned out, Ray's judgment was sound. When Mary returned to her parents' house in late September, she was a shadow of the girl that Lilly remembered. Lilly didn't ask—no one did—what had happened. When Ray asked Ernie to help his daughter, the answer was an immediate yes.

"As I said, Mary is a godsend. But she has no sense of plants."

"What do you mean?" Lilly asked.

"Well, what quantities you should order, for starts." Ernie smiled and shrugged his shoulders. "She can't tell a mum from a marigold, has no sense of how to group them for display or for pricing. When I asked her to sort the plants this morning I thought she was going to cry, so I told her to watch the front of the store instead."

"Her mother's one of the best gardeners I know," Lilly said. "I'm surprised that Mary didn't inherit some of that knowledge."

"I don't remember Mary well, but what I do remember is a young woman who wouldn't give her mother the satisfaction of wanting to learn about gardens."

"I hate to admit it, but you're right. She was, what we would call back in the day, a troubled youth," Lilly said.

"It seems now some sort of trouble has come to

her, which is unfortunate. She's settling in here and is a great worker. But we're going to need to teach her about plants."

"That we can do, that we can do. Tell me. How can I help?" Lilly asked.

Lilly spent a half hour working with the plants. At first she sorted them by size so that Ernie could price them. Then he gave her free rein to create a couple of displays in the garden center, which she did. She put large mums in the middle and smaller mums around them using milk crates and other boxes. She made sure that the display was able to be reached with the misting hoses and showed Ernie how he could swap plants out as they were sold. She'd added a couple of gnomes and other garden ornaments that Ernie had in stock but didn't sell that often.

"Personally, I love the gargoyles. If I didn't have so many I'd buy this one right here. Maybe making that the centerpiece of the display will help it find a home," Lilly said. She took off the apron Ernie had lent her and walked over to the sink area. She put the apron on the stool beside the sink and washed her hands. She had dirt under her fingernails, but she usually did. She looked at her watch. She had time to go home and clean up before dinner. But maybe she'd make a stop at the Star first.

"This looks great, Lilly. Thanks for your help. I could have done it by myself, but I never would've thought of the way you show the plants off. All the levels, the color combinations. You have a real talent for this, but of course I knew that."

"Ernie, you know how much I love plants. I'm

happy to help you with this sort of thing any time, really. It relaxes me. Maybe I'll help Delia with this blasted haunted house—make a garden arrangement on the front yard of plants that people could take with them. I'd love to find them all a home."

"You could do some sort of raffle," Ernie said. "You know we need to raise some more money for the garden by the elementary school."

The two friends looked at each other and both shook their heads at the same time.

"Bad idea," Ernie said.

"If I volunteer for one more thing I want you to put tape over my mouth," Lilly said.

"As long as you do it for me too. I'm not sure how this whole festival got so out of hand, but it's really huge. I had to buy a second order of T-shirts; did I tell you that? We've got so many runners in the 10K already, and the registrations keep pouring in."

"Who knew that a race would be so popular?"

"Since Nicole made it a scenic run around town, and included the bridge in the run around the beach parking lot, it's become much more of a social activity than a real run. Nice thing is that folks who don't want to run, or walk, are volunteering to take care of the registrations at the elementary school, the entertainment break at the beach, and the end party at the Frank lumberyard. It's going to be a great day, but I'll need to go to sleep for a week after it's over."

"You've gone above and beyond, for sure. Making the Triple B the hub for people to pick up their race paraphernalia was very kind of you."

"No big deal, really. There are a lot of volunteers working on this. You should see the bags we're putting together for folks who want to participate in the rest of the Fall Festival next week. Lots of good stuff. Speaking of which, I have your T-shirt and Delia's. Now, don't look like that, Lilly. You're on the committee. The committee has purple T-shirts, different than the others. You have to wear it on Saturday. If you break ranks, chaos will ensue."

"Don't worry. I'll wear it, though I'm not really a T-shirt person" Lilly said. She'd already decided she'd wear it over one of her dresses, and that she'd don running shoes instead of her typical tennis shoes. She knew she'd be quite a sight, but that didn't worry her. Lilly's trademark had become shirtdresses with full skirts and bold patterns. She wouldn't disappoint on Saturday.

"Good. Now, let me get to those leaves. My helpers are going to meet me at the dump. You know on Saturday morning, before the race—"

"We should go and check the path again before the runners come and make sure that there aren't more leaves," Lilly said. "We've already added that to our to-do list for the day."

"Great minds, we think alike. See you tonight at dinner."

CHAPTER 2

Normally, Lilly would run more errands while she was at the Wheel, but she was tired. And achy. She wanted to get home, take a short nap, and clean up before dinner with her friends. But first a cup of tea and a cookie to sustain her on her walk home.

Goosebush, Massachusetts, was full of rotaries, as many New England towns were. The Wheel was the center rotary in town, where many businesses were located and most roads fed into. It was called the Wheel because it looked much like a ship's wheel—or at least that had been the initial design before more people had encroached on the territory with businesses that disrupted the tidy spokes the founders had envisioned. While some might consider the traffic to be slow, for Goosebush the three cars making their way around was as busy as the town got on a weekday afternoon in the fall. Summer was a different story. Fall was definitely quieter, since most folks went north to look at the foliage. In Lilly's opinion, Goosebush's fall colors against the ocean were a special kind of stunning. But she was just as happy that the rest of the world hadn't figured that out. She liked the slower pace.

Lilly walked to the edge of the rotary and decided to go to her right to get to the Star. The Star Café was the creation of Stan Freeland, a young entrepreneur who had seen the underused old Woolworth building and fallen in love with it. He took the four stories and carved out space for a bookstore, a coffee counter, a restaurant and bar, a theater space, and some artist studios. Lilly was forever grateful that Stan hadn't gutted the building completely, but had instead decided to use the old bones and modernize them. Whenever she walked in and looked to her right she could picture the ice cream fountain that was there when she was a young girl. When she walked through toward the restaurant her mind would flash to the lunch counter that had been back there. Stan's business was booming, and for good reason. Good food, lots of seating, dozens of reasons to go to the Star. A perfect, and vital, combination for a small town like Goosebush.

When Stan had first opened the Star he took a loan from some angel investors who offered him a very low interest rate. He never knew who the investors were, and Lilly never told him that she was one of them. Lilly loved her town and did whatever she could to help ensure its future. Supporting new businesses was one way she did that. Gardening was another.

As Lilly walked slowly around the rotary she heard a noise and glanced to her left. She saw Tyler Crane shout to the woman hurrying ahead of him. The woman turned to confront Tyler, and Lilly recognized that it was Nicole Shaw. Tyler grabbed her upper arm and she pulled away, yelling in his face. He leaned down and yelled at her. The spectacle went on for a few seconds and then Nicole looked around, realizing that people were staring. Nicole was new to town and working for the school system as one of the coaches in the physical education department. She worked with Warwick O'Connor, who sang her praises. Lilly had trusted Warwick's opinion of people, including Nicole, although the young woman tried so hard to please that Lilly could never fully get a sense of what she was like as a person. One thing was certain: she had a temper and it was on full display. Lilly wondered what Tyler had done. She had little doubt he deserved Nicole's reaction, whatever it was.

Nicole turned away from Tyler and he grabbed her again. The next thing Lilly knew, Tyler was flipped over onto his back and Nicole was staring at his prone form. She screamed at him, "Leave me alone!"

Nicole hurried around the rotary. She passed Lilly on the crosswalk. "Are you all right?" Lilly asked her. The young woman nodded her head, but the tears streaming down her face belied the nod. She looked down so that her dark hair hung over her face and rushed past Lilly.

Lilly sighed. She'd never been one for drama in public. Or drama in private, for that matter. She made a mental note to tell Warwick about what had happened so he could check in with Nicole. Lilly didn't like the way Tyler had grabbed her, even though Nicole had obviously been capable of taking care of herself. Lilly wanted her to know that she didn't have to take care of Tyler herself, but wasn't sure how to have the conversation. Since

Warwick knew her a bit more, it was better left to him.

Lilly looked over and saw Tyler stand up and brush himself off. To her chagrin, he walked into the Star Café. She almost decided to forgo her visit, but the thought of hot tea and a kitchen sink cookie convinced her to stay on her course.

As Lilly walked around the Wheel, she couldn't help but notice the orange, green, and purple posters for the two-weekend-long Fall Festival. The posters added pops of color everywhere. Delia had done a good job of creating a buzz for the festival. She'd found a designer to create posters and arranged for volunteers to distribute them. Every shop had at least one in the window. They were on every lamp-post. And some industrious person had even strung a banner with the details across the Star Café for all to see.

GOOSEBUSH FALL FESTIVAL: FROM 10K TO HAUNTED HOUSES OCTOBER 23–31

Lilly wasn't sure how Delia was keeping all of her balls in the air these days, but she was managing. And adding to her plate with ideas like the poison garden in a coffin. Lilly smiled to herself and shook her head. Delia was one of the most organized people Lilly had ever met. Of course, that wasn't really surprising. After all, she'd been trained by the best. Lilly's late husband, Alan, had hired Delia as his grad assistant and entrusted her with finishing his work after he passed on. He couldn't have made a better choice. Not only had she seen his work completed, she had been helping Lilly organize her papers and treasures, was a fixture in the Goosebush

Historical Society, and was still the part-time clerk for the town. Goosebush had needed Delia's attention to detail in the last few months, what with the fallout from Merilee Frank's death and the bodies found in Alden Park. Granted, the bodies were over 150 years old, but still. What a mess.

Lilly gave herself a shake. The dark days were behind them all now. Since the unfortunate events of the end of the summer the town had regrouped. Lilly wondered if the robust attention to the festival was partly in reaction to all the unpleasantness. It gave people a reason for the town to celebrate.

Lilly felt the phone in her pocket vibrate and took it out. It was a text from Delia.

Tyler's going live in a few minutes. He says he's got a scoop about trouble with the 10K. Do you have any idea what he's talking about?

No idea. Do you think we should be worried?

With Tyler it's always a good idea to be a little worried. Check with you later.

Delia was absolutely right. Tyler Crane was a piece of work. He had come to town supposedly to do a profile of Goosebush as it neared four hundred years. But it soon became evident that his focus was more on the recent murders and the corruption that surrounded each. He'd moved in right after Labor Day and had become a fixture ever since. A fixture that Lilly purposely avoided at all costs. She had no interest in talking about the challenges that Goosebush had faced in its recent or distant past. At least not to an outsider. She'd barely said two words to Tyler since he'd been in town, and was determined to continue that practice. Something about him had rubbed her wrong from the outset.

She'd been drafted to the committee that was

planning the Goosebush quadricentennial, though she'd tried to get out of it. But as one of the town elders, she found she didn't really have a choice. Besides, her best friend Tamara O'Connor wasn't about to let her off the committee since Tamara had already agreed to serve.

As Lilly walked along the circle she glanced into the stores, just as happy not to see anyone she knew or knew well enough to stop and talk to. She'd go in and get her cup of tea. As cranky as Lilly tried to pretend she was, she loved going into the Star, trying out one of the amazing baked goods with a pot of tea, and settling in near the bookstore to read and to observe her fellow citizens. As she approached the Star she looked to her left. Coast was clear. No one would enter at the same time and insist on joining her. She did not suffer fools gladly and enjoyed her own company. That was truer as she got older.

She walked into the vestibule and saw that Stan had already hung the heavy black velvet drapes that kept the chill from blowing into the building. It hadn't been that cold yet, but it was windy. Lilly put her hand in front of herself and pushed the drapes back to the right so she could get through. No sooner had she emerged than she heard someone calling her name.

"Ms. Jayne? Lilly? Do you have a minute?" a smiling young man called out to her.

Lilly took a deep breath to gird her loins: Tyler Crane, looking none the worse for wear after his confrontation with Nicole. He was standing by the coffee counter, undoubtedly waiting for one of his overly complicated coffee concoctions he was always posting on social media. She looked him over, with his scruffy beard, brown bomber jacket, and well-worn jeans. He was handsome and charming, two traits that had gotten more than one citizen of Goosebush to open up to him and tell the town secrets. Lilly was glad, for the umpteenth time, that handsome, charming men had little effect on her. Her first husband, Pete Frank, taught her that difficult lesson.

"I'm afraid I don't," Lilly said. "I've got a meeting that I'm running late for." Lilly was lying, of course. She was never late. And she didn't have a meeting, though she would ask Stan to order a book if she needed to come up with an excuse.

"That's a shame," Tyler said. "I guess I'll have to go with the story as is."

"Story as is?" Lilly said. If there were some issue he was going to create a hubbub around perhaps she could thwart his efforts, though for the life of her she couldn't imagine what he could be referring to.

"I've got a story that I'm going to run on Saturday evening as part of a 'what does family mean?' series. I'd like to get a quote from you."

"A quote?"

"About the bodies in your backyard."

"Bodies?" Lilly asked. She blinked twice, but didn't avert her gaze.

"I've heard that your garden has memorial stones in it, and there are bodies underneath that famous garden of yours."

"First of all, I can't imagine where you've heard this or what possible interest it could be of yours. Second of all, I'd be careful about what I print, Mr. Crane. You'd better be very careful of your facts."

"Well, you see, this actually isn't going to be a story

in the paper. This is one of my social media posts—
Live From Goosebush. That's a hashtag. Do you
know about hashtags? Social media stories don't go
through the same vetting."

"And yet they can still cause harm to people's
reputations," Lilly said.

Tyler shrugged. "Life can cause harm to people's
reputations. My job is to tell the truth about this
town of yours. If one of its leading citizens has a
graveyard in her backyard, that's of interest. Of
course, I don't have to post the story. Instead, I
could post an interview with you about . . . well, say
Merilee Frank's murder. The true story behind
your relationship, that sort of thing. Seems like a
fair deal to me."

Lilly gave the young man her iciest glare. To his
credit he did not wilt, though most would have.

"Mr. Crane, from what I've seen of your reporting—and I use that term loosely—I don't think you
know the meaning of the word *fair*. Now, if you'll
excuse me."

"I'm a better friend than enemy, Lilly," Tyler said.
"Probably good you remember that."

Lilly didn't look back as she turned and walked
toward the restaurant. She forced herself to unball
her fists and keep her head held high.

"Lilly, can I do something for you? Your reservation isn't for another couple of hours, but I'm
happy to get you a glass of wine if you'd like. We're
not quite open yet." Stan Freeland had been setting
the tables in the Star Restaurant but he stopped
when he saw Lilly standing in the doorway.

"No, Stan, please don't stop working. I was going

to have a cup of tea and a cookie, but after my conversation with Tyler Crane I don't feel like either. If you don't mind, I'm going to sit here for a minute and compose myself."

Stan walked over and held the back of the barstool as Lilly climbed up. He walked to the back of the bar and grabbed a coffee mug, placing it in front of his friend.

"We don't have the same tea selection in here, but I keep hot water going all day. In between the lunch and dinner shift this becomes the break room for employees. Is Irish breakfast tea okay?"

"Perfect, thank you."

"Would you like me to go out front and get you a cookie?"

"No, no. Tea is fine. The cookie is an indulgence. I'm sorry to be such a bother."

"No bother. Tyler has been having this effect on folks a lot lately. He livestreams from here during the week, and I'll admit it's helped business pick up a bit. Kicking him out would be a drama that I'm not sure I'm up to, but I think I need to consider. You're not the only person who's complained about him this week. I heard he was brawling with Nicole Shaw outside earlier. Not cool, man, not cool."

"I'm not one to gossip, but they were having a fight out on the street. He seemed to grab her, or at least he tried. Next thing I knew she'd flipped him over and he was lying on the sidewalk."

Stan laughed. "Please tell me you took a picture, Lilly, please."

"No picture, but now I wish I had." Lilly stirred her tea and took a sip. "He's threatening to run a story on me Saturday night unless I talk to him."

"He's blackmailing you?" Stan asked. He'd been

straightening things behind the bar, but now stopped and leaned on the edge.

"I suppose technically yes, he's blackmailing me. Of course, he's picked the wrong person, since I don't give into that sort of thing. Nevertheless, I can't help but think how many other people he's pulling information from."

"I wonder if that was what the fight with Nicole was about." Stan started loading up bar glasses from the rack on the bar. "I'm not one to gossip either, but I think Nicole and Tyler were dating for a while. There has been a definite frost on the relationship for the past few days. Whenever he's walked into the Star she's left, no matter what she's doing."

"Nicole was dating Tyler?" Lilly shook her head. She didn't say it aloud, but she'd hoped that Nicole had better taste than that. Tyler was handsome, certainly. That couldn't be denied. But it had always struck Lilly that he had a smooth veneer: too smooth. In her experience, that laid out trouble. Bad trouble, not good trouble. In the case of Tyler Crane, in Lilly's opinion, a good character was missing. Of course, most of this was based on hearsay, but hearsay from reliable sources.

"There's no accounting for taste, that's for sure. Nicole could do much better. It's tough in a small town when you're new," Stan said.

"Especially when you're in a high-profile job like hers. Being a coach on one of the school teams means that you're constantly on, and parents don't understand boundaries." Lilly thought about the stories Warwick shared, and what she'd observed at different town functions. Everyone had an opinion about sports, and Warwick was the face of the town teams. Warwick, and now Nicole. She took another sip of her tea and closed her eyes. Tea didn't cure anything, but it certainly made situations easier to navigate.

"Yeah, that's part of the problem. Nicole doesn't let her guard down, so she's tough to get to know. She and I have been talking about her picking up a few hours a week at the Star this winter. That will help her meet people."

"Is Stella leaving?"

"Stella is going to take a couple of courses at night, so I need some help in the bar."

"I hadn't heard that about Stella. I'm glad." Stella Haywood was the youngest sister of Bash Haywood, the chief of police. Lilly knew Bash would never push his sister, but he had to be relieved that she was going to go back and take some more classes. She'd been working on her degree in fits and starts and was close to graduating.

"I'm glad too, but it does mean that I'm down a bartender." Stan laughed. "You know, getting the Star up and running was a dream and it's surpassed my greatest expectations. But keeping it running? I need to do some planning and think through staffing. It's turning into a real business, a big business, and honestly, Lilly? I feel like I'm drowning a little bit."

Lilly regarded Stan for a minute and paused before she spoke. She was always careful not to overstep with people. But her friend Tamara always reminded her that showing you cared wasn't overstepping.

"Stan, why don't you come for dinner sometime soon and we'll talk about the Star if you'd like. I have some experience in business, and have worked with many people at different stages of growth. I'm good at creating new strategic plans, if I do say so. I don't know as much about the restaurant industry, or the bookselling industry, or the theater industry as you do." Lilly laughed and Stan smiled. "But I'm happy to be a sounding board for your thoughts. I may be able to offer you some advice, or point you in the direction of people who can."

Stan put down the glass he was holding, and smiled at Lilly. "Lilly, what a generous offer. I can't thank you enough. Maybe after the Fall Festival is done?"

Lilly took her phone out and opened her calendar. She was never one for effusive emotions, and wasn't about to start. "How about if I pencil you in for the Monday afterwards? The restaurant's closed that night, isn't it?"

"We have limited service, but it's my night off. I'll double-check my calendar, but that sounds perfect. Thanks, Lilly. I feel better already." Stan smiled at her, and she nodded. "And about Tyler. Would you like me to kick him out?"

"Absolutely not. I will, however, ask you to let me out the back way. He isn't going to be eating here tonight, is he?"

"I'll make sure he can't make a reservation," Stan said, giving her a wink.

CHAPTER 3

When Lilly got home she called out to Delia, but her housemate wasn't there. Or she didn't hear Lilly. Windward, the Jayne family house, was enormous. It had been built on a triple lot by a persnickety ship captain who eschewed all of the unwritten ordinances of Goosebush. Most houses were Federalist style; his house was a rambling Victorian. Most houses had small front yards. His house was set back quite a ways. Few houses had fences or gates. He made sure his house was surrounded by a tall stone fence on three sides and a wrought iron gate at the head of the driveway. The house had stayed in the family for generations, but it had fallen into disrepair during the first half of the last century, when the family fortune had dipped. Lilly was forever grateful that her grandparents had held on, and that it was passed on to her father, who passed it on to her. The success she had had in her business life insured that the house had never been as well maintained.

As much as Lilly wanted to go upstairs and take a

short nap and a shower before she went out to dinner with her friends, she needed to see her gardens first. She walked down the center hallway of the house, casually looking to the living room on the left, to the dining room on the right, past the kitchen and the breakfast room toward the three-season porch that ran along the back of the house. She walked through the French doors and closed them behind her. She and Delia had taken out all of the screens and put in the storm windows at the beginning of October, with the help of the students on the Beautification Committee. She'd paid each of them and invited them over to a cookout as a thank-you. Delia told her that the cookout was enough thanks, but Lilly did not take lightly the help that the students gave the Beautification Committee, and she suspected a few of them could use the extra cash.

Delia and Lilly could, and would, continue to sit out on the porch for as long as possible which, thanks to space heaters, was well into November. She stepped out into the porch and looked around. Delia wasn't there either. Perhaps she was in the greenhouse? Lilly looked over to her left and the door at the end of the porch that led to her gardening sanctuary.

Lilly's greenhouse was not a glass box. Though the structure was thirty years old, she'd built it in the style of grand Victorian greenhouses and butted it up against the stone wall, blocking egress from the front yard to the back. Lilly liked it that way. The ornate iron decorative ironwork was designed to go with the house. Inside were all the modern conveniences Lilly could ever want, but the large room still had an old-fashioned air.

Lilly loved her greenhouse and had installed

solar panels so that it was temperate all year long. She paused, but decided not to go in there. The room had a time vortex for Lilly. Whenever she walked in, no matter what the reason, she emerged hours later, eyes glazed and hands dirty. She stepped to the edge of the porch and opened the door to her backyard. Brisk fall gardening would keep her on task.

Backyard was an inadequate term for the back of Lilly's house. When you walked down from the porch you were officially in Lilly's gardens: winding paths, flowerbeds that varied throughout the seasons, artwork strategically placed throughout, seating areas, a dining area on a patio. To some, the garden seemed haphazard. But for Lilly and her friends who understood, it was an homage to the wonderful parts of Lilly's life. The statue in the koi pond? A gift to her from Alan, her late husband. She hadn't loved the piece when he gave it to her, but now it made her smile because it reminded her of him.

She walked past the statue of Saint Fiacre and, as was her habit, bent down to pull weeds or pinch back plants that needed it. She looked at the rosebushes her father had planted those many years ago and was thrilled at how healthy they looked. She and Delia would be preparing the bushes for the winter, but not for a couple of more weeks. Lilly made a mental note to order more materials to build fences around them. According to the almanac, there would be a lot of heavy snow this winter, so she wanted to make sure they survived.

Lilly turned to her left and saw the meditation bench that Delia had placed in her section of the garden. Maybe that was where the poison plant garden would go next year? Typical Delia, the kindest, most gentle person Lilly had ever known, planning a poison garden with the glee that most people reserved for the night before Christmas.

Lilly took a few more steps into the back of the garden, her private section. She saw the three statues dispersed throughout a mixture of seagrasses, short shrubs, and annuals that had receded. While the rest of the garden had mulch, the section had tumbled seashells and stones strewn throughout it. Lilly paused and looked at each statue carefully. The one on the left, the angel with a basket of flowers. The one in the middle, an artist's palette carved out of marble. The one on the right, the broken bust of an ancient Greek.

Lilly futzed in the seashell garden, as she called it, for a few minutes, though it was pristine. She stepped back and wiped a tear from her eyes.

"Well, my darlings, it seems as if we're going to be in the news on Saturday."

"Lilly? Are you out there?" She heard Delia call for her.

"Coming," Lilly called. She put her hands to her lips and blew a kiss at each statue. She walked out the path the other way and stopped by the compost bin to put the weeds and bits and pieces she'd pruned in.

Delia was still dressed as she'd been earlier, with bits of leaves stuck to her fleece jacket and in her hair.

"Did you just get back?" Delia asked.

"I did. I stopped by the Star and ran into that reprehensible Tyler Crane."

"That's a good word for him. I've heard other words lately, stronger words."

Lilly looked at her young friend. "What's the matter, Delia?"

"Oh Lilly, I know you warned me. You told me not to . . . I don't know what to do."

Lilly walked over to Delia and took her gently by the elbow, turning her back toward the house. "Let's go in and have a cup of tea and you can tell me what's bothering you. I'm sure we can figure it out."

Delia took Lilly's hand and gave it a gentle squeeze. "I don't know, Lilly. I've opened a huge can of worms."

Lilly put the electric kettle on and washed her hands in the kitchen sink. She took two of the tins of cookies and put them on the kitchen table and then went back to put the tea together. She looked at the various jars on the shelf and elected to go for an herbal blend that was a combination of lemon, lavender, and a hint of ginger. She sprinkled a spoonful into the bottom of the teapot and poured the boiling water into the pot.

Delia had put her backpack on a kitchen chair and she opened it now, taking out a large file folder overflowing with pieces of paper. She set it down on the kitchen table. She went over to the cabinet and got two coffee mugs and some plates out.

Lilly carried the hot tea over to the table and sat down in her seat. She looked at Delia and smiled. "That's going to take a couple of minutes to steep. Why don't you tell me what's going on?"

"It's about the bodies in Alden Park." Alden Park was one of the oldest pieces of public land in Goosebush. The park had been neglected for years and had become an overgrown eyesore. Last spring the town had come together to start to clear the park and restore it, but that plan had met more than a few obstacles since. The latest had been the discovery of what at first looked like a pond that had been filled in with debris, most of which had rotted. Layers of dirt had been added over the years as well. Filling in the pond corresponded to the town records. But after some digging it became apparent that the debris layer had covered a dump site, which held up the work. A local college had taken Delia's offer up to excavate the dump site as a summer project and catalog the findings, but it had been confusing. All of the items seemed to be related. With the discovery of the bodies of a woman and two children underneath all of the other household items, the project had taken a more ominous tone. The conjecture was that the bodies had been dumped and then all of the household items put on top of them to obscure them, which they had. The timing must have been tight, since the bodies were not part of the town records. With the age of the items, it was surmised that the bodies had been there for at least 150 years.

That lack of clarity on who those bodies were hadn't sat well with Delia and she continued to research the possibilities even when everyone else had given up. She'd stopped talking about it a few weeks ago, and even Lilly had thought she'd let the mystery go. She should've known better.

"What about the bodies?" Lilly asked.

"Well, you know, it was pretty boggy down where they were found. They were able to run some tests and figured out that they were all related."

"Yes, I remember. A grown woman and two children. Could be assumed that they were a mother and her children, but there are other possibilities."

"Well, see, here's what I did to narrow down those possibilities. I submitted the DNA to one of those ancestry tests."

"You did what? Wouldn't the medical examiner have done that already?"

"Since the bodies were so old, the medical examiner didn't take on the case. The college was going to, but there isn't a lot of funding there, so I told them that I would pay for the testing. I thought it would be an interesting way to try and close up the loop and add it to the history of Alden Park."

"But it didn't close the loop?"

"No, far from it. The results were sent to me. I agreed to share them with the students who worked on the site last summer, but since I'll be writing the paper about the site and the find it made sense for me to see them first. Have you ever heard of the Howland family?"

"Of course. He came over on the *Mayflower* and settled in Goosebush. He's one of the founders, as a matter fact. Cole's distant relative, and the reason Cole feels obliged to be at every meeting about the quadricentennial celebration of our town."

"Well, see, that's the problem. If you look at the family tree and how it's supposed to work, Cole's connection to Goosebush comes from Catherine Howland, the descendant of that family. The story is that she and her family, her husband and two children, left town suddenly. She and the daughter didn't survive the trip. The son and his father ended up in California. The father eventually remarried."

"That's where Cole's from, California, right?" Lilly poured the tea for both of them. She opened the tin of cookies and took one of them out, taking a small bite. "He's related to the son who went west with his father. Didn't we know that already?"

"We did, but you know me. Facts and truth—"

"Facts and truth are two different things. Facts are indisputable. Truth depends on who is telling the story." Lilly smiled at Delia and took a small sip of her tea. Delia's obsession with finding the facts had caused them to argue a few times over the past few months, but Lilly had come to understand that Delia was always going to parse between facts and the truth. She was always going to question the truth.

"Yes, well. The truth that Cole knows is that his relative is the son of Catherine Howland. But the tests that were run? They show that it's likely that a member of the Howland family is the body in the grave. Catherine was the only Howland in Goosebush at the time. I checked. And both of those children are hers. I can't prove it, yet. But one possibility is that the bodies are Catherine and her children."

Lilly put her mug on the table gently and looked at Delia. "Did they have a third child?"

"No. I'd begun to wonder if the bodies were part of the Howland family last summer. Some of the china we found in the dump site were a well known family pattern of theirs. I was creating a timeline for when the pond was filled in, and what else had happened in town around that time, so I started digging deeper into the family history."

"I don't understand," Lilly said. "If she and her children are in the grave, who was the son the father brought out west?"

"I did a little research on the father," Delia said. She took a sip of tea. "A few months after he got to

California he married a woman named Abigail Evans. When you look at the town of Goosebush and the records, she's named in a few places. It's harder to track the history of women, since most of them didn't own property, and they couldn't vote. But I'm trying. She lived here at the same time the Howland family did. I don't know who she was, though. I'm trying to find out."

"Did she leave at the same time he did?"

"Hard to say, but I haven't found her mentioned in articles after he moved to California. I'm doing research on all of them to see if they intersected at all."

"Intersected? Do you mean knew each other?"

"I'm trying to find letters, diaries, anything that sheds light."

Lilly took a sip of tea and pursed her lips. "Delia, I know you only like facts, but how's this for a story," Lilly said after a minute. "What would have happened back then if a man killed his family, moved west. He met someone, or took her with him. They had a son. And he passed the son off as from the Howland family. It seems like it might have been possible for him to get away with it, especially if no one suspected anything."

"Why would he do that?"

"The Howland family name carried some weight. And they were wealthy. Maybe he wanted to make sure his son could make a claim to any family fortune in the future."

"That's a big leap," Delia said. "But it may make sense. Especially since the bodies are related. But if that's what happened, it would mean Cole isn't a Howland."

"Which means his claim to Goosebush heritage is

faulty, right? Catherine Howland's husband moved to Goosebush when he married her." Lilly tried to get the image of Cole's face when he heard the news out of her mind. "I can't imagine that would sit with him very well, can you?"

Delia looked at Lilly and shook her head. "Let's slow down. We're making huge leaps and we need more facts before we say anything. Obviously."

"Agreed," Lilly said, taking another sip of tea.

"But here's the problem. Tyler Crane left me a voicemail. He said he wants to confirm that the bodies in Alden Park were members of one of Goosebush's founding families."

"Oh my—"

"What should I do?"

"Don't call him back. If you see him, tell him you don't know anything about the bodies. Buy yourself some time. I don't like Cole much, but no one deserves to hear he isn't who he thinks he is from Tyler Crane."

Lilly texted Roddy when they were getting ready to go to the Star for dinner. She and Delia had decided to walk, and she wanted to know if he wanted to join them.

Love to. Meet you out in front of my house, he texted back.

Roddy Lyden had moved next door last spring. He was a perfect next-door neighbor for Lilly. He was determined to bring his house back to its former glory, which meant working on his gardens in his backyard. He'd enlisted Delia's help in researching what the house had looked like in its prime, but he was in the deconstruction phase now. Workers had been over next door tearing up weeds, removing stumps, reinforcing stone walls, and getting the yard in good enough shape that it would survive the winter and be ready to bloom in the spring. Falls in New England were glorious, but winters were long, so Roddy was playing beat the clock with any work he was doing on the outside of his house. He also had a slew of workmen inside the house, trying to correct some of the home repairs that had been badly done over the years.

Since the first thing Roddy tended to in his yard was controlling the vines that kept strangling his own garden and wandering under the garden gate into Lilly's, he'd gained her respect. He'd also become a good friend over the last few months, and fit right into the Garden Squad, the name that Ernie had started to give their small group of friends. Roddy spent a great deal of time at Windward, especially now that the interior of his house was a construction site. Renovation work had been moved up when a leak in both the roof and the upstairs plumbing required an army of attention.

Lilly added a cardigan and a pair of light gloves to her bag to prepare for the walk home. Her light jacket might have been sufficient, but better safe than sorry. She walked out to the front hall where Delia was waiting for her. Delia had dressed for another season entirely and was wearing her black boots, a puffy coat, and a floral scarf.

"Delia, would you rather drive?" Lilly said. "I'd hate for you to freeze on the walk."

"I'm fine," Delia said. "The walk is brisk, but refreshing. I took a nap this afternoon, though, and I was cold when I woke up."

"A nap is always a good idea," Lilly said. She herself had taken to adding a nap to her daily routine. Closing her eyes for twenty minutes made a world of difference. Lilly opened the front door and stepped back to let Delia pass. She followed her and turned around to lock the front door. Lilly remembered a time in the not-very-distant past when she never locked her front door. Of course, she rarely left her house either. Much had changed in the recent months, mostly for the good. Still, Lilly doublechecked the locks and then followed Delia down the front path.

"Roddy should be out in front of his house. Yes, there he is," Lilly said. They both walked down the sidewalk where he was waiting. Lilly was forever grateful that someone had insisted on sidewalks at some point in Goosebush town planning. They made getting from here to there much easier, and a lot safer.

"Ladies, lovely to see you both. I feel as if it's been an age," Roddy said, smiling at them both. He was tall and handsome, and Lilly reflexively smiled back. "I'm very sorry I wasn't able to help you with the leaves this afternoon. I had an electrician come in to give me a bid on some work. I hope the raking wasn't too arduous."

"I think Cole is importing leaves and putting them on the path so we won't be able to use it for the 10K," Lilly said.

"We don't have any proof of that," Delia said. "But something's up. We're going to go over there really early Saturday morning for a touch-up. We can get some more brooms, since that seemed to work best."

"Count me in," Roddy said. "I've got the weekend cleared." The three friends started walking slowly toward town. Delia walked in front and Roddy offered Lilly his arm, which she took.

"Why did you have an electrician come through?" Lilly asked. "More problems?"

"The roof leak is under control for now, though a new roof is going to have to be put on in the next year or so. But the upstairs plumbing problem required a couple of walls to be opened up, which showed what has been described to me as a fire waiting to happen. Apparently, most of the wiring is original on the second floor, and it has been strongly suggested that it all get replaced."

"Oh Roddy, I'm sorry," Lilly said.

"I'll admit, all of this is moving my timetable up a bit, but I'm glad the house is safer to live in. I may move to a hotel for a week or two so that the work can be done all at once, but I'm hoping it won't be longer than that. I'm going to take your suggestion and get new storm windows installed as well. The rooms have been a little breezy of late."

"Do you have a general contractor helping you with all of this?" Lilly asked.

"Ernie is serving that role," Roddy said. "He knows so many of the people I need to call in, by coordinating all of the pieces I have no doubt the work will be done well, and on schedule. Delia, I believe you're helping as well?"

"Ernie and I are testing out a couple of project software packages, and we're using your house as one of our test cases. Ernie's idea is that he can create some templates for folks so they have an idea of what a renovation project takes."

"When did you take that on?" Lilly said.

"A couple of weeks ago. But Ernie's been talking about it for months. Since he's moving and planning on renovating his new house, he thought that it would be a good time to start. But Roddy's project is smaller, or at least it was supposed to be. I should figure out a way to add the 'your electrical systems are a fire hazard' to the matrix," Delia said. She hurried forward a few steps, took out her phone, and started to voice-record some notes for herself.

Roddy and Lilly slowed down a bit to let her do her work, and started chatting about Lilly's philosophy behind bulb planting in the fall for gratification in the spring.

They arrived at the Star at the same time as Ernie did. Roddy hung back a bit and updated Ernie on the meeting with the electrician. By the time they reached the table the conversation was finished, and they were ready for a fun evening with friends. Tamara and Warwick were already sitting, and there was a bottle of red wine open on the table and a glass of beer in front of Warwick.

"I ordered a bottle of red that Stan recommended," Tamara said. "But I'm not going to drink the entire bottle myself."

"You won't have to, my friend," Ernie said. He picked up the bottle, looked at the label, and nodded. "I love this vineyard, though I haven't had this particular wine before. Stan has excellent taste."

"I'll try some," Lilly said, settling into her place. She knew that Roddy preferred to look at the menu first. She'd noticed that he took his food-and-drink pairing very seriously. Roddy was much more of a foodie than he let on. The plans for his kitchen were for a cook, and Lilly looked forward to finding out if he was accomplished in the area of cooking, or if he was working on his skills.

Ernie poured Lilly a glass of wine, and then poured himself one. Lilly took a sip and smiled. Stan did have excellent taste. She let her menu sit on the table while Ernie opened his. Recently she'd begun to let Ernie read over the menu first and she'd listen to his suggestions. It helped her decision-making to limit the choices to one or two.

"Are you ready for the meeting tomorrow, Lil?" Tamara asked. Tamara and Lilly were the same age and had been friends for over sixty years. Tamara looked fifteen years younger, but Lilly didn't begrudge her that. She watched as Warwick took her hand and gave it a squeeze, and was once again thrilled that her friend had found a second great love of her life. Warwick had become one of Lilly's dearest friends as well.

"The four-hundredth meeting?" Lilly said. "I'm ready, yes. How did we get on this committee again?"

"Ladies, please. How could Goosebush have a major event without one of you on the committee?" Warwick said.

"I'm not sure we both need to serve," Lilly said.

"But we'd never abandon the other one," Tamara said, giving her friend a look that dared defiance. "This committee's going to be herding cats, for sure. Thank you for being willing to host tomorrow, Lilly. The alternative was Cole's house."

"Where you would have been served Colonial fare on pewter plates. With his family crest, of course," Ernie said. Everyone laughed, but Lilly and Delia both looked at each other. Delia went back to studying the menu.

"At my house they'll have a Star smorgasbord, chosen by Delia," Lilly said. "I'm assuming you'll all be there?" Lilly looked over at Ernie.

"Oh, I'll be there for moral support," he said. "Now, let's talk about the dinner menu. Stan has added butternut squash ravioli with a Gorgonzola sauce that I, for one, need to try."

CHAPTER 4

The meeting took place in Lilly's dining room. Since it was a weekday meeting, the number of attendees was limited to those who could free themselves up on a Friday afternoon. When she was planning the meeting, Lilly had promised it would be more of a housekeeping agenda to plan future meetings, think about subcommittees, and figure out ways to get more people involved. The idea had been to have some sort of plan in place by the end of lunch, but people had been talking for over an hour. It was clear that the goal was not going to be met. Not even close.

"Let's recap the ideas on the table," Meg Mancini said.

"Not again," Cole said, dismissively pushing his plate away from him. Lilly wasn't sure if he expected a maid to swoop in and clear the place setting. If he did, he'd be sorely disappointed. Lilly had someone come in to clean once a week, but aside from that she and Delia ran the household.

Delia was too busy taking notes to clear the table and Lilly wasn't about to wait on Cole.

"Yes, again," Lilly said. She'd been grateful to Meg for taking on the reins of running the meeting. "We've got several ideas on the table, a real potpourri."

"That all may work together really well," Ernie said. "I love Delia's idea of honoring the Wampanoag tribes that lived here before the English settlers arrived."

"And the ideas of spotlighting groups who tend to be forgotten, like the African-American community that settled here and were part of the shipbuilding community in the 1800s," Meg said.

"But of course, the original settlers, the people who made Goosebush Goosebush, need to be center stage," Cole said.

"Not necessarily center stage," PJ Frank said. PJ ran the Frank lumberyard and had become an active member of the Goosebush community. His family had been in Goosebush for as long as Lilly's had, though the Frank family fortune had a rockier journey, especially in recent years. PJ was unlike his father in many ways, which was a good thing for PJ. His father, Pete, had begun dating his second wife, PJ's mother, again. Since Lilly was Pete's first wife, it was all a little incestuous, but that's what happened in small towns. Lilly was well past the drama and she and PJ were friends. "There are so many facets of Goosebush. I think our four-hundredth needs to be a time to talk about the history of the town, the entire history, and also to look forward."

"When you say the entire history, what do you mean by that?" Fritz Stewart asked.

Lilly looked at Fritz. She forced herself to keep her face neutral. "The entire history," Lilly said.

"Goosebush isn't perfect and has some blemishes that we shouldn't try to cover up."

Fritz shook his head. "Why do we need to focus on the bad stories these days? When I was a boy we learned the positive side of history, the parts that made you proud. What's wrong with that?"

Delia looked up from her computer and smiled at Fritz. "Fritz, you and I have had this conversation a million times," she said. "The stories you were told supported your worldview. It wasn't the experience of other people. It's all right to talk about that. The fact is that there are remarkable stories that don't get told, and this is the opportunity for us to tell them. They don't have to be happy stories to be meaningful."

"Besides, the stories are going to be told. We're neglecting our duty if we aren't as inclusive as possible in this celebration," Meg said.

"Tyler Crane has been doing a lot of research into the town," Lilly said. She looked around the room and noticed that everyone responded in some way. No one smiled. "I'm not sure I admire some of his research methods, though." She thought about the story he was threatening to publish, but pushed it aside. She needed to decide if she wanted to dissuade him or not.

"That man is a menace," Cole said.

"He is that," Meg said. "The best thing we can do is to cut him off at the pass. Let's own the stories of Goosebush. The good, the bad and the ugly." She looked down at her watch. "Delia, you've been taking notes, thankfully. Would you mind sending them out to all of us? It's getting late and we should probably have another meeting soon. Maybe Delia's notes will clarify next steps."

"I suggest we take the simple path and focus on the first settlers," Cole said. "My great-great—"

"Cole, let's talk about it again next time," Lilly said. "I'm going to suggest two things. First, that we schedule another meeting for right after the Fall Festival. We all have too much going on over the next week to focus on this."

"I have plenty of time," Cole said.

"Then you need to volunteer for something," Ernie said. Everyone laughed. "Seriously, Cole, we're all proclaiming ourselves town elders by forming this committee. That means you need to show up and support the work that's going on. Even if it means raking some leaves."

Lilly pretended to take a sip of tea to hide her smile. She looked at Cole over the rim of her teacup and watched him fume.

"I'll send out a Doodle poll to set up the next meeting," Tamara said. "What's the second suggestion, Lilly?"

"That we make Meg Mancini the chair of the committee," Lilly said.

"Seconded," Ernie said quickly.

"All in favor?" Tamara said.

Cole was the only person who didn't raise his hand.

"Thanks for hosting the meeting, Lilly," PJ said as Lilly walked him out the front door. He leaned forward and gave her a kiss on the cheek. "I love seeing the work you're doing on the house."

"We haven't done anything lately," Lilly said.

"You've painted the old breakfast room. The dining room has new lights up in the crown molding. You've—"

"All right, all right, I've been having some work done." Lilly laughed. "Ernie's been making gentle suggestions."

"And letting you know about tradespeople who could use some extra work," PJ said. "Don't worry— your secret is safe with me. I won't tell anyone what a big softie you are."

"I am not a softie," Lilly said, trying her best to look stern.

"I disagree. And I wanted to thank you again for supporting the idea to have the end of the 10K party at the lumberyard. Most people don't even know we're there, so this is going to be great promotion for us."

"It is the perfect location," Lilly said. "You've got the room, for one thing. I hope it hasn't been too much trouble getting it ready for the event."

"No, not really. We've been getting ready for a few days, clearing lumber, creating spaces for folks to sit. The concessions are arriving this afternoon. I wish we'd spent a bit more time gussying up the outside, but there's too much to do."

"Gussying up outside?" Lilly asked.

"Yeah, we've got some dead flower boxes and a couple of sick planters. Hopefully, there will be so many people there no one will notice."

"I'm sure it will be fine," Lilly said, smiling.

"I'm sorry to volunteer you to chair the committee without checking first," Lilly said to Meg. They were in the kitchen. Lilly was loading the dishwasher while Meg wrapped the leftovers. "I was afraid that Cole was going to volunteer."

"And we'd all be wearing Pilgrim costumes. I get it," Meg said. "Thanks for thinking I'm up to it."

"Please, you're more than up to it," Ernie said as he carried another tray of dishes in from the dining room and set them next to the sink. "Tell me what you need me to do to help, Meg. I'm here for you."

"Thank you, Ernie. I'm thinking of you and Delia both as cochairs. Time to give Tamara and Lilly a break, though I hope they still stay involved."

"Thank you, Meg," Tamara said, bringing in more plates from the dining room. "I love the idea of not being in charge. Now, I hate to eat, meet, and run, but I need to get back to the office. Ernie, do you need a ride back to the Triple B?"

"I do, thanks. Are you all set with cleanup?"

"We are. But please, take some leftovers, both of you." Lilly walked over and grabbed a few of the sandwich packages Meg had been putting together, handing them to her friends. Air kisses and hugs went around the room, and then Lilly walked them out the side door.

"Meg, I'll finish cleaning up," Lilly said. "Delia had to go online to teach her class, but she'll get the notes out this afternoon."

Meg put the sandwich plate in the sink and turned to Lilly. "If you're sure. I need to do some food shopping so we can have a nice meal tonight. Ray and I had gotten lazy being on our own, but now that Mary's home I like to try and eat together once in a while."

"Are you enjoying having her home?" Lilly asked gently. Like many New Englanders, Meg was very private in her feelings except with close friends. And even then, her guard was up.

"I am, though she isn't the girl who left ten years ago," Meg said. She turned on the water and sprayed the plate the sandwiches had been on. She took the sponge and started to wash it. She intently focused on a spot that wasn't there.

"Ten years is a long time," Lilly said.

"She's been through hell," Meg said. She turned towards Lilly, tears streaming down her face. "She hasn't told me everything, but what she *has* told me . . . I don't know why she didn't tell me while it was going on. Her marriage was terrible, worse than I could have imagined."

"Oh Meg, I'm so sorry to hear that," Lilly said. "But you're there for her now."

"We never should have turned our backs on her," Meg said.

"You didn't turn your backs," Lilly said.

"Of course we did. Not overtly, not dramatically. But we both made it clear that we didn't approve. She stayed with him longer than she should have. I'm not sure what made her leave, even now. All I know is she called me one night and asked me to come get her. And that it's partially our fault she waited so long to make the call."

"Don't do that to yourself, Meg. You've got her home now."

"We do. But she and Ray are so much alike." Meg put the plate on the rack and dried her hands. She wiped her eyes and turned to Lilly. "Sorry to dump this on you, Lilly. But you and Ray are friends, and I think he could use a sounding board to help him process all of this. He wants to help Mary, but he doesn't know how to do that."

"I'll reach out," Lilly said. She impulsively stepped forward and gave Meg a hug, which was returned. "And please, Meg, remember I'm here if you need someone to talk to. Anytime."

"Okay, here's what you ordered," Ernie said. He lowered the tailgate on his truck and gestured to the piles of soil and mulch, and the flats of flowers. They were all barely visible under the anemic street-lamp, so Lilly took the flashlight out of her pocket and turned it on. "Tell me why we're here again?"

"PJ mentioned that he wishes they had more time to gussy up the outside before tomorrow, so I thought we could do it for him."

"The Garden Squad strikes again," Tamara said. She was wearing dark jeans and a black hoodie. She slipped on some gardening gloves, and then moved her hips around to stretch them out. "It's been a while."

Lilly, Tamara, Ernie, and Delia, the self-appointed Garden Squad, had come together last spring to start dealing with some of the gardening eyesores around Goosebush that could be solved in the dead of night quickly and easily. Originally they did their work clandestinely to avoid getting permission from the powers that be. But they came to prefer doing the work under the cover of darkness so that no one knew it was them.

The amazing thing was, these days it wasn't always them. Over the course of the summer, other gardening projects had been done secretly, and not by the Garden Squad. Old, unused concrete pots at the beach had all been replanted. Bushes along the side of roads had been neatly trimmed. Weeds around stop signs had been replaced with tall grasses. Guerrilla gardening became a town sport, though no one claimed to play. Between that and the work of the Beautification Committee, Goosebush was looking better than it had in a long time.

"We should have added this site to the committee work for the Fall Festival," Delia said. She reached into the truck and grabbed a bag of soil. "We did work at the elementary school and the beach to make sure they looked good."

"We've been doing work at both those sites all fall, so it was already on our minds," Lilly said. "Honestly, this work will take us an hour at most. I appreciate you all coming out to help. Delia and I could have done it on our own."

"What, and miss out on our Garden Squad merit badges?" Tamara said. "I don't mind. Warwick is out at a game tonight. I was going to invite myself over anyway."

"And this is as easy as delivering it to your house," Ernie said. "Besides, I miss spending time with you dames. We've all been so busy lately."

"Too busy," Tamara said. "I don't know about you, Ernie, but this getting my house ready to go on the market is really tough. More emotional than I thought it would be." Tamara took a flat of flowers and carried them over toward Delia, who had started pulling dead plants from flower boxes.

"It is emotional, isn't it?" Ernie said. "Bob and I bought the house together and remodeled it. Lots of memories."

"I bought my house before I married Warwick. Raised all four of my kids there," Tamara said. Tamara had been a young widow when she met Warwick, and he adopted and loved her three daughters as his own. Tyrone had surprised them all with his arrival a few years later, when Tamara was in her forties. He'd been spoiled rotten by everyone, including Lilly, and had shown signs of lacking direction. Lilly's late husband was Tyrone's beloved "Uncle" Alan, whose illness had sobered him and he'd become a thoughtful young man, pursuing a master's in public policy. Lilly had a lot of memories of that house as well. But change was good. Wasn't it?

Tamara moved over to the planters and started pulling the plants that Lilly pointed out to her. "Do you both regret buying the houses?" Lilly asked. She went over to the truck and took out a flat of seagrasses, laying them beside the flats of flowers. Sometimes she wondered if she and Ernie shared a gardening brain. These were exactly the plants she would have chosen.

There were three houses on Shipyard Lane, all built at the same time with the same silhouette. It was rare that any of the houses went on the market, but when two came up for sale in August, Ernie had bought one. Tamara and Warwick bought the other one. Both houses needed work, but Ernie's needed a complete overhaul.

"No, not at all," Ernie said. "I've been thinking about Bob, and how much he would love the remodeling project, and the water view. He always dreamed of having a water view. We redid so many houses during our years together I'm thinking about him all the time. I always oversaw the construction elements. He was the designer. I'm trying to channel him while I'm thinking about what the bathrooms and kitchen should look like, but it's not working. I'm missing him, that's all."

Lilly reached over and gave Ernie a hug. She understood missing a deceased husband, that was for sure. Ernie returned the hug and took a deep breath.

"It's all good," he said. "We'll just have to have design dinner parties, that's all. I need input. Fortunately, or unfortunately, the house is such a mess that I won't get to that until early next year."

"We can—" Delia started to say, and then a bright light shone on them from across the street. They all looked over and saw the light move closer. Once it got into the streetlight they saw Tyler Crane on his bicycle, holding a large flashlight. He swept it across the four of them.

"The midnight gardeners, I presume," Tyler said. "This night has been full of surprises." He pulled his phone out of his pocket and took a picture. "Thanks for a new story idea, folks. Lilly, you know what to do to stop it, right?" He turned and rode away. They heard him laughing even after they couldn't see the flashers on his helmet anymore.

"Should we go after him?" Delia asked.

"He's not worth the effort," Tamara said. "Did you see his bike? He had two baskets on the back, both full. I wonder what he's been up to tonight?"

"No good, I'm sure," Ernie said. "Lilly, what did he mean by his 'you know how to stop it' remark?"

"Nothing," Lilly said. She focused on replanting the flower boxes, throwing the topsoil down with a little more force than was necessary.

CHAPTER 5

"Knock, knock," Roddy said. The side door to the kitchen was open and he let himself in. "Good morning, ladies." Roddy was dressed in jeans, short black boots, and a Goosebush fleece. She saw the top of his purple volunteer T-shirt underneath his chambray button-down shirt. He made the ensemble look elegant.

"Good morning, Roddy," Delia said. "Would you like some coffee? I've filled up three to-go mugs for us, but there's a bit left over. How are you this morning?"

"Intrigued," he said, taking a mug and pouring a bit of coffee into it. He didn't finish the pot. "Tyler Crane has been very active today, and promises to unveil the identity of the Goosebush midnight gardeners."

"It's only six-thirty," Lilly said, looking up from the basket of food she was packing. "What did he say?"

"He just posted a picture of the Frank lumberyard, with the flowers circled. The caption said something about uncovering the identities. Did he catch you in the act?"

"He did, though we neither confirmed or denied. He rode off on his bicycle before he talked to us. We didn't even hear him come up," Delia said.

"I'd imagine that's why he rides a bike," Roddy said. "Tell me—why wasn't I invited on this midnight run?"

"It was more like a ten o'clock run, and it was very last minute," Lilly said. "You should have come over for dinner. We would have dragged you along."

"Late meeting with the storm window person, discussing the installation schedule."

"That's exciting," Delia said. "Remind me later and I'll update the spreadsheet."

"Let's make sure it happens, first," Roddy said. He swallowed the rest of his coffee and put the mug in the dishwasher. "Though I'm optimistic it will."

"We should probably get going," Delia said. "The Jeep is packed with brooms, tarps, and other things we may need. Hopefully, we won't need to do too much."

Lilly drove the Jeep through town, with Roddy riding shotgun. Delia was sitting in the backseat, typing on her phone.

"What are you doing?" Lilly asked her, looking in the rearview mirror.

"I'm social mediaing. There's a hashtag, Goosebush10K, that folks are using. I'm seeing what's out there already and adding to my story."

"What do you mean by *your story*?" Lilly asked.

"A story is a series of short videos or posts. I'm posting a lot to try and drown out the Tyler vitriol."

"Tyler vitriol?" Roddy asked.

"Yeah, he's not only posting about the midnight gardeners. He's promising to preview five stories about the dark side of Goosebush's families by noon. He says he's going to start as soon as the runners start."

"What a miserable human being he is," Lilly said. Her knuckles turned white on the steering wheel. She took a deep breath and forced herself to relax.

"Lilly, one of the posts he did this morning says he's going to unearth a secret lily. I assume he's talking about what he was threatening you with last night," Delia said.

"He threatened you?" Roddy said, sitting up a little straighter.

Lilly sighed. She waved at one of the volunteers who was setting up a water station on the running path. They'd need to get the path cleared and then get over to the beach to do their volunteer duty there, but it was slow moving through town this morning. It was too early in the morning for this level of hubbub, in Lilly's opinion. The world of races was new to her. She was amazed by the excitement people were showing to exercise en masse. To each their own, she supposed. She'd much rather spend the morning in her gardens.

"He's going to post a story about the bodies I have buried in my garden," Lilly said. She glanced over at Roddy and shrugged. "An unfortunate story this time of year, it being close to Halloween and all. It will get more attention than it deserves. But stopping him isn't worth submitting to whatever extortion he had in mind."

"Do you have bodies in your garden?" Roddy asked gently.

"Not bodies, per se," Lilly said. "But there are some ashes. Both my parents and my late husband were cremated and we did burials at sea in these marvelous sea salt urns. But I saved part of the ashes and put them out in the garden, with memorials. It's a little macabre, perhaps. But it gives me tremendous comfort to have them nearby. And it's more efficient than going to a cemetery every day with flowers. At home, they always have flowers."

Delia reached over the front seat and gave Lilly's shoulder a squeeze. "I like having Alan nearby," Delia said. "I go out and talk to him a lot. Especially this semester, while I've been getting used to teaching. I hope you don't mind that."

"Not at all, darling Delia, not at all."

Roddy paused, not sure of what to say. "Tyler thinks you'd do anything to keep this out of the news," he said. "And he's trying to leverage that."

"For what he passes as news with these horrible social media posts he does," Lilly said. "Yes, I suppose he does. He doesn't know me very well. The worst that will happen is people think I'm eccentric, and at this point I'm trading on that reputation and doing what I can to promote it. Take a look at my outfit if you need proof." She reached down and pulled up the skirt of her dress, which was covered with pumpkins, leaves, and bats. She'd had it made especially for the next two weekends.

"If you're one of the five stories of the day, who are the other four? Did he say what they were?" Roddy asked, still serious about his friend being threatened.

"No, he said he'd be previewing the stories with posts. He probably has them scheduled already," Delia said.

"The real question is, are all the subjects of these stories as self-possessed as you are, Lilly? Or is he going to ruin some lives today?" Roddy asked.

"He's going to try, from the sounds of it," Lilly said. "Tell you what—let's find Tyler after we're done with these leaves. Maybe we can persuade him to hold off for a few days. Delia, do you have any idea where he is?"

"The last post he did was ten minutes ago, but it was generic. Probably a time filler he scheduled. The last live video he did was a half-hour ago, and he said he was heading to the beach."

"Great, we'll head to the beach later. I'll try and dissuade him from ruining the day."

"I'll be happy to help you with that, Lilly. I've been good at dissuasion at different times in my life," Roddy said.

Lilly parked at the edge of the lane. Sure enough, there was a fresh batch of leaves covering the path. Fortunately, there wasn't a wind. The cleanup would be easier since the leaves could be pushed to the side. It looked like someone had already started to do the work. There were piles along the tree edge of the lane. But the lane was empty. For now. In a few hours there would be dozens of runners, and slipping on leaves wasn't part of the schedule of activities.

The three of them piled out of the car, and went to the back to grab rakes and push brooms. Lilly took the broom and swept a few feet. The leaves came up and she pushed them to the side.

"The broom works and will be faster," Lilly said. "I'll do this end. Roddy—take the middle and Delia, take the other end. We want to clear it enough that a runner won't slip, but let's not obsess."

"What, me obsess?" Delia said. She gave Lilly one of her rare smiles and went to the end of the path. Roddy walked to the middle and started to push the leaves into one of the existing piles.

Lilly started to sweep, exorcising her frustrations with Tyler Crane with each push of the broom.

"Delia, call the police," Roddy called out.

"What's the matter?" Lilly called to him, hustling over. Roddy stood up from the pile of leaves he was bent over and walked to Lilly, stopping her from getting too close.

"It's Tyler Crane," Roddy said. "He's under that pile of leaves."

"Is he—"

Roddy nodded. "He's dead."

CHAPTER 6

While Delia called the police using the traditional route of 911, Lilly used her own shortcut and called the chief of police, Bash Haywood.

"Bash, I'm on the egress path near Cole Bosworth's and Fritz Stewart's houses. You need to come here, right now."

"Lilly, what's happened? Are you all right?"

"I'm fine, but Tyler Crane isn't. Roddy found his body under a pile of leaves. He's dead."

"Oh Lilly, not again," Bash said. "Don't touch anything and don't let anyone near the scene. I'm at the race registration. I'll be right there."

Not again? What did Bash mean by that? Sure, she'd been at the scene when other bodies had been found, but she hadn't been the one who found them. She'd been the second person at the scene.

Lilly's phone rang again and she looked down at the display.

"Hello, Tamara," she said. She was whispering

into the phone, but realized she didn't need to. No one was there yet.

"What's going on? I heard Bash say your name and then he took off like a bat out of hell, lights and sirens blazing."

"What was he doing there?"

"Bash signed up for the race," Tamara said. "He was checking in. It's nuts around here, but under control. The race starts in less than an hour. Are you all right?"

"I'm fine," Lilly said. "But, now Tamara, I don't want you to react or to tell anyone else what I'm about to say, do you hear me?"

"I hear you. I've got my game face on. Go ahead."

"Roddy found Tyler Crane under a pile of leaves. He's dead."

Lilly heard a Tamara take a deep, quick breath. "Well, that's something," Tamara said.

"It is that," Lilly said. "Needless to say, keep your eyes and ears open for anything odd."

"Oh my, I need to go. Mary Mancini showed up and it looks like she took a tumble. She's covered in *leaves*. I'll make sure she's okay."

"Leaves. Oh dear. Take pictures, lots of pictures. Of everyone, not just Mary. Tamara, have you heard that Tyler Crane threatened to preview five stories during the race today?"

"That's all people have been talking about all morning. Portia Asher's here, rallying the troops, making people focus on the festival and not the Tyler Crane gossip."

"Even more reason to pay attention to what people are saying," Lilly said. "I've got to go; I hear the siren."

* * *

Bash Haywood took control of the scene, even though he was wearing his running clothes. He was, unfortunately, getting good at controlling homicide scenes. He asked Delia to block one end of the path and Roddy was stationed at the other end. Lilly was standing close to the Roddy end of the lane, but she was within speaking distance of Bash. Just in case.

"Bash, I know this is a terrible question to ask given the circumstances, but what about the race? Do we need to cancel it?" Lilly asked. She glanced down at her cell phone to get the time. "It's due to start at eight-thirty. That's a half hour from now. The runners won't run on this path until the end of the race, but they will be running past here to get to the beach. We need to cancel it now if that's going to happen."

"Is this lane part of the route?" Bash asked. He looked at both ends of the path. Officers had arrived and were officially blocking it, though Delia and Roddy stayed at their posts.

"It is, though it will make Delia happy if runners need to do a full loop," Lilly said.

"What?"

"Something about the full 10K. The path was a shortcut over to the lumberyard so that people wouldn't have to go all the way down to the intersection and then double back to Mission Road."

Bash nodded his head. He pressed the transmitter on his chest and spoke into the microphone that was connected to the earpiece he wore. He turned his back to Lilly to have the entire conversation. After a minute or two he took out his cell

phone and had another conversation with someone else.

"Okay, Lilly, here's what we're going to do. Delia
spotted Tyler's bike at her end of the lane, so we
want to divert folks from that side. We're going to
do some quick reconnaissance on this other end of
the lane, but we can divert the runners away from
that side of the street. Hopefully, we can keep a lid
on this for the time being until all the runners get
through."

"Hopefully. Maybe people will think that the police cars are for security for the runners."

"Maybe," Bash said. "We think canceling the race
would cause more commotion, but once the word
gets out there's bound to be folks who wander over
and want to see what's going on."

"*Commotion* is a mild word for what's going to
happen next," Lilly said.

Lilly walked over to Roddy after the medical examiner had arrived.

"What's going to happen?" Roddy asked, looking
over his shoulder. "The runners are going to arrive
shortly."

"How shortly?" Lilly said, looking at her phone.
The race was going to start in ten minutes.

"I've always found that there are serious runners
who try to best their own time, even at these types
of events. Say this is the 8K marker. If people are
running six-minute miles, then someone will be
running by in forty minutes or so."

Lilly looked around at the police tape that was

being strewn about. "I'm going to check with Bash to make sure you can leave, but I think you should head over to the beach. Take the car. Keep an eye out, take pictures, make notes."

"Why? What are you thinking?" Roddy said.

Lilly looked around the lane. Leaves gently fluttered in the breeze. The bright blue sky cracked open and the rising sun warmed the fall day. It was going to be a beauty. But not for Tyler Crane. Lilly glanced over her shoulder at the pile of leaves.

"I'm thinking that this case is going to get a lot of attention. Let's try to help Bash as much as possible, don't you think? The sooner the better getting this solved."

"Well, then, I won't feel as guilty about the pictures I've been taking," Roddy said. "Or the videos."

"Neither will I," Lilly said. "Delia and I will meet you at the lumberyard later on. Tamara and Warwick are at the elementary school. Ernie's at the beach. Keep an eye out. We'll check in again later."

Bash approved Roddy leaving and going to the beach to cover his volunteer shift. Lilly gently suggested that Bash set up some sort of screen at that end of the lane so that the runners wouldn't be able to see as they ran past. A flurry of activity ensued, so Lilly walked to the other end of the lane to talk to Delia. She'd been moved across the street and was standing there checking her phone when Lilly walked up.

"Look what I found," Delia said, barely glancing up. Lilly looked at her friend and realized that the phone wasn't the only thing that Delia was focused on. A small, furry head popped up between the zipper of Delia's hoodie. The tortoise-colored head turned toward Lilly and meowed.

"Who is that?" Lilly said. She held her hand close to the kitten's nose so that it could smell her. The kitten took a moment and then leaned in toward Lilly.

"I don't know," Delia said. "I've been looking online to see if anyone's missing a kitten, but no one has posted anything. I saw her sitting over there, on a rock. She started crying, so I picked her up."

"Is she all right?" Lilly asked.

"I don't know—what do you think?" Delia said, unzipping her sweatshirt and handing the kitten to Lilly.

Lilly took the tiny body and held it close. "She's awfully thin, isn't she?"

"And dirty. Poor thing," Delia said, reaching out and petting the kitten's head. The purring reached a new decibel level and Lilly handed the ball of fur back to Delia. "Where did Roddy go?"

"To the beach. To do his volunteer shift and to pay attention to anything odd he noticed," Lilly said. She smiled at the involuntary affection Delia was showing the kitten.

"Your idea or Bash's?" Delia asked, zipping the kitten back up in her hoodie.

"Mine, though Bash would have thought of it. Might have already. Who knows who is there already? What have you been up to, aside from rescuing lost kittens?"

Delia looked up and gestured to the yellow police tape that was being strung across the lane. "They've asked me to stay for a bit longer in case they have more questions."

"That's odd," Lilly said. "Roddy found the body and they let him go."

"But I found the bike and the broken camera."

"Broken camera? Do tell," Lilly said.

Delia looked around and leaned over toward Lilly. "His bike was over in the bushes. Right there." Delia gestured with her head. Lilly looked over and saw the police tape around the bike in question.

"How do you know it was his?" Lilly asked.

"I'd seen him riding around town," Delia said. "Plus it had the double basket on the back."

"Were the baskets empty?" Lilly asked.

"Yes, and before you ask, I took pictures. I also found a camera at the end of the lane. It had been smashed, maybe with a rock."

"Was the camera damaged beyond repair? Could you see pictures on it?" Lilly asked.

"Lilly, what are you talking about? I didn't touch the camera, of course. Tyler was—is—dead. The camera may be evidence."

"Of course, you're right," Lilly said. "I admire your restraint, Delia. My curiosity gets the better of me."

"I did get some close-ups of the camera," Delia said. "Without touching it. It looked like the memory card was missing. The flap on the camera was open."

"Odd, don't you think? Why wouldn't someone take the camera? Why would they take the memory card only?"

They both heard a *bing* from Delia's phone, so

Delia turned it back on and checked her notifications.

"Shoot," Delia said. "I was worried about that."

"About what?" Lilly asked.

"Tyler Crane just posted a story. A picture of the library. 'He keeps the family secrets.'"

Lilly read the story that Tyler had posted. She refreshed the screen and to her horror the story now had over fifty likes.

"So they aren't full stories, just miserable dribs and drabs of gossip. This story just posted?" Lilly asked. "But that means that Tyler couldn't have posted it because he's . . . you know."

"Dead. I know. There are two possibilities. One, that someone has Tyler's phone and posted the story."

"He's been posting live videos all morning. I wonder how long he's been . . . been there."

"Not long. He posted a video from here around seven o'clock." The kitten meowed again and Delia went back to rubbing her head.

"Do you know if they found his phone?" Lilly asked.

"I don't think so, no. It wasn't around the area. I did look."

"What's the other possibility? How did the story get posted?" Lilly asked.

"I mentioned it earlier. My guess is that Tyler had scheduled the posts ahead."

"Killing him wouldn't have stopped them?" Lilly said.

"No, but someone may not have known that," Delia said, rubbing the head of the small kitten gently. "What should we do?"

"Check in with Bash and let him know about the posts and the video. Then give Tamara a call. Maybe she can come by and pick you up. The vet is open, so go there first. You should get that kitten home, with some food and a litter box."

"Bash may want to talk to me more about Tyler's posts. I've been in touch with his publisher about other Goosebush stories. His publisher, Scottie something, may have more information."

"You need to tell Bash that. Wait until Bash contacts the publisher, but then follow up. Maybe he—"

"She."

"Maybe she can shine more light on what Tyler's game plan was with these five stories today."

"Maybe she can stop them," Delia said. "If Bash needs to talk to me for longer, will you take the kitten?"

"I will. Tell him all you know. The stories could be a motive for Tyler's murder. It would be helpful to unschedule them, if that's possible."

"Why do I think this won't be nearly that easy?" Delia said. "Come with me to talk to Bash, okay?"

"Of course," Lilly said. She draped her arm over Delia's shoulder and they walked across the street together.

Bash gave Delia permission to leave soon, so she texted Tamara and agreed to meet her at the Frank lumberyard for a pickup. Tamara needed to drop off anything that was left at the elementary school, since they were starting to shut down race registration and preparing for the next phase of the Fall Festival.

"Hmm . . ." Delia said.

"Hmm what?" Lilly asked.

"Tamara says that Portia is overseeing the turnover of the space."

"What does that mean?"

"I have no idea. If Portia's in charge, should we worry?"

"Should we worry indeed," Lilly said. She took her own phone out of her pocket and called Tamara. Lilly much preferred talking to texting.

"What's going on?" Lilly asked.

"Not much. Hold on for a sec, so I can hear you better," Tamara said. She was back on the line in a few seconds and whispered, "I don't want anyone to hear me. No one knows about Tyler being . . . Tyler's untimely demise. But folks have been reading his posts over the past couple of hours and a lot of people are riled up."

"Anything of particular interest?" Lilly asked.

"Nothing much. I'm writing things down. My brain is on overload and I'm tired. I know you told me to keep it to myself, but I did tell Warwick."

"Of course you did," Lilly said. "I didn't mean him when I said anyone."

"I know you didn't. Anyway, a couple of police officers arrived a few minutes ago and Warwick is giving them the registration information. They're being very thorough."

"That's good. Are you able to leave?"

"We're being encouraged to leave, but Portia wants to move some hay bales while we have help. The police are fighting her on it, but she's digging in."

"Tell her that we'll get to it, but she should head

over to the lumberyard to help set up. Are you okay with coming to get Delia and the kitten?"

"What kitten? She asked for a ride home and told me she'd explain once I got there."

"She found a kitten in the woods. Poor thing is skinny and has matted fur. I don't know how long she's been out in the wild, but she likes people so I don't think she's feral. Anyway, she's going to take her to the vet and then home."

"Tell her I'll be right there. I didn't know a fur baby was in need. Poor thing. I'm going to load up the car and leave Warwick to deal with what's going on here. We'll figure out the rest later."

"Bring Portia with you to the lumberyard. They will need help setting up, since I'm not sure when I'm going to get there."

"Has Bash asked you to stay?"

"No, but he hasn't asked me to leave," Lilly said.

Bash asked Delia some more questions and then he let her go to the lumberyard to meet Tamara. Lilly walked Delia to the edge of the lane and watched as she and her feline friend walked along the edge of the road. Delia was a fast walker, so hopefully they'd get to the lumberyard and leave before the influx of racers came.

Lilly waited until there was a lull in the activity before she walked over to Bash.

"Bash, do you still need me to stay?" Lilly asked him once they were alone.

"I think we're in good shape. We got Roddy's statement and the ME confirms what he said. Roddy saw a foot sticking out, brushed leaves to find an arm, took a pulse, and then stepped away from the crime scene."

"I heard him call to Delia to phone 911 and I walked toward the pile of leaves, but he stopped me and told me that Tyler was dead. I wonder how he could tell it was Tyler?"

"The body was lying face up," Bash said. "He had a couple of head wounds, but he was recognizable."

"Do you think he had a heart attack or something?" Lilly asked.

"He may have," Bash said. "The medical examiner couldn't say one way or another, but this will be treated like a suspicious death."

"Of course," Lilly said. "Heaven help me, I assumed it was murder. What's wrong with me?"

"The scene isn't clear," Bash said. "We're going to move forward assuming it was and collect evidence. But as far as the public knows, cause of death is unconfirmed."

"Is it public?" Lilly asked.

"It will be. I called his publisher to let her know what had happened, and to ask her to check and see if his social media was going to keep posting all day."

"Is it?"

"She can't be sure. He used all sorts of programs and she has no idea of his passwords. She says she had no control over his social media feed."

"If he was murdered and the goal was to stop him from posting a story . . ."

"Then someone is going to be very frustrated," Bash said. "I know I don't have to tell you to keep all of this close to your vest."

"Of course not," Lilly said.

"Keep me posted of anything you hear, okay?" Bash said.

Lilly nodded at Bash and smiled at him. He really was growing into his job. He was also getting a lot of practice in difficult situations lately.

"I'm going to meander down to the lumber-yard," Lilly said. "Stay in touch, Bash."

"You too, Lilly," he said, turning back to the crime scene. Lilly took out her phone and snapped some more pictures before she left.

CHAPTER 7

As Lilly approached the intersection where she was going to turn right, she saw dozens and dozens of people running and walking toward her, veering to her left, the long way around to the beach. She'd known that there were a lot of people registered for the race, but the sea of humanity in front of her felt overwhelming. She dug her phone out of her pocket and took some pictures. For whatever reason, and it could have been exhaustion, the festive line of runners coming toward her, the sun in the sky, or the activity of her morning catching up with her, Lilly felt tears welling up in her eyes.

"Ms. Jayne, ma'am, are you all right?" A handsome young man in a purple volunteer T-shirt had been stationed at the intersection to make sure runners stayed on the correct path, since there were four to choose from. He left his station and came over to her.

"I'm fine," Lilly said, smiling at him. She brushed the tears from her cheeks and put her sunglasses back on. "I've had a morning, is all. I'm sorry, you have me at a disadvantage. You know who I am, but I'm not sure I know who you are."

"I'm Chase. Chase Asher, Portia's grandson."

"Chase, of course. I haven't seen you in years. Not to sound clichéd, but you're all grown up!"

Chase laughed. "I hear that a lot. I'm moving in with my grandmother at the end of the semester, but I thought this weekend and next would be a fun way to get to know some people."

"You're right about that. I see she drafted you to be a volunteer. I'm surprised you aren't with her down at the school."

Chase laughed. "I love my grandmother with all my heart, I really do. But if I was with her, she'd be introducing me to everyone with a 'have you met my beautiful grandson?' I do love her, but it can be a lot to deal with."

"I can imagine," Lilly said, laughing. Portia described her grandchildren as the applause of her life, and was thrilled that Chase was moving in with her for a while.

"Where are you going, Ms. Jayne?" Chase asked.

"To the lumberyard to help set up," she said.

"I'm heading there myself in a couple of minutes. What's say you grab a drink of water, and I'll walk with you?"

He handed her a paper cup filled with water. She took it and nodded. Lilly was suddenly very tired. Chase gently took her by the elbow and guided her over to the lawn chairs that were set up on the island in the middle of the intersection. He took one of the five-gallon bottles of water and set it beside her. Then he went back to his station, distributing water and cheering people on.

Lilly sat, watched, and drank water. Chase took

longer than five minutes, but not much. Another volunteer had joined the team, so Chase walked over to Lilly.

"You ready?" Chase said. He picked up a box and balanced it under his arm. He held his hand out to help Lilly up. Though she didn't really need his help, not really, it would have been rude to refuse. Together they broke away from the crowd and started to walk toward the lumberyard.

"This way is a shortcut," Lilly said. She walked him past the main road, up a block and down a path that ran between houses.

"I've never been down here," Chase said.

"When I was a little girl, I biked all over Goosebush," Lilly said. "There's not a road I don't know in this town."

"Were you down by the path that the runners were supposed to go down?"

"I was," Lilly said.

"Did they decide to not have the runners go down there because of Tyler?" Chase asked.

"Because of Tyler?" Lilly asked quietly.

"Yeah, I overheard him yesterday. He said that he was going to set up a remote on that path tomorrow."

"A remote?" Lilly asked.

"He was going to set up a camera and do his live feeds from there."

"I wonder why there?" Lilly said.

"He said something about it being significant to his noon broadcast," Chase said. "He was talking to someone on the phone, I don't know who. I shouldn't have listened in on his call, but I was getting a cup of coffee and I couldn't help but overhear him."

"Did you—do you know Tyler?" Lilly asked.

"Yeah, I do. I mean, I tend to hang out at the Star and he's always there. You can't help but talk to folks, you know? It's a small town."

"It is a small town," Lilly said. "Everyone knows each other."

"Well, sort of. I know people, but I don't *know* people, you know? Tyler figured that out pretty quickly. I wasn't that much use to him on the gossip front, and my grandmother wouldn't give him the time of day. Wow, look, we're here. That's a pretty cool shortcut; I'll need to remember that. Listen, Ms. Jayne, I've got to bring this box of stuff over to the concession table. Are you all right on your own?"

"I won't be on my own for long," Lilly said, smiling. "Thank you for walking me over."

Lilly had no intention of ever running a 10K. Or walking one, for that matter. But she was amazed at how quickly it was all over. The runners started at 8:30. By 10:45 the slowest of the slow runners had straggled into the Frank lumberyard. Lilly kept checking her phone for updates. Tyler's death wasn't public yet. But his account had posted more stories, one as vague yet intriguing as the next.

"Place looks great, doesn't it?" PJ came up beside Lilly and handed her a cookie.

She took a bite and nodded. The parking lot was full, people were drinking samples of beer, eating, and laughing. There were shuttles to take the runners back to the school parking lot, but most people didn't seem to be in a rush to leave.

"The run seems to have been very successful," Lilly said.

"I meant the window boxes and planters. A nice surprise when I came in this morning, let me tell you."

"I hadn't noticed," Lilly said, looking right at PJ and smiling. Sometimes the ease with which she lied scared her a bit. But she'd spent years honing the skill to keep clients' secrets, not knowing how much it would help her in retirement.

"The midnight gardeners struck again," PJ said. "I wish I could tell them thank you."

"I'm sure they know," Lilly said. "Tell me, have you been reading the Tyler Crane posts this morning?"

"I have," PJ said. "They've been getting more and more obscure. By the end of the day, people are going to stop talking about the race and start trying to guess who he's talking about." Someone called PJ's name and he waved. "They need me to tap another keg."

"You're going through a lot of beer this early in the morning," Lilly said.

"We are, but it's all part of the party. We're going to have samples available next weekend as well."

"I'm so glad that the brewery is going well for you and Jessie," Lilly said.

"Yeah, it's a lot of fun." PJ looked around at the crowd. "This was a great way to kick off the Fall Festival, don't you think?"

Lilly nodded, smiled. As PJ walked away, she took out her phone again and hit *refresh*.

"Delia, what are you doing here?" Lilly asked. She'd been busy keeping the food tables stocked, and didn't see Delia arrive.

"This was always low on volunteers, so I came back to help. Tamara came with me. She's over there, talking to Ray Mancini. Bash is with them both."

"Where's the kitten?"

"At the vet. We can pick her up in a couple of hours. They wanted to check her out, but they think she'd be better off being at home with us, so they're staying open. They usually close at noon on Saturdays."

"That's nice of them. Of course she'd be better off with us, poor little thing. She needs some TLC. Is she all right?"

"All things considered, yes. The vet says she's about three months old. They're doing a full workup and cleaning her up. I checked with everyone at the office and no one had heard about a missing kitten. Dr. Allen thinks she may have been dumped."

"Dumped?"

"Yeah, apparently people do that with pets they don't want." Delia's eyes filled up and she wiped the tears away. "Can you imagine?"

"The capacity of humans to be cruel is overwhelming," Lilly said. The sound system screeched. Both women turned toward the small stage that had been set up.

"They're going to make an announcement," Delia said. "About Tyler."

"They?"

"Bash. That's what he's talking about with Ray and Tamara."

"Why are they going to make an announcement?"

"To get ahead of the story," Delia said. "His publisher's making an announcement at noon." She took her phone out of her pocket and put it on a stabilizing handgrip.

"What are you doing?" Lilly said.

"I'm doing a live broadcast. I've been doing stories online. You know that, right?"

"Yes, your Goosebush memories," Lilly said. She was tired, too tired to follow all these threads swirling around in her head.

"His publisher called me and asked me to do a live feed about the announcement."

"And you agreed," Lilly said.

"Tamara and I talked it over. Yes, I agreed. We figured it was the best way to drown out these stories Tyler was publishing." Delia looked at Lilly and tried to smile. "How do I look?"

Lilly sighed and then she reached into the pocket of her jacket and took out a mirror. "You need some lipstick, but otherwise, given what's happened today, you look surprisingly well."

The announcement of Tyler's death was met with an appropriate pause, but the atmosphere at the lumberyard picked up again shortly. Lilly looked around, trying to gauge the community. She watched Ray Mancini walk over to his daughter, Mary, who had finished the race at the back of the pack. He hadn't said too much to her before Bash walked over and spoke to Mary. She twisted away from Ray, and walked to the side to talk to Bash. Lilly yearned to hear what they were talking about, but she wasn't close enough to hear.

What Lilly could do, and did, was to take pictures of everything. She also checked her phone and noted that the final four Tyler postings had dropped on social media. Like the others, they were cryptic, but Lilly recognized the one about herself.

WHAT MAKES THIS GOOSEBUSH DOWAGER'S
GARDEN GROW? THIS REPORTER HAS HEARD THAT
THE BLESSINGS OF HER DEARLY DEPARTED HELP
HER IN INTERESTING WAYS. MORE DETAILS TO
COME.

The picture that went with the story was of the gate to Lilly's driveway, through which one could glimpse her garden.

"More details to come." Lilly felt bile rise in her throat. Five stories previewed. All cryptic, all with a promise of more to come. Lilly knew how this story had impacted her and she had nothing to explain or to feel guilty about. *More details to come.*

The day was catching up to Lilly. She looked over at Delia, who had finished her "live" from the lumberyard that included a mention of Tyler's death.

"Delia, how do you think it went?"

"It went well," Delia said. "Thanks for not listening in. I was really nervous."

"I'll always support you in whatever way you think is best," Lilly said. "How are you doing? I didn't know Tyler, but you did. This must be difficult."

"Thanks, Lilly," Delia said. "Tyler and I had spent some time together, and he taught me a lot about social media. We weren't friends, but still. I don't know what happened, but he was too young to die."

Lilly nodded her head. She watched as Bash walked Mary over to his car. Ray followed them and they all got into the car and drove away.

She turned back to Delia, who had also watched the scene unfold. "Did you notice that the rest of Tyler's stories dropped?" Lilly said. "Is that the right term? They dropped?"

"Or posted," Delia said. She opened an app on her phone and scrolled through. She glanced up at Lilly. "What a jerk. Sorry, I don't mean to speak ill of the dead, but still. I wonder what his plan was for the day?"

"Maybe he was going to do live commentaries about each of the stories, and give more details? Do you think that's what the camera was for?"

"No, he would have used his phone. He used his phone for everything. The camera would have been backup, or used for extra footage."

Delia looked down at her phone and tapped a few buttons.

"The vet texted. I can pick the kitten up anytime. They don't need to keep her overnight. They want to know when I can come get her."

"Well, then, we need to get moving. Let me text Roddy and see if he's on his way with the car. Given everything, I'm sure that people will forgive us if we leave early."

"Lilly, are you awake?" Delia said.

Lilly was awake, but barely. Roddy had picked them up and together they'd all gone to the vet. Once they got back to the house, they got the kitten set up with some food and a litter box in the break-fast room, which was Delia's domain. Delia sat on the floor to be closer to the kitten as she explored her new home.

Roddy had begged off lunch, but had agreed to come over for dinner. Lilly made herself a piece of raisin toast with peanut butter and took it and a cup of tea up to her room. She took a notebook out and went through Tyler's feed, writing down all of the posts he'd done and the time they appeared on social media. She couldn't tell which ones were live and which ones he'd scheduled, since he made his scheduled posts seem like he'd just done them. She found a live video he'd done and she made a star by that entry on her list for the time stamp. But then Lilly paused. Was live, live? Or was live still recorded? Social media flummoxed her. At one point Lilly leaned back and closed her eyes. The next thing she knew, Delia was knocking on her door.

"I'm awake," Lilly said. "What time is it?"

"Four. I've got the kitten with me. Can you hold her for a few minutes while I take a shower?" Delia walked into Lilly's bedroom, holding a bunched-up tea towel in her arms.

Lilly sat up a bit in bed and took the towel bundle from Delia. She looked down at the tiny brown and orange head that peeked up. She petted it gently and felt the purrs that rumbled her tiny body. She watched her eyes start to close and felt the kitten relax in her arms.

"Delia, have you been with the kitten this entire time?" Lilly asked.

"Of course. I lay down on the couch in the breakfast room so we'd be together, but she freaked out if she couldn't see me, so I didn't get a lot of rest."

"What do you mean, freaked out?"

"Cried, ran around. She seemed to panic unless I held her."

"Poor little thing, she's been through it. It's remarkable that she's as alert as she is," Lilly said.

"They gave her some fluids," Delia said. "The vet said she was almost starving."

"She won't starve anymore."

"I'm going to put some postings up in case she got loose and her family is panicked."

"That's probably a good idea," Lilly said. The kitten had fallen asleep. "But if no one comes forward, I'm amenable to her living with us, if you'd like."

Delia smiled. "Really? That's wonderful. My parents never let me have a pet when I was little and I always wanted one."

"I had cats and dogs growing up. My last cat passed away right before Alan got sick. I've missed having fur. Go ahead, take your shower. I'll sit with her."

"Thanks, Lilly. I won't be long. By the way, Warwick called. He and Tamara are bringing dinner over. Roddy and Ernie are coming too. They'll be here in an hour or so. I hope that's all right."

"That's fine," Lilly said, leaning back onto the bed. "I'll get ready after you come back and get the kitten."

"Lilly, do you have a preference? Steak tips or chicken?" Warwick said. He was just outside the screened-in porch, tending the grill. Ernie was standing with him, moving some of the foil-wrapped vegetables around on the grill.

"I love both," Lilly said. "Did Delia send out the tofu?"

"She did, but that will go on last-minute," Warwick said.

"Do you need anything else?" Lilly asked.

"We're all set," Ernie said. "We've got a ton of food here, but all the better for leftovers."

Lilly walked into the kitchen, where Tamara and Roddy were assembling salads.

"Do you think we should eat on the porch, or is it too cold?" Lilly asked.

"Do you have that space heater ready to go?" Tamara asked.

"I do."

"Then let's sit out on the porch," Tamara said. "The time we can do that is so limited. Let's enjoy it."

Lilly walked past her friends and gently pushed the swinging door into the dining room. She went to one of the hutches and took out a tablecloth, place mats, and napkins. She carried them back into the kitchen and put them on the kitchen table. She walked over and took a large tray out of the cabinet that ran along the back wall.

"Where are we eating?" Delia said. She came into the kitchen, the kitten following closely on her heels.

"The back porch," Lilly said. She put seven plates on the tray and put the fabrics on top of them.

"I'll set the table," Delia said. "Come on, buddy, let me show you the back porch. But listen, no more going outside alone, got it?"

"That kitten is the cutest thing," Tamara said. "Are you keeping her?"

"Delia is going to let people know we found her, in case someone is missing her. But if no one comes forward, we'll keep her."

"Good," Tamara said. "This house needs some fur again."

"Tell me," Roddy said. "Are we going to talk about what happened today during dinner, or afterwards?"

"During dinner," Ernie said, carrying a tray

heaped with tinfoil packets. He set it down on the kitchen table and walked over to the cabinet to get some serving bowls.

"I have an audition tonight and I don't want to miss anything," he said.

"An audition?" Roddy asked. "Are you a performer?"

"Strictly amateur," Ernie said. "They're having auditions for *A Christmas Carol* tonight."

"Auditions?" Lilly said. "I thought they were doing readings in December at the Star. They're having auditions?"

"There are lots of roles," Ernie said. "Besides, the Goosebush Players could use some new blood. We're thinking that now that the good citizens of Goosebush have seen the new performance space we're hoping to use at the beach, there will be more people interested in trying out, or supporting, the Players. As long as Delores doesn't screw it up."

"Who's Delores?" Roddy asked.

"She's the artistic director of the Goosebush Players. She's also the chairman of the board, for now at least," Ernie said.

"She is a character," Tamara said.

"That's one word for it," Ernie said. "Another word is *exhausting*. Say, Roddy, I don't suppose you're an actor?"

"Not since my university days," Roddy said.

"If you want to get back on the boards, come with me tonight. We could always use a handsome guy with an accent," Ernie said.

Roddy laughed. "I'll think about it."

"The dinner discussion isn't going to be gruesome, is it?" Tamara said.

"The discussion I'm interested in having is about those stories that Tyler posted," Lilly said. "I suspect the legacy of those stories is going to have an effect on Goosebush. I can't help but wonder what his endgame was."

"And if that's what got him killed," Roddy said.

CHAPTER 8

Morning came early, another gorgeous fall day. Lilly had slept in a bit and was busy preparing a Sunday brunch. She heard the front doorbell ring once, then twice more shortly thereafter. The friend ring. She walked out to the front door, peeked through the peephole, and opened the door.

"Roddy, good morning," Lilly said. "Why didn't you let yourself in?" Lilly had given Roddy a key at the end of the summer, so that he could let himself in. After texting or calling first, of course, which he had. Windward was a very big house and Roddy visited often enough that Lilly felt trekking to the front door needed to be minimized.

"I'm afraid I'm ruining your reputation," he said. "There are a few people outside, peering in the gate. I may be featured in some photos, coming in the front door. I thought it best not to use my key." Roddy stepped in beside Lilly and walked to the back of the house with her.

"People are trying to take pictures of graves in

my backyard. Do you really think you having a key to my front door will do any more damage? It's been quite a morning already," Lilly said, taking a right into the kitchen.

"What's happened?" Roddy asked.

"Emails, knocks on the door, phone calls," Lilly said. "Apparently Tyler's stories are an internet sensation. And I'm part of it."

"I'm so sorry," Roddy said. "What can I do to help?"

"You're doing it," Lilly said. "Let's have breakfast and talk. I hope you're hungry. I made a quiche and we have a lot of scones and muffins. Where would you like to eat?"

"How about the porch again? It's lovely out."

"The sun heats it up nicely. The porch is perfect. Do you mind taking the tray?"

"Not at all," Roddy said. "Will Delia be joining us?"

"She will, but I'm not sure when." Lilly took the coffeepot and a pitcher of water and led Roddy out the French doors to the porch.

"How do you do this?" Roddy said.

"What?"

"We were all here until almost midnight, strewn about out here. Now, it's not quite nine o'clock and the porch is clean and welcoming."

"Dishwashers help," Lilly said. "I'm serious. The second load from last night is going through right now. Plus, Delia was up very early. Tyler's publisher gave her a call at six o'clock. The first call of many. I'm not sure what's up, but she cleaned everything between calls."

"We didn't get very far talking about the murder last night," Roddy said.

"No, we all had to recap the day as a whole and that took a while. Then reading the comments and looking at the reposts took up most of the evening."

"Some of those comments were hair-raising, weren't they? I had to go home and take a shower," Roddy said. "Behind the anonymity of social media lurks a dark side of human beings."

"It does. But social media is also good. It helps us connect. Don't look at me like that—I mean it," Lilly said.

"You sound like Delia," Roddy said.

"Good. I try to learn from her. Listen, my friend, we have to keep up with technology. We don't have to go all-in on social media and start our own YouTube channels."

"Our own what?" Roddy asked.

"But technology is part of the world and it's not going away. Don't get left behind."

"You're right, of course," Roddy said. "If it weren't for social media, I'd barely see my granddaughter. I should be . . . I am grateful. But it doesn't replace in-person visits."

"Of course it doesn't," Lilly said. Roddy rarely talked about his daughter and her family, but Lilly knew that they hadn't visited him in his new home.

"Ah, Lilly, it is a helluva thing when your daughter is just like you, and keeps you at arm's distance," Roddy said, as if answering her question. Roddy and Lilly often communicated like this, with short-cuts because of shared thoughts.

"But didn't you say they're coming down next weekend for the haunted houses?"

"They've said so, but I'm halfway expecting a cancellation. Ah, listen to me. Wallowing in self-pity;

not a pretty place to be, surely." Roddy shook his head. "Where were we?"

"Talking about being derailed by comments on social media," Lilly said. Lilly Jayne was a cranky Yankee—crusty on the outside, but full of love once folks got past the crust. A cranky Yankee also respected the privacy fences people put up. Roddy's daughter was his personal territory. "But we let that dark side derail us. Easy to do."

"Absolutely," Roddy said. "I wonder if the objects of the four other stories Tyler hinted at are having the challenges you're having this morning?"

"My story was the most easily identified, especially for people in Goosebush. He showed my front gate, for heaven's sake."

"He did. The other stories could be identifiable, though, don't you think?"

"Only if you know a little about a lot of things," Lilly said.

"What aren't you telling me?" Roddy said.

"That story about bloodlines being complicated? I think that story is about Cole Bosworth."

"Not an idle thought, I'd imagine. Do you want to explain?" Roddy asked.

Lilly shook her head. "Not yet," she said.

"What about the other stories. 'She shares a family name.' 'He keeps the family secrets.' 'She spills the secrets,'" Roddy said. He looked over at the large whiteboard Delia had rolled out of her office during dinner. They'd tried to sort through everything that had happened and create a timeline.

"All of those stories could be about dozens of people. My question is more along the lines of what made him post those stories." Lilly put a slice of quiche on a plate and handed it to Roddy.

"Answer the question for yourself. Why did he post the story about you and your memorials?"

"Memorials," Lilly said. "You are a kind man, Roddy Lyden. He told me that he'd kill the post if I answered some of his questions." Lilly took a bite of her quiche. She wasn't a great cook, but she had a number of recipes at which she excelled. Quiche was one of them. "He offered to not post it if I talked to him about Merilee's murder."

"Did you have other conversations with him? Had he brought that up before?"

"We'd never spoken," Lilly said. "But honestly, I've gone out of my way to avoid him."

"Why?" Roddy asked. He poured himself a cup of coffee and held up the pot to Lilly. She shook her head. She'd had three cups already.

"I'd heard too much about him in too short a time," Lilly said. "Delia had met him and been charmed by him. But she realized early on that he was a user, so she kept him at arm's length."

"A user?" Roddy asked quietly. He stopped eating and looked at his friend. The anger on her face was palatable.

"Roddy, I don't want you to take this the wrong way, but my advice to young women—anyone, for that matter—is to beware of charming men. Tyler was charming. Delia felt that she'd told him too much and had been indiscreet, but caught herself in time. But I have to wonder: Who else did he charm? What other stories did he hear?"

"But he didn't try to charm you?"

Lilly laughed. "Here's the thing about being a

woman of a certain age. We're invisible to a lot of people. And others, they make assumptions."

"Assumptions?"

"That we're in our dotage. Don't laugh, it's true."

"It well may be. I suspect it is. But considering you to be invisible, or in your dotage? That's at their peril. I know what you mean about charming, though. Tyler had a knack for putting you at ease."

"That didn't work with you, though."

"It didn't, but only because—like you—I'd met Tylers my entire life. A couple of observations about Tyler and his work, however?" Roddy dished himself some fruit from the bowl on the table.

"Please," Lilly said, nibbling on a piece of pineapple.

"I spent some time last night looking at his social media feed versus his published stories in the newspaper. On his social media feed, he insinuated, gossiped, and made wild accusations. But in his journalistic work? He was meticulous. He hadn't done serious stories for a while, but he had quite a legacy of work. His stories were well sourced, impeccably researched, and had no hint of personal bias. Honestly, the two sides of Tyler couldn't be more different."

"Interesting," Lilly said. She kicked herself for not looking at the journalist Tyler's work, but was glad that Roddy had. "What do you think?"

"I think that Tyler used his social media posts as leverage. He wanted other information from you, thought that you'd talk to him rather than have that gossip posted. His mistake."

"Yes, but one with little repercussions. It was true enough, but unkind."

"Right. But would you have talked to him the next time he threatened you with a post? Not you, but someone else, with more to lose?"

"Yes, I can see where someone would."

"Here's the next question," Roddy said, looking right at his friend. "What was Tyler trying to get at? Was he working on a story and trying to get people to give him information?"

"He may have been. Was it that story that got him killed, or the hornet's nests he was stirring up by asking questions?"

"You won't believe who I just got off the phone with," Delia said. She walked into the kitchen juggling her electronics, her phone, computer, and various cords in one hand and under her arm, a notebook with Post-its sticking out under her other arm, a fountain pen clipped to the top of her T-shirt and three mugs in her other hand. The kitten was close on her heels. When she saw Lilly she meowed and ran over to her. "Oh, good morning Roddy. I didn't know you were here."

"Good morning, Delia. Can I help you with all of this?" Roddy stopped unloading the dishwasher onto the counter and gently took the notebook and mugs from her.

"Thanks. It would be easier to make a few trips, but I've already gone up and down three times today," Delia said.

"You know, there used to be dumbwaiters in this house," Lilly said. She'd scooped the kitten up and was petting her gently as she sat down at the kitchen table. The kitten settled down into her lap. "My mother had them blocked off, but not taken out. Maybe we should try and find them again. That would be a good winter project."

"We should try to find the original drawings of this house," Delia said. "Returning the dumbwaiters would be so much fun. I'd love to find all the nooks and crannies. The captain who built it liked to have his hiding places, didn't he?"

"He did," Lilly said. "I'm afraid that he wasn't the most ethical of sea captains and hiding places were his norm. It's been said that it took his children years to find his treasures in this house, which is why they held on to it for so long. The drawings would have come from that next generation and been added to by subsequent ones. I'll try to locate them."

Roddy looked back and forth at both women and grinned before going back to unloading the dishwasher. Delia was plugging her computer in and Lilly was making herself a note in her phone.

"Delia, you mentioned that you'd gotten a call?" Roddy said. He handed her a plate for food, since the quiche hadn't been put away yet.

She took the plate and put it down, looking back at Roddy.

"Breakfast," he said, pointing to the quiche.

"Oh, right, sorry," she said, putting a piece of quiche on her plate. "I think I'm going to need a nap today. I've already been up for hours. I'm glad it's Sunday and I don't have to teach tomorrow. I was online, posting some pictures of the race yesterday on the *Goosebush News*."

"I thought that Fritz Stewart ran those sites. Wasn't that the deal, when the Historical Society decided to create them? That you wouldn't have to run them?" Lilly said.

"It was the deal, but what we decided to do is to create a Google drive where people can post pictures and stories and then I go through them, edit, and post them on the different channels. It really is much easier that way and provides a standard voice for the social media. We've even opened it up to folks outside the Historical Society to submit stories and pictures that may be of interest. Anyway, that's sort of what brought about the call. Tyler's editor reached out yesterday to thank me for the posts I did about the race, and the tribute I did to Tyler."

"What tribute?" Lilly asked.

"I did it late last night. A slideshow of him doing some of his social media posts around town. I mentioned that he'd only been in Goosebush for a short period of time, but he'd made an impression. I didn't paint him to be a saint, but I did say he'd taught me a lot about telling stories, which I appreciated. I posted it from my own account."

"That was nice of you," Lilly said.

Delia shrugged. "I know he upset a lot of people, but he really was a good storyteller. In a way, he mentored me and helped me figure out how to create a voice for the *Goosebush News* social media channels."

"Did he know you were getting story contributions?" Lilly asked. "Did he ever want to know about them?"

"He did and he did. But I didn't share anything with him. In fact, he started asking about a few of the stories we hadn't published yet, so I made the drive private so only I could see it, so no one would be tempted to share."

"Interesting," Lilly said. She stopped petting the kitten and picked up her phone to make another note. "Do you know how he knew about the stories."

"No idea," Delia said.

"What did Tyler's editor say?" Roddy asked. "What's her name, by the way?"

"Scottie Sinclair. She called and asked me if I'd follow up on a couple of stories Tyler was working on. She also asked if I'd start doing the lives."

"What does that mean, start doing the lives?" Roddy said.

"He'd do lives on Facebook, on Instagram, and once in a while on YouTube. He'd tease a story or do an interview. Fluff pieces."

"He did a few of them from the Star, didn't he?" Lilly asked. "Stan mentioned them."

"A lot of them from there, but he'd do them all around town. I guess, given what happened, they want to continue to do them."

"And follow up the investigation of Tyler's death, I'd think," Roddy said.

"She did mention that they couldn't spare a reporter to come here, but they did want to stay on top of what was happening."

"How do you feel about that?" Lilly said. "It puts you in an awkward position, doesn't it? A conflict with the *Goosebush News* site?"

"We talked about that too," Delia said. "I figured it was better if I'm on top of the story, since I can thread the needle between fact and gossip better than most people."

"True," Roddy said.

"She also mentioned that she was having trouble putting together where Tyler's work was. He worked from his phone and uploaded stuff irregularly. He never sent her drafts."

"Has she been able to look at his laptop?"

"She doesn't think that will be much help. She said he even wiped his searches every day, and used a cleaner to make it hard to find things on his computer."

"That seems paranoid," Lilly said.

"Or very careful," Roddy said. "I read some of his previous work. He was an investigative reporter who'd worked on some huge stories. He'd won awards for his work. Phones are remarkable these days. He could conceivably have used it for everything."

"That important a reporter? Now he was in Goosebush," Lilly said. "I wonder what he did wrong in his career? I know that newspapers are cutting back, but shouldn't an award-winning journalist be employable?"

"Let me see what I can find out about his career path," Roddy said.

"Scottie also mentioned that they haven't found his phone," Delia said. "There was some other equipment he had that's missing as well."

"How does she know that they haven't found his phone?" Lilly asked.

"Apparently he had a tracking system on it. He told her about it. He told her that if she ever didn't hear from him for a day, she could find him using the tracking system. But she's been trying to use it and the phone is off the grid. She can't ping it."

"Maybe it ran out of battery?" Lilly said.

"More than likely, someone shut it off," Roddy said. "Even if the battery was too low for the phone to work, the signal likely still would. I'd imagine that someone who was concerned enough about the tracking system being installed would have made sure that it could be used under any circumstance."

"Delia, you should let Bash know about your conversation and make sure he knows about the phone," Lilly said.

"Aren't we going to look into it?" Delia said.

"The phone, or Tyler's death? No, I don't think so. No more than curiosity allows. Seems that this is best handled by the police, don't you think?"

"I guess so," Delia said.

"You're right," Roddy said. "Though I am going to look into Tyler, for my own curiosity."

"Nothing wrong with curiosity," Lilly said, lifting up the kitten and kissing her head, then resting her on her shoulder. "Nothing at all."

"You know you have a crowd outside the gate, don't you?" Ernie said as he let himself out of the screened door and down the porch steps.

"Ernie, you almost gave me a heart attack," Lilly said. She'd been pruning some of her bushes to help inspire them next spring and was in her own world. That was not uncommon when Lilly was in a garden, especially her own. She focused on the plants and they always rewarded her undivided attention.

"Sorry, Lilly. I thought you'd heard me talking to Roddy out on the porch."

"Is he still trapped there?" Lilly said.

"What do you mean, trapped?" Ernie asked.

"He came over this morning and he mentioned that a few people had been stopping at the gate. He didn't want to leave the house and become part of a social media post, so he thought he'd wait it out and read the paper."

"He's going to have to wait awhile. There was a gaggle at the gate. I let myself in with the code, and then waited at the end of the driveway to make sure no one snuck in."

"Honestly. Don't people have better things to do?"

"Obviously not," Ernie said. "Though on a beautiful day like today, you'd think people would take advantage."

"You'd think," Lilly said. "I am. Finishing up cutting back some of the plants."

"They look good," Ernie said, walking through the garden path and looking at the bushes. "What are you up to over there?"

"I'm tilling the edges near the garden wall. Now that Roddy's ivy situation is under control, I need to clean up the edges of the garden and make sure that errant leftover ivy roots don't grow back. Roddy's still fighting the good fight on his side of the wall."

"I wish that the key worked on his side of the garden door," Ernie said. Ernie had sent a locksmith over in August, and after a very long day the key to fit both sides of the garden gate was cut. The lock turned, but they realized that a secondary locking system had been installed on Roddy's side of the fence. Three iron bars were fastened to the bottom of the door. At first they seemed decorative. On closer inspection, the bars seemed to be anchored underneath the heavy granite footing. Since the door swung towards Roddy's house, it couldn't open even though it was unlocked.

The story that went with the door had always been that the sea captain who built Lilly's house had built the house next door for his beloved daughter when she got married. The garden gate was keyed on both sides. The daughter and her father had a falling-out and the daughter had returned her key to her father. With the discovery of the bars through the bottom of the door, Lilly had begun to wonder about the veracity of that story. Had the daughter returned the key, or had her husband barred her in?

Delia had added the story to her "what are the facts" research list. It was an ever-growing, but neatly ordered task list that Delia kept working on during her free time. These days that was never, but hopes were that winter break would yield her opportunities.

"Having the garden gate open would make our lives easier if people are going to camp out at the end of the driveway. Hopefully, they'll find better things to do soon. Come over here, Ernie. What would you suggest I do with this corner? Nothing seems to grow here."

"It's so odd. Usually hostas would flourish in a spot like this. Do you think something is eating them?"

"But why here? We do have nibblers, but nothing down to the roots like over here."

"Let's test the soil," Ernie said. "Maybe there's something we should—"

"You won't believe what happened," Delia said, bursting out the door and running down the steps. Roddy followed her, several paces behind.

"Good heavens, there's a lot of drama bursting out of this back door today," Lilly said, dramatically putting her hand over her heart.

"Sorry, Lilly, I know you hate that. But I had to show you this." Delia scrolled on her phone and handed it to Lilly. "Hit *play*," she instructed.

Lilly did as she was told, with Ernie looking over her shoulder.

Lilly watched in horror as Mary Mancini stood screaming at the camera. "Don't do it Tyler, I'm begging you."

"Mary, it's my job. We've talked about this."

"Screw your job. Screw you," she shouted.

"Now Mary, is that a nice thing to say?"

"I swear to—I'm going to kill you if you publish that story."

Tyler laughed. Mary turned around and slipped on the wet leaves, falling on one knee. Tyler laughed harder and turned the camera back to himself.

"Folks, stay tuned. I'll be updating the Mary Mancini story in the next couple of days." Tyler paused and looked like he was ending the video. A faint beep came up, and Tyler looked at the screen. "You again? What do you want now?" he said as the screen went black.

"What was that?" Lilly asked.

"This posted to his stories about twelve hours ago."

"Which means?" Lilly asked.

"Stories disappear in twenty-four hours. He probably was posting it yesterday, but it didn't finish because his phone interrupted it for some reason. Maybe it was shut off before the video was done processing."

"Tyler's been dead for longer than twenty-four hours," Lilly said. "How did this appear? How did you miss it?"

Delia looked annoyed at the question, but she held her composure. "I hadn't checked Tyler's feed. Too many condolence posts. Apparently this showed up at some point in the middle of the night. Which likely means that someone turned his phone on."

"Were they able to locate the phone when it was turned on?"

Delia shook her head. "I tried to take a movie of the post and I called Bash and told him about it. He didn't sound surprised, so he must have already seen it."

"It doesn't look good for Mary, does it?" Ernie asked.

"It doesn't," Lilly said. "Is she working today?"

"It's Sunday. We're closed on Sundays this time of year," Ernie reminded Lilly. Closing was her suggestion, to give Ernie a much-needed day off. He still felt guilty about it.

"Good thing. Poor Mary. She doesn't need this sort of attention," Lilly said.

"Indeed she doesn't," Ernie said, taking his phone out of his pocket. "I'm going to give her a call and a heads-up."

"I can't believe we're having another meeting about this open house," Lilly said a while later. She poured herself some more tea and lifted the pot toward Roddy, who shook his head.

"We're all here, so I want to make sure that the order is complete," Ernie said. "You are, after all, a major stop on the Halloween stroll."

"Oh lord," Lilly said. "What does that mean, major stop?"

"Between you and Roddy, you have a lot of yard, so there's going to be a cookie and cider stop and a mini–haunted house."

"Do Delia and I have to make the cookies?" Lilly asked. She hated that she sounded so churlish, but honestly, this whole event was her nightmare. Lilly Jayne liked her privacy.

"No, Roddy's in charge of the cookies," Ernie said. "Don't look so panicked, Roddy, Stan is ordering them. You only have to make sure you stay stocked up. Are you going to have help over at your house?"

"I'm hoping my daughter and her family will join me, but they haven't confirmed," Roddy said.

"Maybe if you call her and tell her you need her help she'll be more likely to come," Delia said. "People tend to rise to the occasion when they're needed."

"I'll call her this afternoon," Roddy said, smiling at Delia.

"So, we're going to have a haunted house. What exactly does that mean?" Lilly asked.

Delia sighed and looked down at her phone. Ernie looked at both women and gave Lilly an icy stare.

"You know this is supposed to be fun, right, Lilly? The stroll is to get folks to walk through the historic district. To feel welcome there," Ernie said. "Portia Asher's thrilled. She and her grandson have some sort of plan in place—they're not telling anyone what it is. But if she could fit a haunted house on her front yard, she'd do it."

Lilly wasn't swayed by Ernie's rebuke. She knew

she was fortunate. But even so, entertaining the town of Goosebush on her front lawn was not her idea of fun. She did console herself that the activity would help aerate the lawn.

A light by the back door flashed. Someone was ringing the front doorbell. Lilly stood up.

"I'll go answer. You all know me well enough. This isn't in my comfort zone, as Delia would say. But I'll be a good sport. Tell me what to wear, what to do, and when. I'll make an attitude adjustment."

"That's good to hear," Ernie said. "Delia, put the green makeup back on the shopping list."

CHAPTER 9

"Ray, what a nice surprise, come in," Lilly said. She stepped aside to let him pass, and noticed that there were still a few people hanging out by the gate to her driveway. Up until today Lilly had been considering taking the gate down next summer. It both closed off her driveway and the wrought iron fence that ran along both sides meant intruders could get no further than the front yard, but it also looked foreboding. Lilly decided on the spot that the gate and the fence were both staying put.

"Where did you park?" she asked.

"Across the street at the boatyard," Ray said. "Seems that a few other folks parked there too."

"Lookie-loos. That Tyler story did me no favors," Lilly said.

"It didn't do many of us favors. I was wondering if you had a few minutes to talk."

"Of course. Would you like a cup of tea?"

"I'm fine, thanks."

"Well then, why don't we go into the living room," Lilly said, walking to her left and opening the door.

Ray walked in and Lilly followed, closing the door behind her.

Ray settled into one of the club chairs and Lilly sat on the sofa. Though her house was grand, it was decorated for comfort, and she leaned back into the pillows. She noted that Ray sat on the edge of his seat.

"Have you seen that video of Mary?" he asked.

"The one of her on the path, with Tyler?" Lilly asked. Ray nodded his head. "Delia showed me a short while ago. Ernie called Mary to make sure she knew about it."

"Did she?" Ray asked.

"She did," Lilly said. "She told Ernie she's already talked to Bash about it."

"I didn't realize he'd brought her in," Ray said.

"Isn't she staying with you?" Lilly asked.

"She is, but I've been gone most of the day. Following up."

"Following up on what?" Lilly asked.

"The crime scene. Retracing Mary's steps."

"What made you do that?"

"I saw the video about six-thirty this morning. Hustled out as soon as I did. Best if I know what Mary's up against, evidence-wise. That's why I'm here. I'd like you to keep you ears open, use that intuition of yours. Anything you hear, or see, let me know."

"Ray, I'm not sure what you're asking," Lilly said. "I only met Tyler a couple of times. Bash seems to have it all under control as far as the investigation goes."

"That's what I'm afraid of," Ray said. "That he'll settle for the likeliest suspect."

"And you're afraid that will be Mary," Lilly said.

Ray didn't speak, but he nodded. He stood up and walked over to the fireplace on the opposite wall from the sofa. He turned and fidgeted with one of the small sculptures on the mantle.

"She's been through hell these past couple of years," Ray said. "No one could blame her if she snapped—"

"Ray Mancini, you don't mean to tell me that you think your daughter did that, do you? Come back here and sit down."

Ray did as he was told. Once he sat, he slumped forward and put his head in his hands.

"I hate to think it—"

"Then don't," Lilly said. "I don't know Mary well, not anymore, but I can't believe she'd hurt Tyler."

"She threatened him."

"It sounds like he pushed some buttons," Lilly said. "I doubt she meant what she said verbatim. Do you know what their conversation was about?"

"No, I don't. When she came home she took a shower and went to work at the Triple B. She got home late and went straight to her room."

"When you saw the video, you didn't think to ask her about it before jumping to conclusions?"

"I'm sure she didn't mean to do it," Ray said. He looked up at Lilly with bloodshot eyes.

"Ray, Ernie doesn't believe for a minute that she did it. He's worried about people thinking she did, though. You're her father, for heaven's sake. Default to believing her."

"When I was the chief of police, I got so sick of parents who insisted their children were innocents when I'd caught then red-handed. Seems a bit hypocritical for me to start being one of them now."

"Mary's not some teenager; she's a grown woman

who's putting her life back together. For whatever reason, Tyler was making her life miserable. Seems like you should be more worried about that."

"Lilly, you don't understand—"

"What don't I understand, Ray? That Mary deserves the benefit of the doubt? Especially from her father? Go home and talk to your daughter. Listen to her. Believe her."

"But what if—"

"Ray." Lilly gave him a look.

Ray sighed. "No, you're right. I will. But I need you to promise me you'll keep your ears open for any evidence that would help Mary, even if it's in the court of public opinion."

"I will, even if it's just to prove you wrong. But a word to the wise, my friend. Don't mention your concerns about Mary to Meg."

Ray nodded and stood up to leave. He leaned over and gave Lilly a kiss on her cheek. She stood and gave him a brief hug, and then walked him to the front door.

Lilly was walking back out to the porch when she felt her phone buzz in her pocket. She put on her reading glasses and took it out. A text from Tamara:

Call me when you get a minute.

Lilly took a right and went into the kitchen. She turned on the electric kettle and spooned some tea into a pot. There was a time, not long ago, when people called each other. Nowadays they made an appointment to talk. Lilly was on the fence about that. On the one hand, it was an extra step. On the other hand, it gave her time to prepare for calls.

Lilly hit number two on her keypad and held it down to engage the speed dial. Tamara picked up right away.

"Next time I tell you I'm going to move, tie me down until the feeling passes, okay?" Tamara said.

"Considering you haven't moved in over thirty years, and assuming the next time you want to move is thirty years from now, it's a deal. Of course, we'll both be ninety-five by then, so I'm not sure I'll be up to tackling you to tie you down."

Tamara laughed and Lilly went on. "What are you doing? Do you need help?"

"I'm over at Harmon's house, measuring rooms and waiting for the painting contractor to come by," Tamara said. Tamara and Warwick had bought Harmon Dane's house after he passed away in August. It had a beautiful water view and was one of three identical houses that were built on Shipyard Lane a hundred years ago. The houses were large with porches that ran along three sides. Harmon's house didn't need a lot of work, but it needed enough that the move-in had been delayed for a few weeks.

"I thought you'd be packing," Lilly said. She knew that Tamara was going to have a broker's open house this week, and planned to put her current house on the market at the beginning of November.

"I hired that company you recommended to help," Tamara said. Lilly had heard about a company that helped people with moves. They brought people in to help sort, pack, and price anything people wanted to sell. Though the new house was larger than their current house, Tamara had been overwhelmed with all of the furniture, household goods, and paper that she'd inherited from her parents and Warwick had inherited from his. "The kids are over there now, going through the things we don't want to bring, claiming them for their own."

"Is Tyrone here?" Lilly asked. She hoped so. She hadn't seen her godson for months.

"No, he couldn't get away for the weekend. The girls are doing a video chat with him, walking him through the house."

Lilly didn't mention that the girls, Tamara's three daughters from her first marriage, were all well into their thirties. Lilly loved all of Tamara's children and grandchildren, and felt blessed to have them all in her life. If she'd known the girls were going to be at the house, she might have invited herself over. But she'd see them all this weekend.

"When will Tyrone be back? I miss him," Lilly said.

"He'll be home for Thanksgiving," Tamara said. "Hopefully we'll have sold our house by then and we'll be all moved in."

"I'm sure you will be," Lilly said.

"The only way this is being done is if and when Warwick and I stay on task. That's why I'm calling you. He has a game today—"

"Football?" Lilly said.

"No, that was yesterday afternoon. Today is lacrosse." Warwick was the head coach at the high school. Through Thanksgiving he was busy most weekends. "I'm supposed to go to the elementary school to meet some volunteers. Everyone did a great job cleaning up the check-in area yesterday, but because of the police investigation not everything got done. Tomorrow another set of volunteers are going down to get the stone fence set up.

Today another group is coming to lay down the hay bales."

"Lay down the hay bales?"

"The ones they're using to help frame out where the garden will go. I'll send you the details. I said I'd stop by to make sure everything is moving along, but the painter had to postpone and I don't want to reschedule. Could you go down for me?"

"Sure, I guess," Lilly said. She overheard Ernie and Roddy laughing out on the porch. Were they still working on the plans for the haunted house? Lilly shuddered. "It would do me good to get out of the house for a bit."

"Portia Asher is coordinating the volunteers tomorrow, so I want to make sure that everything is ready to go for her."

"Understood," Lilly said. Portia was twenty years older than Lilly and Tamara were, and was a formidable and opinionated member of the Beautification Committee. Heaven help everyone if the site wasn't up to par. Lilly put her phone on speaker and sorted through emails to find out the schedule for the work being done at the elementary school. She looked at the dates and nodded her head. Tomorrow was the stone wall building, and several classrooms of students were coming out to help as part of a field trip. One of the math teachers had devised a lesson plan about the process in order to make sure there was an educational component.

"The group of volunteers are meeting there at three."

"Got it," Lilly said. She took her phone off speaker and held it back to her ear again. "There's so much going on, it's hard to remember what's happening when," Lilly said.

"The Fall Festival has a lot of moving parts," Tamara said. "Tyler's death has thrown another layer into the mix, for sure. Speaking of which, have you heard anything?"

Lilly told Tamara about the social media post with Mary and Tyler.

"Wow. I wonder if Bash was able to track the phone?" Tamara said.

"I don't know," Lilly said. "Delia seemed to think not, since the phone was turned off again when she checked in with Scottie."

"Cookies are always a good way to get in to see Bash. Maybe you could bring him some, get him to talk. Whoops, sorry, have to go. The painter's here. Thanks, Lilly."

Tamara disconnected the call. Lilly took the tins of cookies down and laid them on the kitchen table. Delia tended to bake when she needed to think, so there were always fresh cookies at Windward. She put some on a plate and walked out to the back porch.

Lilly arrived at the elementary school site at 2:30. She'd left Delia, Roddy, and Ernie sitting on the back porch discussing how much dry ice they'd need to order. Dry ice? Lilly shook her head. She'd agreed to wear a witch's hat. The rest of the planning was on them.

She buttoned up her car coat and pulled on a pair of gloves. She resisted layering her clothes for as long as possible, but the cold wind cut through the light wool. She opened the back door and rifled through a bag in the back, coming up with a large cotton scarf that was covered in pink roses of various shades. Lilly didn't love the pattern, which is why it was in the car, but she did love the size. Despite the fact it clashed with her dress, it was large enough to do the job she needed it to do. She unbuttoned her coat again, wrapped the scarf around her neck, and buttoned it back up. Much better.

Lilly put her phone and a notebook in one pocket, her keys and a pen in the other. She walked over to the lot. The space in question was between two buildings: the elementary school and the library. It was a fairly large lot that went back quite a distance. The school had built a fence to keep the students from wandering, which helped with the delineation of the space. For years it had been owned by the town, but it was no-man's-land. Too small to build on, too large to leave empty, especially in that part of town. Recently a movement had been created to make the space into a community garden, but people were slow to respond to the idea. For now, an agreement had been made to create a wall around the space to let people get a sense of the size, and to mark out what the garden might look like.

The 10K check-in had been there, but you wouldn't know it. The site looked a bit trampled, but no trash or other debris from the day before was evident. For several weeks people had been clearing the field of stones and they were all piled to one side. Lilly also noted several bales of hay piled up near the stones. She took out her phone and tried to remember how to access the drawings of the site that Delia had uploaded to a shared drive.

"Hey, Ms. Jayne," someone shouted. Lilly stopped scrolling and looked up. She hated "hey" as a salutation. She could hear her mother now—"hay is for horses, Lilly, not for young girls. *Hello* is adequate, *hi* if you must." Lilly refrained from saying that aloud to anyone, but she always thought it.

"Hello, Nicole," Lilly said as Nicole Shaw jogged closer to her. "Please, call me Lilly."

The younger woman smiled and nodded. Lilly knew she wouldn't call her Lilly—they'd had the same conversation several times. Nicole had only recently moved to Goosebush and was still trying to impress people around town. Warwick spoke highly of her, which was more than enough for Lilly.

"Lord, but it's cold out here," Nicole said. "I was doing a lap and saw you."

"A lap?"

"I'm training for a half-marathon. I do laps around the parking lots and out by the fields here on the weekend. Not too many cars, some interesting hills. A beautiful place to run." Nicole took a swig of her water bottle and then she wiped the perspiration from her brow.

"Running a half-marathon is something I've never done. And, at this point in my life, I probably never will," Lilly said. "The training must be arduous."

"Never say never," Nicole said. "I've got to warn you; I convert folks into running fanatics. Running is a great way to get your mind off your troubles. Though your running season is short up here in Massachusetts, so you couldn't start training till next spring if you wanted to run outside."

"Darn," Lilly said. She dug her hands into her pockets. "Your running sounds like my gardening. Working outside keeps my mind occupied. I don't mind fall, but I don't love winter because it keeps me indoors."

"I'll have to get used to that," Nicole said. "I've never had a New England winter. Where I'm from, anything below sixty is freezing."

"Where are you from again?" Lilly asked.

"Texas. Born and raised."

"I have been to Texas a few times, but never for long."

"Texas is like its own country in some ways, it's so big. I love it, but I was ready for a new adventure. That's why I jumped at the chance to come up here and work with Warwick on his coaching staff." Nicole bounced from one foot to the other, and ran her hands up and down her arms to warm up.

"Any regrets, except for the cold?" Lilly asked. She smiled. Poor Nicole; if she thought today was cold she'd be miserable in February.

A shadow went across Nicole's face, but she shook it off. "I miss my family. And I miss the food, though Warwick tells me he makes a mean barbecue."

"He does," Lilly said. "It takes him hours, but it's worth the wait."

"He says that once football season is over he'll plan one. Though won't it be too cold by then?"

"Warwick barbecues and grills all year long," Lilly said. "I don't know how he bears the cold, but I'm grateful he does. He talked me into getting a grill for my backyard, and I benefit from his expertise, though I have little interest in learning how to do it myself. He has quite the ensemble he wears during snowstorms. I've learned something about barbecue. It's a great way to get people together for food and good conversation, since it takes a while. It's a lot of fun."

"Same as home. That's another thing I miss, good conversations with people I know."

Lilly took a deep breath. "Nicole, forgive me for overstepping, but I think you knew Tyler Crane, is that right? His death must be very upsetting for you."

"I didn't know him well. Oh my, are folks talking about me and Tyler?" Nicole's eyes got larger and Lilly noticed that tears were close to the surface.

"No, not at all. I saw you with him the other day. Outside the Star."

Nicole blushed. "The other day, as in the day I kicked his butt?"

"Yes, that day," Lilly said. "We spoke briefly when you walked by me afterwards."

Nicole sighed. "I honestly don't remember much after that public display. I was so embarrassed. It's probably all around town by now."

"I'm sure it isn't," Lilly lied.

"Well, serves me right. Lay down with the dogs and you get up with fleas, as my grandma used to say. I guess I may as well admit it. Tyler and I were seeing each other for a while, though I think I took that more seriously than he did."

"Oh my, I am sorry," Lilly said.

"What you witnessed was us breaking up," Nicole said. "For the fifth or sixth time. But that doesn't mean I'm not sad he's dead. Even if the man was a snake, no one deserves to be killed."

"No, they don't," Lilly said.

"Listen, I need to get moving again. My muscles are going to cramp up soon. It sure was nice to see you." Nicole bounced backward and then jogged—more like ran—away from Lilly.

Lilly checked her watch. She looked back at Nicole, but the young woman had disappeared from sight. Where had she gone? For that matter, where had she come from?

She turned on her phone and finally found the drawings for the site. She looked at the notes. She looked at the plan for the bales of hay to give the stone wall builders a sense of the size of the garden. Lilly walked closer to the boundaries and noticed chalk lines sprayed into the grass. Stakes had been hammered into the ground and there was string tied to each one, creating a border.

She hoped that someone showed up to help move the hay, since she wasn't about to do it herself. She knew she could always call Roddy, Ernie, and Delia to help, but she'd wait. She walked over to the hay bales to get a better sense of how big the project was. She saw three columns, each six bales high. As she walked along to the side, she saw that there were eight rows altogether. Eight times six times three: One hundred and forty-four bales of hay.

She walked back to the front of the lot, hoping that a volunteer or two had shown up. She looked to her right and saw a tarp covering a mound of materials on the side. Rocks were lined up along all four sides, save a corner that was flapping in the wind. Lilly lifted the corner and peered inside. She saw two stepladders piled on top of each other and a clear plastic case with string and a hammer visible. Tools. Good. They'd need them, especially the ladders. She lifted the tarp up a bit more and saw a large black knapsack. Was this part of the lost and found from yesterday? She pulled it out and almost unzipped it when she noticed the press badge pinned to it, next to the TC initials.

Lilly was curious, but she decided to wait to satisfy her curiosity. For the second day in a row, she called Bash Haywood.

CHAPTER 10

"Bash, I hope I didn't overstep letting the volunteers get to work," Lilly said. Bash and Lilly were talking while another officer took pictures and made notes about the scene. Bash offered suggestions on occasion and kept his eye on the progress.

"As long as no one touched anything over here," Bash said, turning back to Lilly. He tilted his head toward the other police officer. "That's Steph Polleys. She's new. I'd introduce you, but I don't want to throw her off. This is her first crime scene."

"She seems to be doing a very thorough job," Lilly said. So far the tarp hadn't been moved. "No one touched anything, I made sure of that. Of course, we needed the ladders, but then the Marks brothers showed up with their parents and they scrambled up to the top of the hay bales before anyone could stop them. They almost gave me a heart attack, but their father took it in stride. I suppose you have to when you have hellion children. Now Bash, don't look at me like that. Their own mother would tell you the same thing. Poor woman, those boys haven't given her a moment's peace since they started walking, and they haven't calmed down one iota. Anyway, they climbed up and tossed a few bales off the top. Pretty soon everyone got a system going once I showed them the drawings."

"I thought the great stone wall adventure started tomorrow?" Bash said.

"It does. But the Beautification Committee thought it would go faster if we set up a perimeter and laid hay bales on the inside so that the stones had something to lean up against if need be. Honestly, I don't know what the entire plan is. All I know is that Tamara asked me to come down and check on the work."

"And you were the first one here?"

"Well, yes and no."

"Meaning?" Bash said.

"I didn't see anyone when I parked and walked over here. But Nicole Shaw was out for a run and stopped to say hello."

"Nicole?" Did Lilly see a flush on Bash's cheeks when he said her name, or was that her imagination? "What direction did she come from; did you notice?"

"I'm sorry, I didn't. She says she runs all along here and she mentioned hills, so she must run behind the buildings as well. She went off to continue her run and I lost her again when I looked away. She must be pretty fast."

"She is," Bash said.

Lilly looked at him, eyebrows raised.

"We've gone running a couple of times," he said. "Down by the beach."

When Bash didn't continue, Lilly jumped in. He'd tell her what he wanted to tell her in his own time. Or she'd get him to tell her another time, but not standing in a field looking at Tyler Crane's knapsack.

"I'm surprised she had so much energy today," Lilly said. "Yesterday was her event. She must have been running all over the place, making sure things were going well. I would have taken the day off. Of course, I'm not a runner."

"Yesterday she wasn't officially competing," Bash said. "She never checked in here at the school."

"I saw her at the lumberyard," Lilly said. "I'm surprised she wasn't at the registration area."

"She was part of the race, but not running it. Stella was volunteering at the bridge, making sure runners stayed to the right when they went over it. She said she saw Nicole come in from a side street and join the crowd going over the bridge."

"That's odd," Lilly said.

"Not if she was near where Tyler's body was found, and needed to join the race in the middle," Bash said quietly.

Lilly glanced over at Bash, but he was watching Officer Polleys take pictures of the tarp from all angles. Lilly was going to offer to share the ones she'd taken while she was waiting for them, but she didn't think they'd appreciate the offer.

"I'm sure you could ask her to explain," Lilly said. "She really is a lovely person, though I don't know her well. Yes, I think the best thing to do is to ask her."

"Which I did. She said she was checking on some volunteers and took a shortcut back to the bridge."

"See? I'm sure the volunteers can corroborate her story."

"They weren't there. She did call that in, that the volunteers were missing. But no one can confirm timing."

"Bash, I don't want to cause any trouble for her, but you heard about the fight—"

"The fight she had with Tyler the other night? Out on the street?"

"Near the Star. It was quite a ruckus. I didn't hear what it was about, though."

"Steph, how much longer?" Bash asked the officer.

"Five minutes, is that all right?" she asked. She lowered the camera and ran her hands along her pant legs.

"Take all the time you need," Bash said. "I was just asking."

"Ms. Jayne, we're done." One of the Marks boys ran up to Lilly, a huge smile plastered on his face. Lilly turned around and saw several people standing in the middle of the lot, looking over at her.

"That looks terrific," she said. "Bash, if you'll excuse me."

Lilly walked over and a small group of volunteers walked with her around the lot. They all looked at the plans, and Lilly made notes on the adjustments they'd made to keep the hay bales intact while laying them out.

"Any idea what they're going to use these for once the walls are up?" one man asked. Lilly knew him, but his name didn't come to her.

"I suspect they'll be using them next weekend for the Fall Festival, and then I'm not sure. I'll find out. Send me an email to remind me to let you know," she said. She dug into her pocket and pulled out one of her calling cards. "I know I could use some for my gardens and I suspect other people would have a use for them as well."

"Sure would," he said, taking the card. "I appreciate it. Would hate to see them sit somewhere and rot."

"Oh, that won't happen," Lilly said. She smiled at the man and he nodded back. The New Englander in both of them connected. Frugality would not allow perfectly good things, like bales of hay, to go to waste.

"What time are they setting the concrete forms?" someone else asked.

"Concrete forms?" Lilly asked. "The ones behind the stone wall? I thought they were using concrete blocks?" Though stone walls looked nice, it had been decided that a two-foot concrete wall around the perimeter would survive the winter better, and would also make sure folks couldn't easily change their mind about the use of the space over the winter.

"They decided to use short forms instead. A more efficient way to build a concrete wall. They'll set them up and then the kids can work on the walls. They'll fill the forms later in the week. That way the wall will look good for next weekend."

"This is not my area of expertise," Lilly said. A few people laughed. "I know that several people are meeting here at six o'clock tomorrow morning. I'd imagine they'll be setting up the forms and getting the site ready for the students. Anyway, thank you all for coming by today. Many hands made light work, that's for sure. We still have a little sunlight. I hope you all enjoy the rest of the day, and I'm sure I'll see you this week or next weekend."

Lilly continued to make notes and chat with people while taking pictures of the hay bales and the string. She'd show them to Delia. If anything needed to be fixed, they'd need to come out early tomorrow to do it. Lilly should have been paying closer attention to what the volunteers were doing, but she'd been distracted. And she wasn't going to correct anyone's work in front of them, not after the effort they'd all put in.

"That's not another body, is it?"

Lilly turned to the person asking her the question. The woman was young, with layers of varying colored blondish-brown hair framing her face. Her big brown eyes were expertly made up, as was the rest of her face. Lilly noticed that she was not dressed for a lot of outdoor work, but she did have some straw stuck to her sweatshirt, so she must have been helping.

"No, not a body. Just some possible evidence the police wanted to look at."

"Whew, that's good," the woman said. "Sorry, I should have introduced myself. I'm Clara." She held out her hand to Lilly.

"Oh, hello, I'm Lilly," she said, taking Clara's hand.

"I know who you are. My father mentioned you," Clara said.

"Your father?"

"Alex Marsden."

"Oh, Alex is your father," Lilly said. Alex Marsden had lived in Goosebush for a short time, but he'd left quite a trail before he went to jail last summer. "I'd heard you moved into his house. I hope you're enjoying it."

Clara looked at Lilly and tilted her head. "You're the first person who didn't treat me like I have a plague because of who my father is. I appreciate that."

"I'm sorry that people aren't treating you well," Lilly said.

"Oh, they're not treating me badly. They pause whenever they say his name."

"Give people time," Lilly said.

"I will. Anyway, I hear you're the person I should talk to for gardening advice," Clara said. "I love my father, I really do, but he had terrible taste in wives, remodeling houses, and gardens. Have you seen the outside of his house?"

Lilly laughed. "Not recently. But it was rather plain, as I recall."

"*Plain* is one word for it. I'd love to jazz it up."

"Ernie Johnson is going to be your neighbor—"

"He bought the Preston house," Clara said.

"Right. He also owns Bits, Bolts and Bulbs and is an excellent gardener. We're going to walk through his gardens in the next couple of weeks. If you're home, why don't we walk through yours as well?"

"That would be great," Clara said. "I get over-whelmed thinking about it, but I need to step it up if I'm going to keep up with my neighbors."

"Here's my email," Lilly said, handing her a card. "Send me yours and we'll coordinate."

"Thanks, I look forward to it," Clara said. "It looks like they need you back at the tarp, so I'll be going. See you soon, and thanks again."

Lilly looked over at the tarp area, where Bash was frantically waving her over.

"What's wrong?" Lilly said, hurrying over.

"Do you know how to shut this thing off?" Bash asked. He had on blue evidence gloves and was holding a tablet out to her. Lilly looked closely and watched as the tablet had more and more notifications appear on the top line.

"What's it doing?" Lilly asked.

"I opened the cover and it came to life. The screen said *time's up!* and then boxes started opening and closing," Bash said. Officer Polleys was pale and standing off to the side.

"The tablet must be connected to the internet all the time," Lilly said. "That makes sense, I suppose. For a reporter, I mean. That way he could work anywhere. Close the cover again. That will probably do it."

Bash did as she suggested. They all stood for a few seconds, but of course the tablet wasn't going to tell them it was shut off. Lilly took out her phone and opened the apps Delia had shown her.

"Tyler's official work site doesn't seem to have any new stories," Lilly said. "Oh, wait. What's this?"

Lilly turned so that she and Bash were standing side by side. She pointed to the post that had appeared on Tyler's feed.

"Read it aloud," Bash said.

"'Small-town police forces are more like an extended family than anything else. That's why I didn't go to the police to get help. I didn't see the point. My friends, what would you do about this?'" Lilly hit the *play* button on the video below.

The video was of a wall, and then the camera lens was shifted so that Ray Mancini was visible walking toward it quickly.

"I'm going to say this once, and only once, Crane, so listen up. Come near me or mine again and I'll kill you. Do you understand? Don't laugh. Don't ever laugh at me. Cause the thing is, I could do it and I could get away with it. People know me in this town and we take care of our own. Remember that." With that, a hand swept to the side of the camera and then the lens tumbled around until it landed face up on the ground, lovely tin ceilings filling the frame.

"Oh dear," Lilly said. "I'm sure Ray didn't mean to—you know, I could probably erase that," Lilly said. "Or I could call Delia and she could walk me through it."

"Can't do that," Bash said. "Besides, it's on social media now. It's out there."

"Do you think this is how the story posted this morning?" Lilly said.

"Not sure. Looks like this posted on Facebook and then automatically posted on Instagram, so I doubt it. He may have scheduled the post, or my turning on the tablet did it. I suspect it's the latter. Looks like I have a long night in front of me," Bash said. "Thanks for your help, Lilly. You might as well head home."

"Okay, Bash, if that's what you want."

"It is."

"Well, then, I'll be going. Good night, Bash. Let me know what I can do to help. By the way—Officer Polleys, is it? I'm Lilly Jayne. It's very nice to meet you."

Once she was in the car, Lilly wished she'd brought a bag of cookies to Bash. No matter. She'd bring them to him tomorrow, after she'd talked to Delia.

Lilly was stopped, getting ready to turn out onto the main road when her phone rang. She looked behind her. No one was there, so she pulled her phone out and hit the speakerphone.

"Hello, Delia," she said. "You won't believe—"

"There was another post," Delia said quickly. "It was about Ray—"

"I saw it," Lilly said. "I was there when it posted, I think. Are you home? I'm on my way."

"I've been bicycling around where I found Luna, putting up signs, asking if folks know where she came from."

"Luna?"

"Yeah, that's what I'm calling the kitten. There was a full moon last night, did you notice?"

"I hadn't, but I'm not at all surprised. Luna is a lovely name. I thought you posted about finding her online."

"I did, but I thought I'd go old-school and put up some posters. Not everyone's on social media, Lilly."

"You don't say."

"I'll be home in a bit."

"Why don't I come and get you?" Lilly said.

"I went by to talk to Cole Bosworth," Delia said. She'd taken the front wheel off her bike so it could fit into the backseat of the Jeep.

"What about?" Lilly asked.

"To ask him if he knew anything about Luna," Delia said. She settled into the passenger seat and buckled up. "He didn't."

"That's all you went by to talk to him about?" Lilly asked.

Delia sighed. "I was going to talk to him about the bodies in Alden Park, but I didn't know how to bring it up. I thought I should wait until you were with me. You're good at bringing up awkward conversations naturally." Lilly laughed. "You know what I mean."

"I do. I can't help but wonder if Cole knows that the 'what makes a family' post Tyler teased may have been about him."

"I don't think so. He invited me to come back another time to look at the family documents he's been working on. Apparently, he has quite the collection."

"How did he get started researching his family?" Lilly asked.

"His father left him some documents and he's been doing his own research," Delia said. "I guess he and his father didn't get along too well, because Cole didn't really look at it until a dozen or so years ago, after his mother died."

"He moved to Goosebush about ten years ago," Lilly said.

"Exactly. He said that connecting with his family roots has become his reason for being. That's how he phrased it. His reason for being. How could I tell him he may not be a Howland after he put it that way?"

"I'm glad you didn't tell him," Lilly said, taking a left turn. "We should let Bash know first."

"I thought you were staying out of this." Delia said.

"It's getting complicated." Lilly told Delia about Ray's visit that morning and about opening the tablet, triggering the recent post on Tyler's feed. Delia took out her phone and looked at her social media channels.

"When did Bash turn on the tablet?" Delia asked.

"Around four thirty."

"Four thirty-seven?"

"Sounds right."

"Hmm. His turning the tablet on may have completed the post. What did you say the boxes said?"

"Time's up? Something like that. Bash would know. He thinks it posted to Facebook as part of what happened."

"I'd love to look at Tyler's setup and figure out what happened."

"Maybe we can offer your expertise to Bash." Lilly slowed down and turned her blinker on before she went in her driveway. She hit a button on her sun visor and the gate opened. She turned in the gate and noticed a figure run in behind her. She stopped short and put the car in *park*. She got out and turned around, prepared to berate the visitor.

"Oh Lilly, I need your help." Meg Mancini stepped toward Lilly, tears streaming down her face. Lilly leaned into the car.

"Delia, close the gate and park the car. I'm taking Meg inside."

CHAPTER 11

Lilly handed Meg a box of tissues and let her compose herself. She went over to the sink and filled a glass of water, handing it to Meg.

Delia came into the house through the back porch and Lilly heard her say hello to Luna. They both came into the kitchen.

"Oh, sorry," Delia said. "Do you want to be alone?"

"No, Delia, please stay," Meg said. She blew her nose gently and looked down at the kitten. "Who's this?"

"We're calling her Luna," Lilly said. "Delia found her yesterday. She may be lost, or someone dumped her. Anyway, we're taking care of her."

Meg reached down and the kitten put her head into Meg's palm and rubbed it.

"What's going on, Meg?" Lilly said.

"Bash called Ray and asked him to come down to the station," Meg said, pulling Luna into her lap. "He went, of course."

"You didn't go with him?" Lilly asked.

"No, I didn't. I was so angry with him I could barely contain myself."

"Why?" Delia asked. She was changing Luna's water.

"Our daughter Mary's been through it. Ray and I both feel guilty about not knowing how bad it was for her. Ray's way of coping is to be angry and threaten people. Including, apparently, Tyler Crane. Mary saw some post and got hysterical. That set Ray off and he and I started fighting. Then Bash called."

Lilly took her phone out of her pocket. She scrolled to the post and handed Meg the phone. "Push the *play* button," she said.

Meg did as she was told. And then hit the button again. And again. She finally looked up at Lilly, all color drained from her face.

"Oh no," Meg said. "You don't think—"

"Of course not," Lilly said. "What's wrong with you people, expecting the worst of each other? I do think we should go down to the station, though, don't you? Where are you parked?"

"At the Star. I was going to go there, but decided to take a walk to sort through my thoughts and ended up here."

"That's fine," Lilly said. "I'll drive."

"Let me feed Luna and I'll come with you," Delia said. "I want to ask Bash if he'll let me look at Tyler's computer, tablet, whatever."

Lilly, Delia, and Meg were asked to wait when they got to the police station, and wait they did. The officer at the front desk offered them tea or coffee, and they accepted the offer. They broke into the bag of cookies Lilly had brought for Bash, but Lilly was careful to leave a good number for him.

After forty-five minutes or so Ray wound his way through the sea of desks and walked out the gate to the front of the station.

"What are you all doing here?" he asked.

"Waiting for you," Meg said.

"Ready to bail you out if necessary," Lilly said.

"Not necessary. At least not yet," Ray said. "You saw that ridiculous post?"

"*Ridiculous* meaning your behavior?" Meg said. "Threatening someone like that. You should be ashamed."

"I am, Meg, I am. For many things," Ray said. He looked at Lilly and then back at his wife. "Yes, I was an idiot. Bash had some questions for me on the timing."

"Which was?" Lilly asked.

"What?"

"When did he make that video?" Lilly asked.

"Thursday night. At the Star. There were several witnesses, as it turns out. He texted me on Friday, warning me that he was going to post it, suggesting we talk."

"Did you? Talk?" Lilly asked.

"We'd planned to after the race on Saturday. We had a meeting set up for one o'clock."

"Which obviously you didn't keep," Lilly said.

"No one mentioned the fight before the post went up?" Delia said.

"It was hardly a fight," Ray said. "I didn't touch him."

"You only threatened him," Meg said.

"Meg, I didn't—"

"Ray, you have to get control of your temper. This isn't like you—"

"Meg, Ray, I suggest you both head home and discuss this there. Unless Bash wanted you to wait around?" Lilly said.

"No, I'm free to go," Ray said. He looked chagrined.

"I'll talk to you both tomorrow," Lilly said, more gently. "Meantime, Delia and I brought Bash some cookies."

"Bash, thank you for seeing us," Lilly said.

"Cookies were mentioned," Bash said.

"Indeed they were. Here you go," Lilly said. "There were more, but we ate some while we waited for Ray."

"Were you afraid I was going to throw him in jail?" Bash said.

"Meg came by and we offered to come down with her," Lilly said. "She was understandably upset."

"Sorry about my tone," Bash said. "Been a long day. These cookies are the first thing I've had to eat since breakfast."

"Oh, Bash, I wish I'd know that. I would have brought you some leftover quiche."

"Whenever you come visit me, bring me a picnic," Bash said. "I'm joking—these cookies are great."

"Bash, Lilly told me about the tablet posting when it was turned on. I can't figure out how that happened," Delia said.

"Neither can I," Bash said. "I'm going to send it over to a tech tomorrow to take a look."

"Or Delia could look at it," Lilly said.

"We really need to follow procedures on this one," Bash said. "Even if Tyler's ends up being an accidental death."

"Bash, I can disable the internet and take a look. You'll at least know what programs are running. Make sure nothing else is scheduled. That sort of thing."

"He could have scheduled a post to Facebook," Bash said.

"Except he didn't. His boss made me an administrator on the page. There weren't any scheduled posts," Delia said.

Bash took out a piece of paper. "Who else is an administrator on his accounts?"

"Technically they belong to his employer. Just Scottie and me."

"Could she have posted that?" Bash asked.

"She could have, I suppose. You should ask her."

"I did, a little while ago. She said she didn't do it. She sent me a link to his video storage and that video isn't in there, according to her. I've got my people going through it all."

"Anything in there besides videos?" Lilly asked.

"Documents. Files of his newspaper stories. Research. Most everything is at least three years old."

"From what I understand, Tyler used his phone for his videos. And for composing posts. But maybe he used his tablet too. We could see what's in his gallery and what other applications he has running," Delia said.

"And by doing so, you could post another story," Bash said.

"Yes, but I'm pretty quick. Once the internet is disabled we'll be good to go," Delia said. "I doubt your tech folks would be quicker."

Bash picked up a pen and tapped it on the desk. "You have five minutes while Lilly and I talk. Wear these gloves and use a stylus." He tossed a pair in front of her. Delia smiled and put on the gloves.

"All right, Lilly, tell me what you know." Bash took a bite of cookie and looked at her.

"Bash, I don't—"

"Lilly, the coroner was about to rule this an accidental death. Then that video went live. Now people want me to arrest Ray."

"Arrest Ray? Who would want that?" Lilly asked.

"Ray was a good cop. Maybe too good for some, if you know what I mean. He ticked more than a few people off in his career. They wouldn't be too sad to see him have to go to trial, even if he wasn't convicted."

"Based on a video?"

"And a hazy alibi. Yes. He'd probably get off, but his reputation would be ruined."

"Oh my," Lilly said. She knew how much Ray valued his reputation.

"It's pretty obvious that one of the five stories Tyler posted yesterday was about Mary. I'm thinking the 'what makes a family, blood or a name?' tease was about her."

"No, we think that was about Cole," Delia said, glancing up briefly. Seeing the look on Lilly's face, she went back to the tablet.

"Cole?" Bash asked.

Lilly sighed. "This story has a lot of conjecture, so keep that in mind." She told Bash about the Howland name and how Cole might not be in the bloodline.

"And you think Tyler knew?"

"Seems likely, but I'm not sure how."

"The other stories—" Bash said.

"All about families. 'He keeps the family secrets,' 'She shares a family name,' and 'She tells the family secrets' are three of them. The 'She keeps her dead relatives close' is me, but the picture of the gate made that clear. I still don't know how he found out."

"You may as well know: Someone told Nicole about the memorial garden and what it meant. Anyway, that's what Nicole and Tyler were fighting about. He told her he was working on a bigger story and needed your help, so he was going to use that as leverage. Not the first time Tyler did that sort of thing, as it turns out."

"Huh, what's this?" Delia said. She looked up at Bash and Lilly. "Tyler had a flair for the dramatic. That's probably what he used the tablet for. He could take it out and make a big production of using it. He could also pretend to by typing on it, and be taking videos. I found something on it interesting."

"What?" Bash asked.

"It's some sort of app Tyler could program. When the clock ran down, it could be programmed to publish a post or send an email, or do whatever he wanted it to do."

"I've never heard of such a thing," Lilly said.

"Neither have I," Bash said. "But it seems like a pretty good way to automate blackmail, don't you think?"

"What do you mean?" Lilly asked.

"I take a video of my tablet as I'm setting the timer. I tell whoever they've got X amount of time before the post is live, or the email is sent," Bash said.

"Or the story is posted," Delia said. "He had the app set up to interface with several programs. That's what all those notifications were."

"Let me make sure I understand this," Lilly said. "He used the tablet to blackmail people. And he was going to blackmail Ray with the video?"

"He did blackmail Ray with it. Ray showed me the text," Bash said.

"What did he say?"

"He said that he needed Ray to confirm a story for him, otherwise he'd post the video. Ray said they planned to meet yesterday at one."

"When the post didn't come up, Ray thought he was free and clear. What was the story?" Lilly asked.

"Ray says he didn't know," Bash said. He closed his eyes and rolled his head back and forth.

"We have to find Tyler's phone," Delia said. "I can keep looking at his online files, but I think the answer is in the phone."

"Yes, we have to find the phone," Bash said. "And hope it doesn't tie the noose around Ray's neck any tighter. Now, Delia, show me what you've figured out."

Lilly watched Delia walk through the applications on the tablet with Bash.

If one of the stories was about her, and one was about Cole, and one of them was about Mary, who were the other two stories about? What did they mean? What would people do to prevent them from being told? Lilly took her phone out and typed in some notes.

CHAPTER 12

The next morning, Lilly was waiting for the coffee to be done brewing when she heard a knock on the door. Three short knocks, a pause and then two more. Ernie's knock.

Lilly walked over and opened the kitchen door. She had never been, would never be, one to shout "come in!" to someone, even though the door was unlocked.

"Good morning, Ernie," she said.

Ernie came into the room carrying two bags in one hand and a large box in the other.

"Good morning, Lilly. I came by to bring some gifts for the kitten."

"Luna."

"Luna. Great name. I assume this means you're keeping her?"

"Delia put signs up yesterday. If no one comes forward, yes, we're keeping her."

"Good. Cats are good company."

"Cats *are* good company," Delia said. She walked into the kitchen with her bag in one hand, cradling the kitten in the other. "Even when she dances on your head at the first sign of light."

"Perhaps you shouldn't let her sleep with you," Lilly said. Both Ernie and Delia turned and stared at her. "If she keeps you up."

"She's a baby, Lilly. She shouldn't have to sleep alone." Delia put the kitten down on the floor.

"Come see what I brought for you, Luna," Ernie said. He began to unpack the bags he brought: a cat bed, a cardboard scratching box, toys. Luna's bounty was plentiful.

"What's in the box?" Delia asked.

"A kitty condo."

"A kitty what?" Lilly asked.

"A two-level contraption that cats can climb on, scratch, and make their own. I got a small one for her since she's a kitten. Theoretically, it will stop her from clawing your furniture."

"Clawing my furniture. I'd forgotten about that. We'll need to get some double-stick tape to put on it. My mother always did that and it seemed to work."

"Good idea," Delia said. She sat down on the floor and took Luna's gifts out and showed each one to the kitten. Luna preferred batting the packaging around.

"Lil, I didn't just come by to give Luna her gifts. I have a favor to ask. Two favors. First, can you spare a cup of coffee?"

"Always," Lilly said. She put three mugs on the table and took the cream out of the refrigerator. She sat down and took one of the scones out of the tin Delia had opened. Ginger lemon. Yum.

Ernie took a sip of coffee. "Delicious. Now for the second favor." He took one of the scones that

Lilly offered him and broke off a small bite. "Lilly, I'm wondering if you'd come down to the beach with me. I'm doing a walk-through with some people to talk about the performance space we're planning, and I need you to hold me back from choking Delores."

Lilly laughed. While she couldn't imagine her friend being violent, if anyone could push him to the edge it was the artistic director of the Goosebush Players, Delores Stevens. Delores lived a heightened life when she wasn't at work at the local bank, and drama oozed out of her pores. She was what Lilly's mother used to call a difficult personality.

"I'll go with you," Lilly said. "When's the walk-through?"

"Tomorrow. I'll text you the details. Thanks, Lil."

"I have a favor as well," Delia said.

"Take care of Luna while you go in to teach today," Lilly said.

"That goes without saying," Delia said. "I have a list of items I'd like you to get out of the Historical Society archives." She handed Lilly a piece of paper. The print was large enough that Lilly didn't need glasses. "Could you go down to the library and make two copies of them for me?"

"Two copies?"

"One for Bash," Delia said.

"What are the items?" Ernie said.

"I hope they will give context to the bodies in the park," Delia said. "I've been trying to find letters, diaries, anything from around the time we think the bodies were put in the park."

"To see if you find any clues. That's smart." Ernie looked down at his watch. "Sorry, I'd love to hear more but I need to get into work and open up."

"Is Mary going to be there today?" Lilly asked.

"That's the plan," Ernie said. "She's got guts, I've got to give her that. I'm going to offer to let her work in the office today, so she doesn't have to talk to folks, but I doubt she'll take me up on that."

"I may stop by later to say hello to her," Lilly said.

"Come by for lunch," Ernie said. "Catch me up on what you've been working on."

"I will if I can," Lilly said. "First I'm going to go by the elementary school and see how the stone walls are coming along."

Lilly parked at the library and walked down the hill. The hay bales were still in place, but an outer layer of activity had been added. The forms had been placed in front of the bales of hay. The stone walls were being built in front of the forms. Theoretically, the stone walls were supposed to be free-standing, but that wasn't working particularly well. Lilly smiled. The different classes were working on different parts of the wall, so the quality was varied.

"What do you think?" Portia said, walking toward Lilly.

"It looks a bit chaotic," Lilly said.

"A bit?" Portia laughed. "I was freaking out about it at first. My grandson's description, not mine. But the kids are getting the hang of it. And we have a crew coming in after school to gussy it up while the concrete is poured."

"Having the concrete walls in place makes the stone walls more decorative than structural," Lilly said. "That takes some of the pressure off."

"The stone walls make it look like it's always been here, or should have been. We can dismantle it all if need be, though I hope that doesn't happen. After the Fall Festival is over we'll get the soil ready for planting. We've got your recipe ready to go."

"That will make this a popular spot," Lilly said, laughing. Every gardener had their own winter mix that they used to get the ground ready for planting the following spring. Lilly's included seaweed, manure, compost, and salt hay. As long as there wasn't a cold snap the smell wasn't too bad. But it wasn't good either.

"Yeah, well, it will keep people from bothering it. And dogs won't use it as a dumping ground."

"Another good reason for the walls. Get everyone used to the space being used," Lilly said. "And discourage the dogs."

"Exactly," Portia said. "I heard there was some extra commotion here last night."

"Someone put Tyler's knapsack under the tarp with the ladders, so I called Bash."

"At least it wasn't another body," Portia said.

"Portia, that's a terrible thing to say."

"You've got to admit, we've had more than our share of sordid stories these past few months. Course, maybe it's that we know more about it."

"What do you mean?" Lilly asked.

"I was thinking about those bodies they found in Alden Park. Poor woman. Didn't they say she likely died from a blow to the head?"

Lilly nodded. "They aren't sure how the children died."

"A terrible story. And for how many years did her family think she ran away with her children? Or moved out of town and was never heard from again for whatever reason. Nobody knew any better. And nobody knew to miss her. How many other stories like that happened here? Folks who died under mysterious circumstances, but no one knew or cared enough to look into it. Family abuse that was ignored because it wasn't anyone's business, or so people thought. Chose to think. Minding their own business and looking the other way."

"Portia, where's all this coming from?" Lilly asked gently.

"My father was not a nice man," Portia said. "Our family was one of the oldest in Goosebush, so everyone ignored what was going on. This is going to sound terrible, but the best thing that happened to us all was the day he dropped dead from a heart attack. When I heard about those bodies in Alden Park? Let's just say, I wondered if under different circumstances that wouldn't have been my mother and me."

Lilly reached over and took Portia's hand. "That's terrible. I had no idea."

Portia gave Lilly's hand a squeeze and then let it go. "No one did," she said.

"You know, Portia, I've been thinking so much about who they were, I hadn't been thinking about how they lived. And died. You're right. We've normalized and glossed over so much over the years. I'm sorry you had a terrible time growing up."

"It all worked out. My mother got remarried, this time to a good man. I married a good man. Raised two good men and two good women. They raised good children. We broke the cycle. Been wondering if maybe Mary Mancini broke her own cycle by coming home, poor girl."

"I don't know—"

"The thing is, it shouldn't be Mary's shame. Good for Ray for calling Tyler out and protecting his family. That's what I say."

"I don't think that Ray did anything to Tyler," Lilly said.

"I don't either. But I admire people who stand up to bullies. Folks like Ray. And like you." Portia reached out and took Lilly's hand, giving it a squeeze. "Good seeing you, Lilly. I'm going to go and encourage those kids over there to think about straightening up their wall. Things are under control here. People are whispering about Ray. That needs to stop. Go and do what you do, my friend. Fix this."

Lilly waked around and talked to some of the students working on the wall. She was impressed by the concerted effort that was taking place, the attempts to make the wall work. Stone walls weren't easy, but everyone was getting the hang of it. More than a few people were disassembling in order to rebuild. Everyone was enjoying themselves.

"Hey, Ms. Jayne, how are you this morning?" Chase Asher stood up from where he was helping four students choose stones.

"Hello, Chase. Nice to see you again. What are you doing here?"

"My grandmother talked me into skipping school and helping out. I'm glad she did. This is a blast, but then I've always liked puzzles."

"Putting stones together is a puzzle," Lilly said.

"Want to give it a whirl?" Chase asked.

"Thanks, but my knees aren't up to it," Lilly said.

"It's so cool that teachers are letting students work on this as part of their school day. Art and math classes mostly, but I met a history teacher who is out here too."

"I suspect getting students outside for a couple of hours is good for them."

"Sure is. I went to a school that made me sit in a chair all day. I was doing terribly. My parents moved me to another school, where I could move around. It made all the difference."

"There are all sorts of ways to learn and to teach. To do any job, really. I'm glad you found one that worked for you. Obviously it worked out. Your grandmother talks about how well you're doing all the time."

"My grandmother loves me. No one loves me as much as she does. I could decide to mow golf courses as a career, and she'd think I was brilliant."

"Actually, that work takes a lot of expertise," Lilly said. "But I hear what you're saying. Unconditional love is a tonic, isn't it?"

"It is," Chase said. He and Lilly stood and watched the students for a few minutes in silence. "You know, I keep forgetting then remembering about Tyler. His being dead. It's pretty sad that no one seems that upset about it, don't you think?"

"It appears that you do, which speaks well of you. Yes, I think that when someone isn't missed, that is a sad thing. That's all we leave behind, really. The good opinions of others."

"Tyler was an interesting guy," Chase said. "But the good opinion of others was not his legacy. Not that he cared about that. What he wanted to do was to leave a legacy of good reporting."

"Is that what he called it?" Lilly said. "I'm sorry, that sounds harsh. But the last time I met him, he was threatening me unless I talked to him."

"Yeah, he did that a lot. He said it was the best way to get folks to talk when he was working on a story."

"What story was he working on?"

"There wasn't one, yet. He was convinced that if he rattled enough cages, a story would emerge. He did what he could to rattle people. Made sure they were important enough to have a story or two to tell."

"Did you tell him stories?" Lilly asked.

"No, I didn't know any. Even if I did, my grandmother would have killed me. Tyler tried to get her to talk, but she threw him out. Said she never trusted men like Tyler."

"I wonder who his charms worked on?" Lilly said.

Chase sighed. "My grandmother told me that if you asked me questions, I needed to be sure to answer them and not hold back. He mentioned that Fritz Stewart was a fount of information. And he dated Nicole Shaw, but she's new to town, so I don't know what she could have told him."

"Anyone else?"

"He said that Delores Stevens was more dramatic offstage than on. Do you know what that means? I sure don't."

Lilly smiled. She wondered if there was more to Delores than her affect, but she filed that question away. "Tell you what, Chase. If you remember anything else, give me a call. I'd love to know what Tyler was working on."

"And if that got him killed," Chase said, taking her card. He went back over to help a group of children shore up their wall.

Lilly slowly walked back up the hill toward the library. She was close to the front door when she saw Nicole Shaw coming out.

"Nicole, off for another run?" Lilly asked.

Nicole looked down at her running suit and laughed. "No, ma'am. This is what I wear to work. Came by the library during my free period to borrow some books." She lifted up the bag she was carrying. It was full.

"Light reading?" Lilly asked.

"Mysteries. Some romance. Nothing too heavy," Nicole said. "Now that the 10K is done, I'm free most evenings. Books fill the time."

"Books are wonderful companions," Lilly said. "But if you'd like other ways to fill your time, consider joining the Beautification Committee."

Nicole smiled. "I specialize in killing plants. Can't even keep a cactus alive."

"The Beautification Committee is about more than gardening," Lilly said. "We take on projects around town that need doing. That stone wall down there? That's one of our projects."

Nicole looked down the hill and smiled. "I could do that," she said.

"Looks a lot different than it did yesterday, doesn't it?" Lilly said.

"Sure does," Nicole said.

"Did you take a look yesterday, while you were taking your run? They'd staked out the outlines for the wall. They used chalk first, then stakes with string. I noticed the chalk on your sneakers and wondered if you'd taken a closer look."

Nicole paled and looked down at her running shoes. Lilly didn't see any chalk, of course. But she'd wanted to see if Nicole would react.

"I did take a look," she said. Nicole kept staring at the wall project down the hill.

"Nicole, did you leave anything at the site?" Lilly asked gently.

"What do you mean?"

"I've been thinking about the tarp yesterday. It was all tucked in, except on the end where I found Tyler's knapsack."

"You found Tyler's—"

"And the thing is, it was a windy day. Very windy. But the tarp hadn't lifted up. It was still covering everything. Whoever left the pack hadn't left it for long. Even an hour or more, and the tarp would have lifted up. Maybe even blown away. You were the only person I saw there, Nicole. I wonder, did you see anyone else?"

"The police asked me the same thing. No, I didn't."

"But you were in the area running, so surely you would have noticed someone else."

Nicole put the bag down and sighed. "Okay, you've got me. It was me."

"It was you, what?"

"I left the bag there."

Lilly nodded. "What happened on Saturday, Nicole?"

"I have no idea. Really. I was checking the route before the event started and I found Tyler's backpack thrown to the side, a couple of streets up from the bridge."

"You didn't call him to let him know?"

"No, I didn't. I looked inside and saw his tablet, a computer, some file folders. Thought it would do him good to panic for a while, so I hid it deeper in the woods. Then I heard about what happened."

"And it was your turn to panic."

"Yes, ma'am. I went back for it yesterday and decided to leave it where someone would find it."

"Was his phone in the pack?" Lilly asked.

"No. Far as I could tell, everything was in the
pack just as I left it."

"You realize you need to tell the police about
this, right? Let them know where you found it, and
when?"

Nicole wiped the tears that were rolling down
her cheeks. "Yes, ma'am. What a mess. You're right,
of course. I've been up half the night thinking
got away because of me. I didn't know what to do.
That's no excuse, I know that. I'll go talk to the
chief. Let me call Warwick first. He'll need to cover
my classes."

CHAPTER 13

Lilly offered to go with Nicole, but the younger woman refused. Lilly walked into the library and made her way down to the Historical Society.

The Goosebush Historical Society took up a corner of the library basement. While it made sense in a lot of ways, since the Historical Society kept supplemental records of Goosebush, the holdings of the society were overflowing. The society had come close to inheriting a house, but the property was tied up in probate and would be for a long time. So they made due with the space they had, creating floor-to-ceiling shelves and file cabinets with a system only the volunteers who ran the society understood.

The list that Delia had given Lilly had the titles of items with a series of numbers next to them. Lilly assumed they would indicate the location. Delia's long-term dream was to digitize the records in the Historical Society so that anyone could access them, but that work took time, people, and funding. Lilly had been helping her write a couple of grants to help with all three.

"Lilly, it's good to see you," Fritz Stewart said as Lilly walked into the Historical Society. "What brings you here?"

"Delia sent me down to pull a few items and to make copies. She's teaching today, so she couldn't come herself."

"They must be important, then. Did she send you down with a list?"

"She did," Lilly said, handing it to him.

Fritz smiled. "You know, it took me years to understand the filing system of this place. But I swear, Delia can locate items without having to look up the code."

"The code?" Lilly asked.

"Yes, see these numbers? The first six numbers are actually pairs. The first two are the time period. The second two indicate what it is. A newspaper clipping, a journal. That sort of thing. The third two indicate whether or not the record has been digitally archived yet. The rest of the numbers and letters have to do with the approximate location of the records. See how she gives me a few possibilities? Delia's usually right."

"Forgive me for saying so, but that doesn't seem very precise," Lilly said.

"It isn't. But we're working on it. Proper archiving and record-keeping. It's that it was a jumble for a number of years, when only a few volunteers worked here and ran it their way. Delia has strong opinions on how things should be done. She's winning me over. Let's see what she's looking for."

Lilly watched as Fritz went into a trance of sorts,

double-checking numbers with a big book on the desk. Working here both fed and frustrated Delia. It fed her in that the information held in the society was discounted from the official records. Letters, family Bibles, pictures, bits and pieces of lives that added to the complexity of people's stories. Delia liked making these stories part of the official record of the town.

It frustrated her because it was hodgepodge of record-keeping. "There's no system," Delia would say.

"Obviously there's a system, since people find things," Lilly would respond.

"There's no science to the system," Delia explained. "People make arbitrary decisions, and that's not how this is supposed to work. Things get lost all the time. It's frustrating."

"Lilly, this may take longer than we anticipated," Fritz said, coming back to the counter with a banker's box. "So far I haven't been able to locate the specific items Delia is requesting. What are they, anyway?"

"I'm not sure," Lilly said. "She called them articles."

"Perhaps from some periodicals of the day? That may take a while. I did find some issues of the *Goosebush Times*," Fritz said, pulling a binder out of the box.

"The *Goosebush Times*? What was that?"

"A ridiculous magazine of sorts. Created by one of the more eccentric citizens. Akin to that Goosebush gossip site that was active a few months back. I flipped through, but there are several issues missing that should be in the binder."

"Are there any other copies of it? Does the library have them?"

"Not of much value to anyone, really. I can't imagine what Delia wanted with them."

"May I see the other issues?" Lilly asked.

Fritz sighed and pushed the box of archive gloves toward Lilly. He handed her a large binder and she opened it. Each page of the *Goosebush Times* rested in a plastic sleeve. Lilly looked more closely.

"Do you mind if I read these?" Lilly said.

"Surely there are better uses of your time," Fritz said.

"Not really, no."

Fritz sighed again. "If you must. But I'm leaving in an hour, so you'll have to be done by then. Mind you, keep them in their sleeves. They are very delicate."

Lilly sat down at the table in the room. She took out her phone and texted Delia.

Fritz can't find the materials you're looking for. Any of them.

She carefully opened the binder and started to read the *Times.*

"You look done in," Ernie said. "And it's barely noon."

Lilly looked up at her friend and smiled. She was at the Triple B, back in the garden center, one of her favorite places on earth. She had taken it upon herself to refresh the displays of mums, pinch back a few plants, and do some misting. The smell of dirt always calmed her down.

"I had a frustrating morning at the Historical Society," she said. She bent over again to line up some more of the pots. "You know those periodicals Delia asked about?"

"You were going down to make copies?"

"They weren't there."

"Maybe they were misfiled?"

"*Periodical* is a loose term for these items. They were a sheet of paper, double-sided. The creation of an anonymous citizen of Goosebush. The *Goosebush Times.* Someone kept them all—they were only printed for few years—and donated them to the Historical Society."

"Maybe the collection got lost?"

"No, the collection was there, minus the issues Delia was looking for, and a few others. I spent an hour reading them. Quite the rag. The articles, three or four sentences each, had enough innuendo to put Tyler to shame."

Ernie laughed.

"Honestly, Ernie, I only read a few issues, but I'm wondering about the man of the cloth with a drinking problem, and whether or not he was the next victim of the thrice-widowed woman who lived by the beach."

"They sound wild," Ernie said.

"Fritz was disgusted that I was laughing as I was reading them. He wouldn't let me make copies of them, but I did take some pictures when he was distracted." She found one of the pictures and handed it to Ernie.

He put on his glasses and read for a couple of minutes. "Oh, you have to send these to me," he said, handing Lilly back her phone. "They're fascinating."

"Aren't they? Whoever published them was a

troublemaker," Lilly said. "Fritz said he'd keep looking."

"But?"

Lilly shook her head. "Not sure. Fritz seemed a little squirrelly about the whole thing. He couldn't look me in the eye. I didn't want to come home, so I came down here, even though it's early for lunch."

"We'll talk to Delia about it," Ernie said. "I've got something that will cheer you up. Come see the display over at Alden Park."

"The display? Oh, right, it's voting this week. I'd forgotten!"

"You must be the only one who has. Did I tell you about the brilliant plan Mary Mancini came up with for voting?"

"I thought voting was online?"

"Not fun enough. We set up the displays in Alden Park, so visitors could get a sense of them in situ. First people come over here and get a festival bag. It includes a list of the festivities for the week, a button, some other swag businesses have contributed. There's also a marble inside."

"A marble?"

"That's how folks vote. They go over, decide which display they like best, and then they come back over here and put a marble in one of those jars." Ernie gestured to a row of quart-sized mason jars that were painted different colors, with numbers on them and cards in front.

"Whoever gets the most marbles wins? That is fun," Lilly said. "How's it going so far?"

"We thought it would be slow, it being Monday and all, but we've had a steady stream of visitors. I've had to order more supplies for the festival bag. At this rate we'll run out by Wednesday."

"How do the drawings look?" Lilly asked.

"I still wish you'd done one," Ernie said.

"I have my own gardens to express myself with," Lilly said. "Other people need the opportunity. How many entries were there?"

"Twelve."

"Twelve? Wow, that's a lot."

"Take a walk with me and take a look. I'll even give you a marble."

"Sounds perfect."

Alden Park had been, at one point in Goose-bush's history, a gem in the center of town. It had fallen into disrepair over the past thirty years and was barely a shadow of its former self. Last spring a cleanup had been scheduled, but the discovery of Marilee Frank's body had derailed that. And then the discovery of the three other bodies had further complicated things. But finally the park was ready to be brought back, though the time lag had given people enough time to form opinions on how it should look, and for what purposes.

One thing that most people agreed on was that a decision had to be made in order to get some work done before the ground froze. And so the competition was announced. The rules were stringent, requiring an in-depth plan that worked within specific parameters. The decision would be announced on Saturday. The renderings were available online, of course, but Lilly liked the idea that people had to visit the park to weigh in. Still, she was surprised that so many people cared.

Lilly had visited Alden Park several times over the past few months, but not for a couple of weeks. She was impressed at the exhibition that had been set up in the meantime. Because it was an exhibition. Twelve easels set up around the park, each holding a large piece of plywood on which a rendering had been laminated. Lilly pulled on the corner of one of the easels. It wasn't going anywhere. The plywood had been screwed onto the easel and the frame was footed with some weights so it wouldn't move.

Paths had been cleared so that one had to move around the park in order to see all twelve boards. Enough of each board was visible that Lilly felt compelled to tour the park to see them all.

She and Ernie stopped and looked at the first two drawings.

"What do you think?" he asked.

"Not very good," Lilly said.

"Terrible, more like. This is what democracy looks like. We didn't prejudge any entries."

"They aren't terrible, they're not imaginative," Lilly said, moving on to the next board. "Though you have to hand it to this person who wants to make this a park for dogs only, with humans only able to visit as long as they stay on the edges."

"Yeah, the doggie watering fountains are fun. But Alden Park needs to be for two-legged animals as well."

They continued to walk. Lilly stopped by one drawing and smiled. "I love this one," she said.

"That's a favorite," Ernie said. "Miranda Dane's. But don't tell anyone I told you. The entries are supposed to be anonymous."

"Miranda? Really?" Lilly looked closer at the drawing, noting the herbs and flowers she'd included. "You do realize this is a poisonous garden, don't you?"

"What do you mean?" Ernie said.

Lilly pointed out the plants, naming them and indicating their toxicity. "You got some of these plants for Delia. This rendering shows them matured and in full bloom. It's a lovely plan, aesthetically. And of course, it could also be considered medicinal," she said.

"Yeah, I doubt the dog lovers will see if that way. Can we keep this between us for now? If she wins we'll need to discuss it, but I'd rather not open up this hornet's nest if we don't have to."

Lilly turned her head at the sound of two voices talking loudly a few feet away.

"Where did he come from?" Lilly asked. Cole Bosworth was standing two boards up from them.

"He or Fritz come here every day to see their drawing."

"They submitted an idea?"

"They did," Ernie said.

"What's it like?" Lilly asked.

"Oh, you'll have to see for yourself."

Lilly slowed down, hoping that she wouldn't have to talk to Cole, but he didn't move, so she and Ernie joined him.

"Lilly!" Cole said. "Good to see you. Tell me, what do you think?"

Lilly looked at the garden plot. It was pedestrian, at best. The main feature of the park was several statues. Lilly looked closer at the renderings of the statues.

"The most important citizens of Goosebush, all memorialized here in the park," Cole said.

"All white men," Lilly said, turning to Cole. "Not a terribly complete story. Our town has a much richer history than this." She pasted a smile on her face, but it wasn't sincere, and both she and Cole knew it. "I can't imagine the town would go for this particular selection."

"The statues can be reconsidered," Cole said. "Perhaps a statue of Catherine Howland is in order. She's an important part of Goosebush history. We'll have a lot more fun working on this project now that Tyler isn't around digging up dirt."

"Tyler's legacy continues, though," Lilly said. "He had some stories queued up to be posted on social media, and they're continuing."

"So there's more to come?"

"Looks like. Anyway, an interesting drawing, Cole. There are so many great drawings here. I'm going to continue the tour. Good to see you."

Lilly walked more quickly, attempting to put space between herself and Cole. She'd learned long ago to listen to people, even if she didn't like them, in case they had good ideas. Her patience with Cole and his myopic view of the world was wearing thin, though.

Lilly stopped at the purple number ten that also had a sailboat on the signage. Lilly looked around and realized each entry had a distinct marker. "Interesting. I just noticed this sign is purple."

"Each sign has a number, a color, and an image. Like modern parking garages. Different folks remember different things, so we wanted to make it easier."

Lilly stepped closer to look at the details of the drawing and a smile broke out on her face. "This is wonderful," she said. Indeed it was. A fountain was in the middle of the park. The center had a statue with water coming out of parts of it. But the drawing showed that there was a water feature built into the ground around the fountain, with bursts of water that would shoot up. Another part of the drawing showed a makeshift skating rink around the fountain during the winter.

"Isn't it?" Ernie said. "I love how alive it feels."

"Alive. That's a good word for it. I have no doubt people would make a point to come by and visit. Whose is this?"

"I'm not going to tell you until you've voted," Ernie said.

Lilly and Ernie walked by the two other boards. Lilly paused before she left the park and looked back.

"What a wonderful idea this was, Ernie," Lilly said. "Getting people to walk around and really see the park. It is so much bigger than people would expect."

"It is," Ernie said. "Though I'm hoping that folks also have a better sense of what's possible here after their tour."

"What do you mean?"

"The restaurant idea? And the huge concert venue? Neither one of them seem like they make a ton of sense, space-wise."

"No, I agree. Though maybe some compromises could be made to scale things appropriately. But my favorite remains the one with the central fountain. Number ten, that has my vote. Now tell me, who did it? I promise I won't tell anyone."

"Roddy."

"Roddy? Really?" Lilly said.

"Don't act so shocked," Ernie said. "Roddy is a man of many depths. I refrained from helping him too much with the plants and flowers, which is why they all look a little abstract. The fountain that turns into a skating rink is the central feature of the park."

"It's wonderful."

"Yeah, I think so too. Speaking of Roddy," Ernie said, pulling his phone out of his pocket to check the time. "I know I suggested we have lunch, but I'd forgotten I'm supposed to meet him for lunch in a few minutes."

"Don't let me keep you," Lilly said.

"Why don't you join us?"

Lilly smiled. "Don't mind if I do."

Ernie and Lilly walked back to the restaurant in the Star. *Star* stood for "Stan's Theater and Restaurant," though the building was much more than that. Lilly still couldn't get over the wonderful restoration Stan had done to her childhood haunt. While she remembered the old grill in the back of the Woolworth with great fondness, she had to admit that she liked the new restaurant better. So did most of Goosebush.

Roddy was sitting in a booth waiting for Ernie, and he smiled when he saw Lilly.

"What a nice surprise," Roddy said.

"I hope I'm not intruding," Lilly said. "This looks like a business lunch." She took note of the rolled-up plans and pad of paper sitting on one side of the booth.

"The business of getting my house finished and getting my gardens ready," Roddy said. "Ernie's been helping me keep track of the projects."

"With Delia," Ernie said.

"Ah, yes. Her software project. I'm afraid I'm a terrible test case for her. I change my mind constantly and don't update the spreadsheets."

"You're doing a pretty good job," Ernie said. "It's all a question of coordination."

"And knowing what to coordinate," Roddy said. "That's where I'm lost."

"It helps me as well. Since we all need plumbers, electricians, carpenters, roofers, and who knows what else, us coordinating with Warwick and Tamara keeps people employed and able to move from project to project with a plan in place. We've got a tight window to get work done. This seems more efficient than fighting over tradespeople."

"It does," Roddy said. "Plus, I'm learning a lot in the process. Between you and Tamara, you have a lot of strong opinions that are helping me form mine."

"Like what?" Lilly asked, smiling.

"Suffice it to say, the idea that I needed to make bold choices now was not lost on me. I was prepared to make do with a galley kitchen but the plans have changed. I'm able to get my dream kitchen, as you know since I've been peppering you with questions about yours."

"Giving you the kitchen you wanted only made sense, given everything else that was being done. And since you wanted to lose that wall, the galley kitchen could change."

"All good, all good. A lot of decisions, but thankfully, again, I am surrounded by people with excellent taste."

"Ernie, what do you mean you have a tight window?" Lilly said. "Your house just went on the market."

"I know. I thought it would take a while to sell my house, it being fall and all, but Tamara tells me I've got a couple of people interested."

"That's exciting," Lilly said.

"It is, but the new house isn't near ready. I've been clearing it out, but for every box of trash, there's a box of treasures. I have to clean out the attic because of the repairs that need to be done, so I'm trying to consolidate things into a few rooms, hoping that Delia will help me go through everything after I've moved in. Every contractor who's come into the house so far remarks on what a gem it is, then points out the seventeen things I need to fix. Right now the kitchen and bathrooms are both gutted, most of the walls have holes in them for new electrics, and I'm losing a battle with leaky windows."

"But you love it," Roddy said.

"I love the process. We—my husband and I—used to do this sort of work together," Ernie said. "I hadn't thought of rehabbing a house since Bob died, but I'd forgotten how much fun it is. Makes me miss him, of course. But I'm having a great time. Or I will, once I figure out what to do with the Preston family archives."

"What do you mean?" Lilly asked.

"Albert must have had a small family with a lot of history. There are pictures, paintings, christening gowns, recipe files. You name it. I can't bear to throw anything away. But Delia says the Historical Society can't take a donation for a while. So I'm trying to sort things."

Lilly felt her phone buzz in her pocket, but she ignored it. Ernie did the same when his beeped with a text. But when Lilly's phone rang, she decided to answer.

"Have you seen it?" Delia said.

"Seen what?" Lilly said. Both Ernie and Roddy

looked at her. She turned on her speakerphone, but lowered the volume.

"Look at Tyler's stories," Delia said. "I'm on my way home."

Lilly ended the call and then she went to her phone and pulled up the app. Ernie and Roddy were doing the same thing. The story Delia was talking about wasn't difficult to find.

The video was a loop of Mary Mancini turning and slipping on the leaves. There was a sound of laughter, and writing on the image: *I could watch this all day, but I have work to do.*

"What a jerk," Ernie said. "Poor Mary. Sorry Roddy, I'm going to have to take a rain check on lunch. I want to make sure she knows about this."

"I should probably call Ray," Lilly said.

"I'll do that too," Ernie said. "I'll also let him know I'm talking to Mary. You let Bash know."

"I will," Lilly said, taking out her phone and sending Bash a text. "Ernie, come over for dinner. Bring Mary if you'd like. You and Roddy can talk then."

"Sounds good," Ernie said, standing up and putting his phone in his pocket. "I'll call you later to see what you need me to bring."

Roddy looked up from his phone. "If someone could explain the value of these stories that disappear and you can't rewatch, I'd appreciate it. I wonder how long it would take to put that image together. Damnit, I can't get the story back."

"I think you can look at them again, but I don't know how. We probably all shouldn't have looked at it at once," Lilly said. "From what I understand, the purpose is to be like a quick whisper of a conversation. But I have trouble understanding the whole thing myself."

"I talked to my daughter about it earlier today," Roddy said.

"About Tyler's murder?"

"No, about the social media aspect of his work. She is a digital marketer, so she knows how all of this works."

"The apps?"

"That, and how the stories get posted. And if it's possible to postpone the postings, if you understand what I mean."

"To schedule them? That's what it looks like he did with the five family stories on Saturday."

"Scheduling is one thing. But I wanted to know if it was possible to schedule something, but then to have to manually do the posting anyway."

"I don't understand," Lilly said. She nodded at the waitress, who filled their water glasses, and she and Roddy both ordered soup and salad.

"Tyler seems to be playing games," Roddy said. "I've been looking at his posts and catching up on these story things. On several occasions, he'd tease a post, but I couldn't find it. But I did notice he'd post something substantial to his feed. I wondered: Might Tyler be the sort of person who would threaten to post a story, but offer to cancel the post if someone told him what he wanted to know? If he had to manually post he would have been able to make a case-by-case decision."

"I see. The only way he could do that, and not make a mistake, would be to have to approve the posts," Lilly said. "Is that possible to do?"

"According to Emma, yes it is," Roddy said. "There are several scheduling programs that would allow for that setting."

"Interesting," Lilly said. "It speaks more to how

Tyler operated than the mechanics themselves, don't you think?"

"I wonder if whoever has his phone is intentionally posting these stories to cause harm."

"Or if Tyler scheduled them and someone is posting them when they turn on his phone. Maybe they're looking for something else, or trying to divert attention."

"A story they're desperate to squelch, probably," Roddy said.

"The question is, did squelching a story make someone desperate enough to kill?"

CHAPTER 14

"This social media business is native to Delia and to my daughter, but I need to catch up on how all of this works. Stan seems to do a very good job of it," Roddy said.

"He does. I thought I understood, but the Tyler posts showing up after he was killed are throwing me off. I'll see you tonight for dinner," Lilly said. "Delia's on her way home and is going to stop by the market." Lilly left Roddy in the restaurant talking to Stan about social media.

Lilly stepped out onto the Wheel. Two doors down from the Star there was a new bakery and she went in. Honestly, since Delia stress-baked she didn't really need to shop for cookies and cakes, but she did like to support local businesses. When she walked in, a wave of vanilla and sugar washed over her. The lighting inside the store had brown tones and the interior decoration was dreamlike, with oversized chairs, signs in offset ornate gold frames, and art pieces not only on the walls, but floating in midair. Lilly couldn't help but smile.

"Afternoon, Lilly," the woman behind the counter said. Lilly looked up and blinked a few times.

"Hello, Kitty. You're looking well," Lilly said. Kitty Bouchard was looking well, actually. Her hair was a shade of soft pink not found it nature, but it suited her. She certainly looked happier than she had the last time Lilly had seen her. Of course, Kitty had just found out who had killed her friend Merilee Frank, so not looking her best was understandable.

Kitty Bouchard was not Lilly's favorite person. Kitty had been on the prowl for her next husband for a few years, and she'd left more than one marriage damaged. Lilly did not admire that behavior. Not in the least. While Lilly did not wish her ill, she did her best to avoid her. But avoiding her was out of the question now since the shop was empty. "Is this your store? It's lovely."

"Mine, with a couple of partners," Kitty said. "We've only been open a couple of weeks but—"

"Kitty, I need a dozen cupcakes, stat." A woman burst into the store along with a column of cold air. "Oh, I'm sorry. You were before me."

"I'm still deciding," Lilly said. She watched as Kitty gathered the cupcakes into a beautifully designed box, making the woman laugh as she took her credit card and charged her an obscene amount of money. The woman left and Kitty turned back to Lilly.

"One of our most loyal customers," Kitty said. "Happily she has four kids and a busy social schedule, so she comes in almost every day."

"If the cupcakes taste as good as they look, I can understand that," Lilly said. She was being sincere. The elegantly piped frosting and dusting of different colored glittery sugars was simple, but elegant.

"What flavor is that?" Lilly asked, pointing to the second row.

"That's our strawberry lemon surprise," Kitty said. She smiled and Lilly noticed that Kitty actually looked happy, a rarity for her.

"Part of what makes the cupcakes special is that we fill each one, and we also brush a flavored syrup. The cake itself is good, but the extra infusions of flavor help them stand out. Here, try this one. It's our mocha special." Kitty reached over and picked up a sample in a paper cup, handing it to Lilly.

Lilly smiled and nibbled. Then she ate the rest of the sample in one bite. She normally wasn't a cake person, but this was delicious. Moist chocolate cake with coffee cream in the center. The buttery frosting complemented it perfectly.

"Amazing flavor," Lilly said, nodding. "I'll take six cupcakes. An assortment. You choose them for me."

Kitty looked pleased as she fussed over the choices and carefully boxed the cupcakes. She put the box in a large brown paper bag that had the store logo on it. Lilly noticed a swoosh of gold on the bag and noticed the pile of bags, stamp pads, and gold pens behind the counter. Handcrafted bags. Another lovely touch. Lilly had to hand it to Kitty. The store was very well done.

Lilly paid for them and left, carefully carrying the bag with the dinner desserts.

She was walking by the jewelry store when someone burst out of the door and almost collided with Lilly.

"Oh my, I'm so sorry," Nicole Shaw said, blushing slightly. She looked down at Lilly's bag. "I hope your cupcakes survived."

"I'm sure they're fine," Lilly said. Actually, she wasn't, but Nicole looked so upset Lilly didn't want to make Nicole feel badly. "Are you all right?"

"Actually, no, ma'am, I'm not." Nicole blinked back tears and looked away.

Lilly reached over and gave Nicole's hand a squeeze. "Is there anything I can do?"

"No, there's nothing. Nothing anyone can do, unless you can transplant some man sense in me."

"Man sense?"

"I really thought he was different. But turns out he was like all the others."

"Tyler?" Lilly asked gently.

"Tyler. I had some jewelry I needed cleaned and repaired. Tyler offered to drop it off here for me. Turns out he didn't do it, even though he said he did."

"What do you mean? Do you think he stole them?" Lilly guided Nicole to the side of the store against the front window, out of earshot from people walking by.

"No. Maybe? No. I think he was probably investigating them. They were unique pieces."

"Investigating them? What do you mean?"

Nicole sighed. "The pieces were gifts. From my ex-fiancée. He's the real reason I came up here. The breakup wasn't good. It was his idea. He insisted I keep the jewelry he gave me. He'd designed them especially for me. He usually came up with something after we'd had a particularly awful fight. Recently I've been realizing I not only wouldn't wear any of it again, it was a reminder of a sad time in my life. I was sending them over to be cleaned and to get them appraised. Like I said, Tyler offered to take them in for me. But then he texted me a pic-ture of the open box and asked me where I got all of that loot. His term. He said he wanted to hear the story."

"What a jerk," Lilly said.

"That's a nice word for it," Nicole said. "I don't know when I'm ever going to learn not to trust men. He really threw me for a loop. I must have scared him a bit, the way I reacted, and he promised me he'd bring them in like I asked. Idiot that I am, I believed him. I hadn't had a chance to come by until today."

"Is that what you were arguing about the other day?" Lilly asked.

"That and other things," Nicole said. She looked away from Lilly and down to the ground. "He used me for all he was worth, then tossed me out like an old pair of socks once I stopped helping him."

"Helping him?" Lilly asked quietly.

"He'd asked me to look into some . . . some sto-ries he was writing. He figured I'd be better at get-ting information from folks, being new and all. I had no idea how he was going to use what I told him, though."

"What did he do—"

"He called it gathering information, but back home we called it blackmail, pure and simple. Well, not really simple. Let's leave it at that. I wasn't the only person who was getting him tidbits, but when he told me he was going to run a story about—"

"About what?"

"About you," Nicole said. "I'm so sorry. I heard the story about the memorials in your garden and told Tyler. That was my fault."

"Where did you hear the story?" Lilly asked quietly.

"Pete Frank. He and I were talking one day. I mentioned that my cat had passed away, and I wasn't sure what to do with the ashes. He told me about your gardens. I'm so, so sorry. He didn't mean anything by it. He really didn't. Me and my mouth, running on and on."

Pete Frank, back to complicate her life again. She had no doubt that he didn't mean any harm, but still.

"Don't worry about it, Nicole," Lilly said. "When Tyler said he wanted the story, what do you think he meant?"

"He collected stories and information. I was on to him, though. He figured out what caused people pain, and then pressed on that pain point until he got what he wanted. The morning he died, he sent me a text that said 'I'm thinking about posting a sparkly story later today. Call me.'"

"Did you call him?"

"I tried. He didn't answer."

"What time was that?" Lilly asked.

"Seven o'clock or a little afterwards. I was on my way out to make sure the checkpoints were all set up, otherwise I would have called him out in person."

"Then you found his backpack."

"Yes, a while later. I went by the path where the runners were going, and found his bike. I took the backpack out of the basket. Honestly, I was going to use that as leverage if I needed to. Hold it hostage until I got my jewelry back. You must think I'm terrible."

"Not at all," Lilly said. And she didn't, much to

her surprise. She found herself liking Nicole and wanting to help her. "You didn't see Tyler when you found his bike?"

"No, but he must have been there." Nicole ran her hands over her arms to warm up. "Under the leaves."

"Did you touch his camera?"

"I didn't see a camera. I just took the backpack."

"Have you told Bash Haywood all of this?" Lilly asked.

Nicole blushed again. "Not all of it, no."

"Do you still have the text?"

"Yes, why?"

"Bash should be looking for the jewelry. Go over and tell him everything. Show him the text, the call records from Tyler. Everything."

"Chief Haywood is getting more and more reasons to think less and less of me."

"He's a professional," Lilly said. "He's heard it all before."

"I sure would have liked him to have a higher opinion of me," Nicole sighed. She looked down at her watch. "I've got time now. I'll go over and speak to him."

Lilly walked with Nicole to the crosswalk. Nicole kept walking around the Wheel, but Lilly went right, heading home. She turned back and saw Nicole turning toward the police station. She made a mental note to call Bash later.

Lilly let herself into the front door of her house and made the long walk into the kitchen. Delia was there, unpacking grocery bags.

"Hello, Lilly. What have you got there?" Delia asked.

Lilly lifted the bag so that Delia could read it.

"You went to the Cupcake Castle?" Delia said. "Kitty's store?"

"I didn't know it was Kitty's store before I went in. You might have warned me."

Delia laughed. "She owns it with a couple of other people, but she's the one in the store most of the time."

"Does she do the baking?" Lilly asked.

"The baking is vanilla and chocolate cupcakes. They make a few dozen every morning. Kitty does the fillings, the frosting, and the syrup. Once they sell out, they close. Usually they're closed by three o'clock."

"I'll admit that I wasn't going to buy any, but then I tasted the mocha one, and I was sold. I got six for dinner tonight. What are you doing? Where's Luna?"

"Luna's sleeping on the cat bed Ernie brought by. I lined it with one of my scarves."

Delia was taking out pans, bowls, pots, and spices. She always pulled everything out before she started cooking, and organized it all in a way that made no sense to Lilly, but worked for Delia.

"I'm going to make a couple of lasagnas. One sausage, the other seafood. I got some bread and salad as well. A simple dinner that will provide some leftovers, I hope. The rest of this week is pretty busy."

"It depends on who comes to dinner." Lilly smiled. "I told Ernie to invite Mary. She may not want to come, but I wanted to make sure she knew she was welcome."

"Especially after the latest Tyler story." Delia shook her head.

"Roddy and I were discussing one of the ways these stories may be getting posted."

"You and Roddy? Using your social media expertise?" Delia smiled at Lilly, then she went back to organizing her dinner preparations.

"Hush now. There are people worse than we are at this. We were wondering if the person with the phone is trying to do something, and keeps posting by mistake?"

Delia stopped and considered that for a moment. "That could be what's happening. I've been wondering if someone is finding Tyler's posts and deciding to sow the seeds of discontent. And to throw blame on Mary."

"So they know what they're doing. This feels to be particularly cruel to Mary, don't you think?"

"Maybe she's the easiest target?"

Lilly told Delia about her conversation with Nicole while they both assembled the lasagna ingredients. Lilly started the white sauce for the seafood lasagna while Delia browned the sausage.

"Wow," Delia said. "Do you think Tyler stole her jewelry?"

"I'm not sure," Lilly said. "He may have kept it for leverage against Nicole. Or maybe he was using it to entice someone else? We're all assuming that Tyler was a reporter who would do anything for a story. It seems that he was that in the past. I've been assuming he was onto a big story. But perhaps he was less honorable these days, and was willing to blackmail for more than information."

Delia stopped turning sausages and looked at Lilly. "That could explain why he came to Goosebush. Small town, lots of secrets."

"It seems to me that he was targeting folks with either wealth or power," Lilly said.

"But why Mary? She doesn't have either."

"Adding a laugh as she was falling? That was the work of a man who liked to cause humiliation," Lilly said. "Maybe humiliating Mary was sport for him."

"People can be awful, can't they? Meg is beside herself, worried about Mary. And about Ray," Delia said.

"Did you talk to Meg today?"

"Yes, I called her when you couldn't get those copies of the *Goosebush Times* out of the archives. That isn't the first time this sort of thing has happened."

"What sort of thing?"

"Missing materials. I don't want to speak ill of anyone, but I think Fritz is trying to control the narrative."

"Explain what you mean by that," Lilly said. She turned off her burner and moved the pot onto another one to cool.

"Fritz only likes happy stories," Delia said. "Surely you've noticed that."

"I have," Lilly said, pouring some water into the electric teakettle. "He's always been like that, though it seems worse of late."

"Ever since we started to catalogue what was in the archives. The thing is, our Historical Society doesn't have the official records. Those are in the library. We have the letters of folks who lived in Goosebush, family Bibles, journals. More personal information. And most of it isn't sunshine happy. It's about the struggles of regular people, or the issues of inequality some people faced. Fritz doesn't like that. The stories don't always fit into what he thinks Goosebush is, or was."

"It can be difficult for people to understand that not everyone has had their same experiences in life. Especially people like Fritz, who have lived a fairly charmed existence."

"But has he?" Delia said. "Do you know that his wife and son were killed in a car accident years ago when they were on vacation in Canada? He's got some family money, but he's lost a lot on some investments lately. That's why he canceled his trip to Europe last summer."

"How do you know all that?" Lilly said.

"His wife and son? He mentioned them once when people were teasing the two of us about being single. The investments? I noticed that he was online a lot and he didn't clear his cookies, so I'd go back and look at his web history."

"You spied on him?"

"I gathered information. I didn't tell anyone else about it."

Lilly prepared the tea things in silence. Delia was one of her dearest friends. She was a brilliant researcher and a protégé of her late husband's. But there were times when Delia's clinical eye on humanity was challenging to Lilly's sensibilities. Lilly also collected information about people, but never dispassionately.

"So, Fritz doesn't like sad stories. Do you think he is getting rid of materials that don't support his worldview?" Lilly asked.

"I do," Delia said. "I didn't want to say anything, but I had to tell Meg. The issues of the *Goosebush Times* I asked you about? They were all around the time of Catherine Howland's leaving Goosebush. The official family letters mention her moving west with her family, and she and her daughter dying of a fever during the trek. But last night I read another letter a friend of hers wrote shortly after the news of the death broke. Her friend said that it may sound terrible, but now her friend was finally at peace, though she hoped that her brute of a husband bore no part in her death, or in the death of her little girl. She mentioned that at least she'd no longer be part of the idle speculation of that terrible rag, the *Times*. She also mentioned that 'that terrible woman' had left town. She doesn't name 'that terrible woman,' but I was hoping I could figure it out. I thought it would be worth looking at some of the issues around the time she left town. I wanted to get some context for what else was going on around town."

"I read a few of the issues that were in the binder. They were fascinating. I didn't understand them, but they were fun to read," Lilly said.

"Probably not for the people in the stories," Delia said. "It was an anonymous paper, printed once a week for a couple of years. Speculation is that it was a group of women—part of the Garden Society, as a matter of fact—who published it. One of the members had access to a printing press. It was full of gossip about people in town. There were also some political articles."

"And it stopped being printed? What do you think happened?"

"I hadn't given it much thought, until now," Delia

said. "The issues were part of a huge collection that was recently donated, and we're still going through it. I hadn't stopped to read all of the issues yet. I wish I had."

"I took some pictures of the issues that are still there. Maybe they can help. It does seem odd the issues you were looking for were gone. If Fritz has been taking items out, I wonder why?"

"I thought it was to tell the happy stories," Delia said. She turned the heat off the sausages and turned to look at Lilly. "But now, after your Nicole story? I wonder if he was giving materials to Tyler."

"If that's true, then Fritz may have been helping Tyler with a story about Catherine Howland. He was on the same track as you were. Wouldn't that have hurt Cole?"

"Maybe that was the point," Delia said. "Cole treats Fritz like an addled old man half the time. The other half he treats him like a servant. Maybe Fritz was getting payback."

"Another interesting theory," Lilly said. "You know what you need to do?"

Delia nodded. "I'll call Bash. Don't start assembling the lasagnas without me."

"No worries," Lilly said, pouring herself a cup of tea. "I wouldn't dare."

"Thanks for the late lunch, Lilly. And the cupcake." Bash Haywood pushed his chair back a bit from the dining room table, but made no effort to stand up. He hung his hands down to the side and pulled his right one up quickly. "What the—"

"Sorry, I should have mentioned that Luna has

the run of the house," Lilly said, laughing. "She likes to cuddle hands."

Bash looked down and smiled. He picked the kitten up and rested her on his shoulder. She quickly nestled into his neck and closed her eyes.

"Are you a cat whisperer?" Lilly said. "You put her right to sleep."

Bash laughed. "We've always had at least two cats. Right now we're up to three, and I told Stella no more. Is this the kitten Delia found on Saturday? Good thing Stella didn't see her first. She's a beauty."

"No one has come forward to claim her, so it looks like she's ours," Lilly said. "She's been to the vet and has a clean bill of health."

"That's good. If anyone comes by looking for her, I'll let you know. But it looks like she was dumped."

"People can be terrible, can't they?" Lilly asked. "Letting a baby like that fend for herself."

"They can be. I hate to speak ill of the dead, and I'm not saying he deserved killing, but from what I'm learning about Tyler Crane? He was one of the terrible ones."

"He had been a good guy at one point, though," Lilly said. "Roddy was looking at his old stories, and he had quite a reputation as a great reporter."

"He did, until his methods for getting those stories resulted in a lawsuit. The newspaper he was working for settled, but he was let go. He wasn't able to get another job," Bash said.

"Until this one," Lilly said.

"Yeah, though his current employer isn't really a hard news source. More of a social site. Tyler was a bit of a celebrity reporter there. He gave them credibility; they gave him a job."

"What do you think of my theory of why he came to Goosebush?" Lilly asked.

"Blackmail? As good a reason as any. I tend to agree with you. Though folks claim he told them he was on to a real story."

"I wonder if it was the Catherine Howland story," Lilly said.

"Would that be a big story?" Bash said.

"He wanted to talk to me about Merilee Frank's murder. All the bodies were found in Alden Park. Maybe he'd tied something else into the story, or threatened to."

"Great, another possible motive," Bash said.

"At least it gets Mary off the hook a bit," Lilly said.

"She's been off the hook with me for a while. She admitted to seeing him. But that second story today, it shows her falling and running away. Then Tyler had time to create the story that got posted, with the music and all. It had to have taken a while. Mary had called a car to pick her up and take her to the registration site. We finally found the driver and he verified that he saw her running out of the path. He thinks he saw Tyler waving at her."

"What took him so long to come forward?"

"He shouldn't have been driving the car," Bash said. "His older brother did the rideshares. That morning his brother was sleeping off a hangover, so he was doing the driving."

"That means Mary's off the hook."

"But Ray's still on it. He's got some holes on his

timeline I need to fill. Especially if his daughter called and told him what had happened."

"Did she?"

"Neither one is saying, but there was a call between them."

"Shoot," Lilly said. "Any luck finding the phone?"

"No. It gets turned on, but only for a few seconds. Every time it looks like it should be where Tyler was killed, but we've gone over the area with a fine-tooth comb. I even did a search of Cole's house, but I didn't find it."

"Why Cole's house?"

"It looked like it was there the last time it was turned on, but it wasn't. Trust me, we looked. Short of having an officer sit there twenty-four-seven, I don't know what to do."

"It sounds like the killer is playing games with you," Lilly said. This idea went against the thought that someone was futzing with the phone by accident.

"We need to find Tyler's phone," Bash said. "That's the key to this whole thing. Anything else you need to share with me?"

"I'm assuming Nicole came by and talked to you about her jewelry?"

Bash nodded. "She did. We'd found the box, but had no idea who it belonged to. I told her I'd get it back to her as soon as possible."

"Do you think that could have been a motive?"

"Hate to admit it, but yes. I wonder if Nicole was the 'she spills the secrets' story that Tyler was talking about. And she was strong enough to kill him. The medical examiner says that he was struck on the side of the head, probably with a branch of some sort, and then he fell and hit his head on one of the stones that lined the side of the path."

"Does that mean it could have been accidental?"

"He could also have fallen, and then been hit by the branch. It could have been accidental, sure. But that doesn't seem likely."

"A lot of people could swing a branch, especially if they were riled up," Lilly said. "Nicole's not the only one capable."

"But she does have a temper," Bash said. He smiled for a moment, then his face looked grim again. "She has to stay on the list."

He got up and walked around the table, handing Lilly the sleeping kitten. He leaned down and gave her a kiss on the cheek. "Thanks again, Lilly. For the food, the information, and the conversation. Let me know if you find out anything else."

"I'm not looking for any other information," Lilly said.

Bash laughed and the kitten jumped a bit. "You may not be looking, but you're finding. Stay in touch, Lilly."

"According to Scottie Sinclair, Tyler loved the idea of bringing power structures down," Delia said. They were all sitting around the table on the back porch, too full to move into the dining room. The porch was three-season, but the last week of October was pushing it. Still, everyone wore layers and Lilly had a blanket tucked around her legs. The space heaters helped take the chill off the room.

"Sounds like Tyler was also interested in having those power structures pay him off," Tamara said.

"Delia, you knew him better than any of us. Do you think he was in search of a story? Or a blackmailer looking for victims?" Roddy asked.

Delia looked down at the kitten in her lap and petted her for a few moments before looking up and around the table at all her friends.

"I don't know," Delia said. "Tyler was . . . well, he was . . ."

"Obtuse," Lilly offered.

"That's a good word for it. I hate to admit it, but I have trouble reading the motivations of charming men. That's why I usually avoid them."

"No offense, Roddy and Warwick," Ernie said.

"You're charming too, Ernie," Delia said. She smiled around the table. "The three of you are all charming, but I trust you. That's different."

"We're grateful for your trust," Roddy said. "And for the compliment. I thought my charming days were well behind me."

"As if," Tamara said, tapping him lightly on his arm. "I'm glad we got our hooks into you before you charmed your way into other dinner invitations. We keep your social calendar pretty full."

"I can think of few places I'd rather be than here with all of you. Though if I'd known Kitty Bouchard could bake like this, perhaps I would have said yes to one of her dinner invitations." He picked up a piece of cupcake and popped it into his mouth. Ernie had cut the cupcakes into eighths and they were all sampling them.

"You'll have to make due with visiting her store, then," Ernie said.

"Oh no," Roddy said. "I don't want to encourage her in any way."

"Fine, then, we'll buy the cupcakes," Tamara said. "These really are fabulous."

"Back to the matter at hand," Lilly said. "I'm worried that Ray Mancini is going to get blamed for Tyler's death. And to protect Mary, he's not going to fight it."

"I'm worried about that too," Ernie said. "So is Mary, I think. She's stoic, but this is hard on her."

"I'm sorry she didn't come over tonight," Lilly said.

"She really appreciated the invitation, but she wanted to go home. I give her a ton of credit—she isn't hiding. At all."

"What would she be hiding from?" Warwick asked.

Delia looked uncomfortable and shifted in her seat, but she didn't offer anything to the conversation.

"People like Tyler don't need to have a story that will cause you trouble in order to do their work," Roddy said. "They only have to find the stories you'd rather not have told. Mary may not have done anything wrong; she probably didn't. But she had a story she didn't want told and Tyler found it. Same thing with Nicole, most likely."

Everyone looked at Warwick, who nodded. "It's her story to tell, but suffice it to say she didn't move to Goosebush for the job. She moved to get away. But I don't think she has it in her to kill anyone."

"Neither do I," Lilly said. "But she's on the list of Tyler's victims, which puts her on the list of Tyler's possible killers."

"You're on that list too, Lilly," Tamara said.

"I am, I suppose. For the record, I didn't do it," Lilly said.

"I can vouch for her alibi," Delia said.

"Thank you, friend," Lilly said, smiling.

"People like Tyler tick me off," Ernie said. "Bullies, pure and simple."

"Nothing pure, and nothing simple, about it," Lilly said. "Without his phone, it's hard to know what Tyler was up to."

"Then it's fairly obvious what we need to do," Roddy said.

"We have to find his phone," everyone said at once.

CHAPTER 15

Lilly spent Tuesday morning in her garden. It was another clear fall day. Cold, but not freezing. Mentally Lilly always considered November 1 the end of the gardening season, so she had five days left. Saturday was Halloween and the haunted house, so it was really only four.

Lilly raked up the leaves that had fallen in her garden beds, carefully tending to the underlying plants. She took out her notebook and made lists of what needed to be done where, before the first frost of the season. As she went around the garden she talked to the plants, thanking them for a wonderful season.

"You need some extra nourishment this winter," she said to the roses.

"Let's cut you back some more," she said to the hydrangeas. "You were looking a bit leggy this summer. We may not get as many blooms next year, but that's fine. You can grow into yourself again. I'm sorry I let you go for a couple of years. I was being selfish."

And on it went, Lilly lovingly tending to her gardens and moving some of the potted plants into the greenhouse for the winter. She stopped and paused at the memorials in the garden. Her parents, and Alan. Of course Pete knew about them. He'd been married to her when her father died, and had helped dig the hole for the bush they planted over his ashes. She doubted that Pete meant her any harm by telling the story. Far from it. But as she gathered the piles of leaves and added them to the compost pile, she thought about the discomfort she'd felt at the public airing of her personal business. For others, shame would be attached to the discomfort. A powerful motivator.

Lilly felt her phone buzz in her pocket. She took off her gloves and retrieved it.

"Good morning, Roddy," she answered.

"Good morning, Lilly," he said. "I'm calling to make sure you remembered our appointment this morning?"

"What appointment?" Lilly said. She knew she didn't have anything on her calendar, but that didn't mean she didn't have a meeting.

"I mentioned it last week and should have followed up with you. Especially with all that's going on. I'm going to walk my gardens and make a list of things that need to be done. I'd love to know if there are any plants or bushes we need to put in this fall."

"I remember. Was that today? I'm happy to come over," Lilly said. "How's the bulb planting going?"

"Done," Roddy said. "I'm glad you talked me into it. I'm already looking forward to seeing what comes up in the spring, even if we only planted a small batch."

"Let me finish here and then I'll be over. We need to get this garden gate sorted. It would be so much easier to cut through that way."

"I've been trying to find a solution," Roddy said. "I'd rather not take up that entire slab of granite, but will if it comes to that. I did find the original key—did I tell you that? I've been uncovering a ton of treasures."

"You'll need to show me the treasures as well."

"I'd be delighted to. Oh, did I mention that Mary Mancini is coming over at eleven? I called and asked her to come by and take an order as we walked through the garden."

"I'll be there," Lilly said.

Lilly went out her front door and locked it behind her. Thankfully, the privet hedges gave her a sense of privacy and no one was camped out by the front gate today, as far as she could see. She walked to her right, across her yard, through a gap in the bushes and into Roddy's yard. She walked along the side of his house into his backyard.

Whereas Lilly's house had walls on three sides that made her backyard impossible to access, Roddy's was wide open. That said, in recent years there really hadn't been a reason to visit back there. The large tree that had been the focal point had been taken down, and the gardens had been allowed to lie fallow. Even the grass had given up, resulting in patches of dirt, weeds, and yellowing anemic attempts at green. Roddy had been determined to change all that, but he'd lived in his house for less than six months. At this point, both inside and out were at the chaos stage that came right before order was restored.

When Lilly arrived, Roddy was nowhere to be seen. She texted him that she was there as she walked around. She went over to the rusty wrought iron table in the middle of the patio area. A set of plans was unrolled on the table, held down by four large stones in either corner.

Roddy's garden was rumored to have been designed by Florence Winslow. Florence was one of the little-known figures in Goosebush history that Delia had discovered. She was an African American woman, a descendent of slaves, who had moved to Goosebush in the mid-1800s. Officially she had worked for one of the great garden designers of the area, Forest Hunter, but Delia's research indicated that she did a lot of the designs herself, especially the smaller gardens that didn't bring the acclaim of the other Hunter jobs.

The original garden design had looked like a ship wheel, with the tree in the center and spokes and paths dividing the garden into eighths. The design had taken up the entire backyard, which was not small since Roddy had a double lot. The design had been lost, but was still faintly visible from the attic windows.

Delia had provided Roddy with as much information as she could find about the gardens. But this drawing? Delia hadn't done that. Lilly took out her reading glasses and looked at the plans more carefully, picking up the stones and turning the pages to see more detail.

"What do you think?" Roddy said. He came out of the French doors that led out to the garden, kicking it closed behind him. He was carrying a tray full of glasses, a pitcher, plates, and other accoutrement. Lilly cleared a spot on the table for him to set down the tray.

"These are stunning," Lilly said. "You have an amazing sense of detail."

"Thank you," Roddy said. "But I will admit, the actual plants that need to be planted are why I need you here. I know what I want this to look like, but I need experts to help me figure out what should be planted where, and with what other plants, to give me the look I want."

Lilly smiled. "There's a lot to consider. How one choice will affect another. Shade and sun. But the vision you have is clear, so it will be fun to figure out. By the way, I saw your drawing for Alden Park. Also stunning."

"I thought those were supposed to be anonymous," Roddy said.

"I was with Ernie. He didn't tell me until after I'd decided which one to vote for," Lilly said. "Of course, if I'd seen this I would have known already. When did you become a garden designer?"

Roddy laughed. "Hardly that," he said. "When I was young my mother gardened, and I'd help her. Then the family fortunes turned and we moved into a large apartment complex. So we'd visit gardens. She'd draw them and encouraged me to do the same. I found I enjoyed it. When I traveled, I'd take pictures to send to her, of course. But I'd always do a drawing of the gardens I visited as well. I'd watercolor them when I got home. She saved them all, bless her. I still find the process very relaxing. But I may have found another project to interest me. We have a few minutes before Mary comes by. Come in the house and take a look."

Roddy walked Lilly to the front of the house, making sure that she avoided the various drop cloths, buckets of tools, and debris piles along the way. The floors were all covered with red paper to protect them.

"When did all this happen?" Lilly said.

"When the roof started to leak and then it's all been downhill from then," Roddy said cheerfully. "Honestly, I know it's a mess, but I'm having a wonderful time. We've found three boarded-up closets. I've been collecting the things in here."

Roddy turned to his right and walked into one of the rooms. There were several six-foot tables set up with items lined up on them. Roddy kept walking, but Lilly looked over at each table. Books, framed pictures, kitchen utensils, tools. A couple of dolls with china heads, the bodies long since rotted. Bundles of letters, tied in faded ribbon. Small knick-knacks of varying types.

"You found all of this in the house?" Lilly said.

"Yes, all of it," Roddy said. "My things are in storage. Not sure what I'll do with all of this, but it's fun to look at. Look at this." He lifted a sheet off one of the tables. Lilly saw a large dollhouse on the table, a replica of Roddy's house.

"That's amazing," Lilly said.

"I found this in one of the boarded-up closets," Roddy said. "Along with those dolls, some pieces of costume jewelry, and other bits and bobs. There was a note inside the dollhouse: 'To Eleanor on her fifth birthday. With love, Grandfather.' "

"Eleanor was my grandmother's cousin," Lilly said.

"Ah, so it is from the old captain. I'm wondering

if he sent these gifts to his grandchildren, and his daughter hid them rather than give them to them?"

"I've been thinking about that locking system on your side of the gate," Lilly said. "The family lore has always been that the daughter didn't want to see her father. But what happens if we reframe how we look at it? Maybe her husband didn't want her to see her father?"

"And he barred the door so she couldn't open it. And if her father tried, he'd think she had locked the door. A terrible thought. I've been trying to preserve the stonework around the gate, but I'm reconsidering that. It looks as if the pieces of iron are being held down by the stone itself, so it has to be moved. I know we don't have to have the gate able to open, but I don't like what it represents."

"I agree," Lilly said. "More terrible family stories. We all have them, but I'd love to end the locked gate. Let the captain rest in peace—about that at least. Anyway, the dollhouse is lovely. Are you going to give it to your granddaughter?"

"I'm going to offer it to my daughter, but it's likely that some of that paint has lead in it. I've decided I'm going to make one for my granddaughter that's safer for her to play with. I've started working on it already. I'm hoping to have it done by Christmas."

"That's lovely. Are you going to show it to Emma this weekend?"

"I'll show her this, yes. But not the one I'm making. I'd rather that be a surprise."

"Are they coming this weekend?" Lilly said.

"Yes, they are," Roddy said, smiling. "Which means I need to get the house in better shape by then, but that's easily done. Believe it or not, the work is almost finished here on the first floor. Painting is scheduled for tomorrow. The kitchen counters are going in tonight, so there will be running water if the plumbers show up on time. The floors were all redone before I moved in, so it will be in decent shape before my family sees it."

"I look forward to meeting Emma and the rest of your family," Lilly said. The doorbell rang and Roddy went to answer it. Lilly looked at the dollhouse again, thinking about her great-great-grandfather and the daughter he'd lost. She'd always assumed it was his fault, the estrangement between the two. But what if it wasn't? What if the estrangement was the fault of her husband? Given the time, she may have had little say in the situation. Did she even know her father had sent this over? Or did her husband hide that from her?

Families and secrets. What a legacy of pain they left behind.

"Thanks for doing this walk-through with us, Lilly," Mary said. "I think I've learned more about gardening in the past two hours than I have in the weeks Ernie's been trying to teach me at the store."

The three of them were sitting out on Lilly's back porch. They'd done the walk-through of Roddy's gardens and tried to sit outside at his house, but the air was a bit too brisk, so Lilly had suggested the move. She'd taken the opportunity to walk Mary through her gardens to show her examples of what they'd discussed.

"I've always been an experiential learner," Lilly said. "Textbooks never worked for me. I needed to dive in and learn. It's one thing to show you plants, but when you see them in a garden and understand how all decisions work together, that's something else."

"Having a passionate teacher also helps," Mary said. She smiled and took a bite of her lasagna. "Thanks for lunch as well. This is delicious."

"It really is," Roddy said, helping himself to another piece of the seafood lasagna.

"Delia always makes extra food so we can rely on leftovers for a while," Lilly said. "Fortunately, she's a great cook."

"I appreciated the invitation to dinner last night," Mary said. "It meant a lot. Thank you."

"You have a permanent rain check," Lilly said. "You're always welcome."

"Maybe my folks and I can set up a dinner date soon," Mary said.

"I'd love that," Lilly said. "You know, your father and I have been friends for a long time. We went to school together. He's one of the best men I've ever known."

Mary smiled. "I know he's a good guy," she said. "We don't always get along, but we're working on it. It's just that . . . well, he's pretty clear on what's acceptable and what isn't. I always hated to disappoint him, and I'm afraid that's all I've done lately."

Lilly was tempted to say "I'm sure that's not true" or "you couldn't disappoint him," but she refrained. She never thought it was good form to pander to people, and she wasn't about to start now. That said, if she could do something to help Mary and her father, she'd do it. Their estrangement obviously caused a lot of pain.

"Do you like working at the Triple B?" Lilly asked.

"I know that Ernie likes having you there. You've improved his work life tremendously."

"I do, actually. I enjoy helping people figure out how to improve their houses in different ways." Mary looked down at her plate and pushed the food around.

Lilly looked at Roddy. He lifted his shoulders slightly and took another bite of lasagna.

"Any ideas for this porch?" Lilly said.

"What do you mean?" Mary said. "I love this porch as it is."

"I do too," Lilly said. "But we're coming up to the time of year I can't sit out here. I've turned it from an open porch to a screened-in porch. Adding the storm windows makes it a three-season porch. I'm wondering if I could make it into a room I could use all year long."

"When did you start thinking about that?" Roddy said.

"Last night when I couldn't get to sleep. I always think about gardening or remodeling my house when I have trouble going to sleep. Maybe I'm a little jealous of all the work everyone else is doing on their homes."

"Is there a crawl space under the porch?" Mary asked.

"Of sorts. This is actually where the coal was delivered back in the day. See that patch of wood? That was the trap door. The area beneath here is connected to the old basement. It was originally dirt, but was dug up a few years ago and concrete was poured. It was poured under here as well. The porch was lifted and a more solid foundation was built underneath. We did that twenty or so years ago, and blocked this part of the basement off from the rest of the house."

"Well then, you could insulate it pretty easily. Run some heating ducts out here. Get more weatherproof windows that still allow you to have this open, airy feeling. Maybe a gas fireplace in the corner. It would be important to maintain the character of the room, but it could be done."

Lilly looked around and smiled. "That sounds wonderful. I can picture it already. I hate to add to your plate, Mary, but would you write down your ideas?"

"Sure, I'd love to," Mary said. "I used to act as a general contractor for the business my husband— my ex-husband—and I ran." Mary looked down at her plate again and sighed.

"I wish I'd known that," Roddy said. "Ernie's been helping me with the projects on my house, but I would have loved to hire someone who knew what they were doing."

"I'm not licensed here," Mary said. "I haven't even talked to Ernie about my past experience. He didn't ask me about it; hired me on the spot. As a favor to my parents, I'd imagine."

"Maybe it started out that way, but you've helped him out tremendously. You should let him know about your expertise. He'd use it to expand his business," Roddy said.

"Yeah, well, I haven't talked about what I used to do with anyone. Or about what happened. Maybe I should, though."

"Mary, I'm a firm believer in not having secrets if at all possible," Lilly said. "They become toxic."

"They do indeed," Roddy said. "Though sharing

secrets must be done carefully. Ernie Johnson is as fine a man as I've ever met. I'm sure he'd be happy to learn about your expertise."

"I know he's a good guy. You all are." Mary took a deep breath and looked up at Lilly, keeping her eyes focused on her. "My parents never liked my husband. My father didn't trust him. He threatened to do a background check on him before we were married. In hindsight, I wish he had."

"Mary, what happened?" Lilly said, gently. She sensed that Mary wanted to tell her story.

"He didn't abuse me, at least not physically. But he did convince me that he was the only person in the world who really loved me, who understood me. I cut myself off from my family. I sent cards, made phone calls on holidays. But I hadn't seen them for years.

"My husband traveled a lot. He was gone as often as he was home, but that was fine. The business was going well and it kept me busy. We renovated houses, even flipped a few. Then one day last spring I was in the office catching up on accounts payable when the FBI arrived."

"The FBI?" Lilly said.

"Yup. Seems that my husband had been investing in some shady deals, so they came in and took over everything. They froze all of our assets."

"We had something similar happen here," Lilly said.

"I know, my father told me. But that's not the worst of it. I kept working, trying to keep the business afloat. I mortgaged everything so that I could get my husband out on bail. Then I found out the bad part."

"It gets worse?" Roddy said.

"All summer long I never stopped believing him, you know? I thought that he'd made a mistake, been trapped in something bigger than he was. But then his wife showed up."

"His what?" Lilly asked.

"His wife. Mother of his two children. They'd been married for fifteen years. They separated for a while, that's when we met. But they never got divorced."

"He's a bigamist," Roddy said.

"Amongst his other lovely traits, yes. But wait, there's more." Mary sighed and wiped her eyes. "Everything was in his name. I mean everything. His wife claimed it as property due her. I was so humiliated I didn't fight it. I lost it all. My whole life fell apart in less than three months."

"Then you came back to Goosebush," Lilly said.

"I didn't mean to," Mary said. She wiped the tears from her eyes. "But I was packing up my stuff and found the birthday card my mother had sent me. She sent me one every year, but I'd stopped opening them. This time I did and I realized how much she still loved me. I called her and told her I needed to come home. Less than twenty-four hours later, she and my dad were at my house, helping me pack up my things."

"Do they know what happened?"

"About the FBI, yes. About the bigamy, no. I can't bring myself to tell them."

"But Tyler found out, didn't he?" Roddy asked gently.

Mary nodded. "He threatened to tell everyone unless I started feeding him stories."

"What sort of stories?"

"Gossip. He was especially interested in the people on the four-hundredth anniversary committee. Both of you. Cole Bosworth. He wanted me to get my mother to help him."

Lilly got up. "Mary, may I give you a hug?"

"Please," Mary said.

Lilly put her arms around Mary. "Mary, the shame of all of this isn't yours. You need to tell your parents what happened."

Mary nodded. Lilly let go and Mary stood up.

"I already told Bash," Mary said. "He told me that he wouldn't tell my dad, but he suggested I do it since he was bound to find out."

"Good advice," Lilly said. "The story is yours to tell."

"And the secret was mine to keep," Mary said. "But not for much longer."

CHAPTER 16

After Mary left, Roddy helped Lilly clean up and then went back to his house to meet with the gas company. He hadn't been gone long when Delia got home.

"How's your day been so far?" Delia said.

"Busy. I walked through Roddy's garden plans with him and Mary Mancini. She came over for lunch and gave me some great ideas for turning the porch into a usable room. She's going to write them up."

Delia looked at Lilly, who fixedly was repackaging leftovers into smaller containers. While others may have pried, Delia did not. Lilly would tell her what she needed to know when she needed to know it.

"I had a cup of coffee with Meg Mancini," Delia said. "She suggested that I drop by Fritz's house for a visit."

"And accuse him of stealing?"

"No, not that. She wants to wait until next week, after the festival, to take any action. She's added a second volunteer to all of his shifts in the meantime. No, she wants me to look around. Try and throw him off guard."

"What does that mean?"

"Meg calls me the archivist police force. She thinks that my dropping by will freak Fritz out enough that he returns the items he took, if he took them. She'd rather give him a chance to return them than to call him out publicly."

"That seems like the kindest way to deal with the situation."

"I'm not sure I'm good at kind. And I know I suck at subtle. You have to come with me," Delia said.

Lilly was going to argue, but what was the point? Though Delia was kind, she had strong opinions on rules and how they should be followed. And subtle was not in her young friend's wheelhouse.

"Let me take a quick shower. I've been gardening all day," Lilly said. "Then I'll go with you to visit Fritz."

"Why Delia, Lilly! What an unexpected surprise." Fritz Stewart met them at the door wearing a pair of magnifying glasses and archival gloves in addition to his regular uniform of trousers, a button-down shirt, boat shoes, and a knit vest. His hair was wild and his beard needed combing.

"Hello Fritz, sorry we didn't call ahead. I need to talk to you about some missing files from the Historical Society. May we come in?" Delia said.

"So much for subtle," Lilly whispered into Delia's ear as Fritz stepped aside to let them it. It was a good thing that Lilly spoke when she did, because she lost her words the minute her eyes adjusted and she could see inside Fritz's house. The old Colonial had a center staircase, with a hall behind it that was lined with wooden file cabinets. Lilly looked to her left and saw into what must have been a dining room at one point, but was now piled high with boxes, papers, and files. Fritz guided them into the room on the right. This used to be a living room. Lilly remembered coming to visit with her mother in years past. But now? Now it was another filing room with a couple of chairs and a couch. Fritz picked up a pile of files from the couch and deposited them on one of the chairs.

"Have a seat. I'm sorry that I can't offer you refreshments, but I'm in the middle of a project."

"I can see that," Lilly said, looking around.

"Oh this," Fritz said. "This is ongoing. Ever since my brother Edwin passed on and left me his share of the family papers. Might I ask you both to wear some archival gloves? I'm afraid this is all a little fragile. I do my best to keep the house dry and at the proper temperatures, but it's difficult." He handed Lilly a box of archival gloves and she took two out and put them on. She handed the box to Delia and nodded her head, indicating that Delia should do the same.

"I'd imagine it is," Lilly said.

"Edwin was quite the collector," Fritz said. "Not only of our family papers, but of his wife's. Generations of things passed on, and no one else left to give them to. It's all a bit overwhelming, I have to admit."

"You should consider passing it on to the Historical Society," Lilly said.

"I need to go through it first and decide what I need to keep," Fritz said.

"You mean decide what you want other people to read," Delia said.

"What do you mean?" Fritz asked. Lilly noticed he looked away from her while he asked the question.

"We've talked about this, Fritz. You only want to share the happy stories. I'm sure that in all of this"—Delia gestured to the room at large—"there are some skeletons to be uncovered. An adopted baby who was the illegitimate child of someone. Shady business deals. Parts of the family history you'd rather have forgotten."

"And what is wrong with exercising some editorial restraint on my family history? What business is it of anyone else's?"

"No one's history is just their own," Delia said. "We all intersect with each other. Don't you get that? One part of your family history could help answer another family's missing piece. No one has a right to edit that."

"On that we need to agree to disagree, Delia," Fritz said. "As we always have. And likely always shall. But surely you didn't come by to lecture me, did you? What can I do for you?"

"I came by to talk to you about some missing items from the Historical Society," Delia said.

"What missing items?" Fritz said, blinking several times.

"The issues of the *Goosebush Times*, for example."

"That rag. Hardly worth the storage space it takes up," Fritz said.

"Not your decision to make, Fritz," Delia said. "Did you take them out of the library?"

"I did not," he said.

"Then you won't mind if I look around for them?"

"I most certainly would mind. You have no right—"

"And you have no right to decide what should and should not be read—"

"I have every right—"

"Says who?"

"Says me, that's who, young lady. I'm three times as old as you are and know more than you ever will about what's worth remembering and what isn't. I've spent a lifetime trying to forget more than you'll ever know. Now I'm afraid I need to ask you to leave." Fritz stood up and Delia followed suit. Lilly stayed seated.

"Fritz, I'm looking around this house and I can't imagine you getting rid of anything. You may not like the story some of these items have to tell, but I can't imagine you getting rid of them," Lilly said.

Fritz sat back down. He took his magnifying glasses off and rubbed his eyes. He put his head in his hands and kept it there.

"What happened, Fritz?" Lilly asked gently. She pulled on Delia's sleeve and the younger woman sat down again.

"That terrible young man, the one who died—"

"Tyler Crane."

"Yes, Tyler Crane." Fritz lifted his head and looked at both Lilly and Delia. Then he closed his eyes. "He started to come into the Historical Society, asking questions, reading up on the history of Goosebush. He told me he wanted to write a series of articles about the place, and I thought, why not? The town could use some good press."

"So you started giving him information," Lilly said.

"Indeed I did. Then he started to request some items. I took note of what they were and started to read them for myself after he left."

"What were they?"

"Some of the journals of our more disgruntled citizens. Letters from around the time those bodies must have disappeared. The ones in Alden Park. Pictures of the houses that were destroyed in the fire of 1912. That sort of thing. Unhappy stories."

"You took it upon yourself to make them not available to him," Lilly said. "What did you do? Did you destroy them?"

Fritz shook his head violently, and sighed. "No, you're right about me. I could never, would never destroy records. No, I started misfiling them so that no one could find them."

"You misfiled them?" Delia gasped. Lilly bit back a smile. In Delia's world, misfiling was one of the greatest sins.

"I kept a list," Fritz said mildly. "I hadn't had a chance to refile them."

"You kept a list," Delia said. "Where is that list?"

"In the Historical Society, of course. I put in in the sign-out volume from 1997."

"Why there?" Lilly asked.

"No one would think to look for it there, that's why," he said.

"All right then," Lilly said. "That's where we'll find it. Now that Tyler's not able to ask any more questions, we can put things back where they belong."

"That we can do," Fritz said. "A terrible thing happened to him, of course. But he really was a most unpleasant young man."

"He was that," Lilly said gently. "Tell me, did you

see him the morning he died? Did he come by here to talk to you, by any chance?"

"No, I'd made it perfectly clear he wasn't welcome here. Besides, even if he had come by, I was at Cole's house. We had an early walk. We wanted to get out before the runners ran amok. Then we went back to Cole's house for breakfast. I'm sure he'll remember."

"Fritz, thank you for letting us barge in on you," Lilly said. "Delia and I'll be going now."

"Yes, well, I'm sorry for the fright I gave you, Delia, about the missing documents. I know we disagree, but you care about our history as much as I do. Just in different ways."

Delia stared at Fritz silently, so Lilly jumped in. "She does care about it, very much."

"I've been mustering up the courage to ask a slight favor of you, Delia," Fritz said.

"What is it?" Delia asked. The question sounded like a hiss, and Lilly knew she needed to get Delia some fresh air.

"I need some help cataloguing all of this. I'm afraid I started using one system and then I switched to another one. You have such a methodical brain. Would you consider . . . would you mind coming over and helping me sort through all of this?"

Delia looked around and shrugged. "I'll be happy to. I'll have more time over winter break. Would that be all right?"

"That would be fine," Fritz said. "That would be fine."

* * *

"That was nice of you, being willing to help Fritz," Lilly said.

"Did you see his house? Who knows what treasures are in there? I'm trying to save them, that's all." Delia started the car and turned around in Fritz's driveway. "To Cole's house?"

"Let's go by the path first," Lilly said.

"Where Tyler died? Why?"

"I want to take a look, is all."

"Hoping you'll find his phone lying out there?" Delia teased.

"Something like that."

The two women climbed into the Jeep and drove over to the path. They parked at one end, the end they found Luna on. They got out of the car and walked to where they'd found Tyler that morning. Lilly stood in the spot where he died and looked around. Delia stood next to her.

"What are you looking for?" Delia asked.

"I'm just looking," Lilly said. "Every time I've been here I've been so intent on raking the path I've never really looked around. You can actually see several houses from this spot, not just the abutters."

"Especially with the leaves off the trees," Delia said. "It is probably much more private in the summertime, don't you think?"

Lilly looked around and nodded.

"It was probably much more private before those two trees were taken down," Lilly said, pointing to the lot across from the path where two stumps opened up a clearing that showed off one of the newer houses in Goosebush. On the lot of what used to be a standard Colonial now stood an oversized house that went right up to the boundary line.

It was after that house was built and the trees were taken down, that Goosebush tightened up its building codes.

"What a monstrosity. They said they took the trees down because they were dying, but I think they did it to give them a better view of the marshes," Delia said.

"Undoubtedly," Lilly said. "I wonder what else they had a clear view of."

"Not what happened here last weekend," Delia said. "They went on a cruise for the month of October. Don't you remember her talking about it?"

"That's right." Lilly nodded. She immediately recalled Mrs. Porter discussing the trip while shopping for travel books in the Star. "Cole's house is right there."

"Do you think he saw anything?" Delia said.

"I'd imagine Bash checked it out. Besides, you could only see something if you were looking out of that side window there. What does that go to?"

"I don't know, but I saw the curtain move, I think. See that flash? Maybe he's got a suncatcher," Delia said.

"Yes, because Cole is the type to have suncatchers in his windows," Lilly said. "Unless they had them in Colonial times?" Lilly turned toward Cole's house and waved.

"What are you doing?" Delia asked.

"If he's watching us out the window, he'll come out. And that will tell us that he can see this spot."

"Why would he—" Delia stopped talking when Cole stepped out of his back door and crossed the lawn toward them.

Lilly plastered on a smile. "Because Cole can't bear to be embarrassed. And being caught spying on us is embarrassing."

Cole finally got closer to where they were.

"Hello ladies," he said. "What brings you out here?" The access path was four feet lower than the houses on either side, with a stone retaining wall, so Lilly and Delia had to look up.

"We were discussing plans for next spring," Lilly said, gesturing to the path.

"Next spring?"

"Yes, the Beautification Committee is taking on new projects, and we are considering leveling this path so it can be more easily accessed by vehicles. Not cars, necessarily. But bikes. And motorcycles. That sort of thing." Lilly kept the smile plastered on her face and watched Cole turn three different shades of purple before he was able to speak again.

"That can't be legal," Cole said.

"Legal? Of course it is. Since this is public land, we'll need to go through the proper channels, of course. The point is, we need to maintain it and to let people know they have the right to use it," Lilly said. "Delia and I both agreed that we need to do something here to change this up so that the only thing that this path is remembered for isn't Tyler's death. I'd hate for this to become a memorial to his fans."

"A memorial? That would be terrible," Cole said, looking around as if hordes of people were about to descend. "It's bad enough that that buffoon Bash Haywood insists that I had something to do with it. He's searched my house—did you know that? A terrible invasion of privacy."

"Are those lilacs on your land, Cole?" Lilly asked, knowing full well the answer, but wanting to see if he knew.

"They are," he said, looking over at the straggly bushes on his left.

"You know, if you took some time tending to them, they could provide a wonderful natural privacy barrier for you," Lilly said.

"The roses on the other corner of your lot would do the same thing," Delia said.

Cole looked around. "Do you ladies have a moment or two to spare? I'd love to get some gardening advice. My flowers have not been doing well these past couple of years. My fault, I'm afraid. I forget to water them. Perhaps they are beyond hope."

"Nothing is ever beyond hope," Lilly said. Delia climbed up the retaining wall at what looked like a natural set of steps. She turned around and offered Lilly a hand.

"Give me a minute so I can walk around to the street. I'm well past the age where climbing retaining walls makes any sort of sense."

CHAPTER 17

Lilly met Cole and Delia in the middle of his backyard. The site made Lilly sad. The lawn was perfect, the shrubs were trimmed. But there was no life, no personality.

"I have a service come in to take care of things," Cole said. "They offered to look at the outer edge of greenery, but I told them to mostly deal with the inside of the yard. It looks terrific, doesn't it?"

"Like a golf course," Delia said.

Cole smiled and nodded, missing the contempt in Delia's voice. "That's what I was going for."

"The bushes along the side? They were all planted years and years ago, likely for privacy. If you start tending them, they'll grow in and you won't be able to see anything on the path," Lilly said. She walked them all over to the lilac bushes and made a mental note to call the Sayer brothers. "When they're healthier they'll be denser, even when they've lost their leaves. I'd imagine now you can see anything that happens out here."

"I can, though not a lot of people use it. Especially since . . . well, you know."

"Tyler died out there," Delia said.

"Yeah, that."

"Funny you didn't see anything that morning," Lilly said. "You have windows on that side of the house."

"Only in the mudroom and the kitchen," Cole said. "And I wasn't in the kitchen. I never go in the kitchen if I can help it. Fritz and I had taken a walk, and we came back. He made some coffee and the next thing I knew the police were here."

"It must have been very upsetting," Lilly said.

"You have no idea," Cole said. "It was going to be bad enough having hundreds of people running by, but that would have lasted for a day. The way it turned out, people have been out here all week."

Lilly made a tsking sound. "Very upsetting," she said again.

"Cole, you mentioned that you had a copy of your family tree?" Delia asked. "Would you mind if I took a look at it? The Catherine Howland lineage post-Goosebush isn't well-documented."

"Of course, of course," Cole said. "Come right in." Cole led them to the back door. Delia turned around and looked at Lilly.

She shrugged her shoulders. Getting inside the house wasn't a terrible plan, for curiosity's sake if nothing else. Lilly saw Delia take her phone out of her pocket and turn it on, snapping a few pictures in the direction of the path as she walked.

Cole held the door for them as they walked into the mudroom. Whereas Fritz's house had been packed to the gills, Cole's house was almost austere in decoration. The lack of personality made Lilly wince. Every piece of art, every item on every step looked like an homage to Colonial times. Even the furnishings in this part of the house reeked of that era, with hard wooden benches instead of chairs sitting next to a short wooden table. No wonder Cole didn't like to spend time in the kitchen, Lilly thought. She did glance to her side and saw the tall windows that ran along the side of the house. She walked over and, sure enough, the view of the path was clear. Well, fairly clear. The windowpanes were small and of wavy glass. Cole took authenticity to the nth degree.

He led them into the dining room and invited them to sit at the table. "Be right back," he said, leaving the room. As soon as he was gone, Delia jumped up and started snapping pictures. She looked out the door of the room and across the hall.

"That looks like his study," Delia said. "I don't see a window on this side of the house, do you?"

"I see a covered window by that awful tapestry," Lilly said. "This room feels like several historical eras vomited their worst decor, don't you think?"

"It's pretty bad," Delia said. She continued to snap pictures. When she heard Cole on the stairs, she quickly went back to her seat.

"Here it is," Cole said as he entered. He was carrying a large roll of brown paper and had a huge binder under one arm. He took the roll of paper and gently laid it on the table.

Delia took out her archival gloves and stood up to help him. He looked at her quizzically. "We were visiting Fritz," she said. "He gives them to his visitors."

"Ah. Well, you'll find a bit more order here. This

is something I've been working on for the past dozen years or so."

Cole unrolled the paper with Delia's help. Lilly realized that far from an historical document, this was Cole's family tree, laid out by the man himself. Lilly could tell that he'd created it because of the red box at the bottom of the tree, ringed in red, which said *Cole Bosworth b 1950*.

"Do you mind if I take pictures?" Delia asked.

"Of course not," Cole said.

"What are these numbers in the corner of each box?" Lilly asked.

"That's the biography number," Cole said proudly. He took out the binder he'd been carrying under his arm and laid it on the table. "I've been writing the biography of each family member."

"You've been writing them?" Lilly asked.

"With citations, of course," Cole said. "And referrals to other documents."

"May I see?" Delia asked.

"Of course," Cole said. He handed Delia the volume and she opened it to one of the entries. She looked up and found the entry on the sheet that Cole had created.

"We may have lost her for a while," Lilly said to Cole. "She loves this sort of research. Especially when it's methodical."

"Fritz's house must give her hives then," Cole said.

Lilly laughed. "It gives her ideas of how to clean things up," she said. "This is your father's side of the family? Do you have your mother's side done as well?"

"Her family history is far less interesting," Cole said. "And not nearly as noteworthy."

"All family histories are interesting and noteworthy," Delia said, looking up sharply. She went back to her reading.

"You and my mother would have gotten along famously," Cole said, laughing. "In fact, I wouldn't dare look into this history while she was alive. She didn't have much good to say about my father's side of the family. I had no idea that he traced all the way back to the *Mayflower.*"

"Didn't he mention it?" Lilly said.

"He wasn't around when I was a kid," Cole said. "He died twenty years ago. He never mentioned it."

For an instant, Lilly saw the boy who needed to belong that Cole hid with his *Mayflower* bravado.

"Wow, you've done amazing research," Delia said. "Do you mind if I ask you a few questions? How did you make this connection?" She pointed to two squares on the map.

Cole put on his glasses and took the book from Delia. He flipped through a few pages and then turned to her. "When you look at the data files from—"

Lilly's phone buzzed at that moment. She took it out of her pocket while Delia and Cole discussed databases.

Are you already at the beach? I came by to pick you up, but you're not home.

I'm at Cole Bosworth's house, Lilly texted back. **Pick me up. I'll be waiting outside**.

"So sorry," she said, standing up. "I need to do a beach walk with Ernie. Delia, are you okay getting home on your own? I'll leave you the car."

"I'm fine, as long as Cole doesn't mind me staying," Delia said.

"I'm delighted, delighted. Thank you for coming by, Lilly. Do you mind seeing yourself out?"

"What were you doing there?" Ernie asked as he picked her up outside Cole's house. Lilly caught Ernie up on her day's activities. She didn't tell him Mary's entire story. That was Mary's to tell. But she did say that they'd had a good talk.

"Yeah, she took an extra-long lunch. She just got back to the store. She said she'd stopped by her parents' house. She looked better than she has. Lighter somehow. She wanted to talk, but I told her we'd have to chat later. I didn't want to put this meeting off any longer."

"Make sure to give her time to talk."

"Sounds cryptic," Ernie said.

"Her story to tell. But you should know that she thinks a great deal of you."

"Thanks, that's nice to hear."

"All right. What's the goal of today?" Lilly asked.

"We're walking around the performance area that's being proposed for the beach. You know, the one that the Goosebush Players may have access to. Delores insisted on a tour."

"And you want her input?"

"Oh, heavens no. The goal is to keep Portia and Delores from coming to blows. To keep Delores's expectations realistic. And to come up with plan B for the parking lot space if this feels like it won't work for the Goosebush Players. In other words, another day in paradise," Ernie said. He turned to his friend and smiled.

*   *   *

Ernie drove slowly over the bridge and turned to the left to park. The parking lot was very large. At the other end, away from the bridge, there was the public bathhouse, where people could get concessions or use the showers to rinse off before they got back in their cars during the beach season, which went from Memorial Day through September. In the summertime, residents needed a sticker to get over the bridge. Out-of-towners could park for the day, but it cost them twenty-five dollars during the season. Nevertheless, the parking lot was always full. The Goosebush beach was too beautiful to resist.

Ernie drove down to the bathhouse end of the parking lot and parked. They both sat in the car for a few seconds, watching Delores and Portia arguing near the site of the proposed performance space.

Lilly stepped out and did what she always did when she was near the beach. She took a deep breath of sea air and held it for a few seconds. Never mind that it was low tide and the bayside of the beach was "fragrant." Never mind that the wind whipping over the dunes was fiercely cold. This was why Lilly lived where she did, to be able to take in this air whenever she wanted to.

"Good afternoon, Lilly," Delores said. She was in full artistic-director mode, with a flowered kerchief tied around her hair, a red floor-length cape gathered around her, and dark cat's-eye glasses featured prominently on her face.

"Hello, Delores. Portia, good to see you," Lilly said.

"We barely have daylight left for our discussion," Delores said.

"There's no discussion," Portia said. "You're getting a courtesy tour of the space."

"But surely, my concerns need to be accommodated if this is to work," she said.

"What concerns are those?" Ernie said.

"There is no back stage," Delores said. "And a concrete slab is hardly sufficient to our needs."

"The thought is that staging can be brought in as needed," Ernie said. "The slab is more of a delineation for people to understand where the performance area is. It will also have electricity conduits built in and speaker locations."

"Unsatisfactory," Delores said, raising her voice. "This is an opportunity for a great theatrical space. Instead it's barely fit for—for—"

"For community theater," Portia said. "Like the Goosebush Players. We're hardly the American Repertory Theater, Delores. I think that this will be fun for the summer. Lighter fare. A great opportunity to—"

"Suffer outdoors," Delores said. "Where are the private dressing rooms?"

"There will be tents set up," Ernie said. "And there's a space for a couple of campers as well."

"Tents? Campers? That will not do. Not at all," Delores said. She walked around the area and made dismissive gestures, muttering about camping.

"Delores, I'm sorry that you feel that way," Lilly said. "We were hoping the Players would be part of the summer season here. But there are several other organizations interested. I'm sure we can fill the weeks."

"And not include the Players?" Delores said.

"You don't sound interested, Delores," Lilly said. She turned to her friend. "Ernie, I didn't dress for this breeze. Could you take me home?"

"Of course, Lilly," Ernie said. "But would you

mind helping me for a minute? The Goosebush Glee Club is putting in a bid, and I promised I'd get them some better measurements for risers."

"The Goosebush Glee Club? What would they possibly do here?" Delores asked.

"Sing. Entertain people. Get them interested in coming to the rest of their concerts," Portia said. "You know, try and grow their audience. Something you don't seem to understand how to do, Delores."

"How dare you—"

"I'm on the board of the Goosebush Players. That's how I dare to," Portia said. "Head on home, Delores. We'll talk at the next board meeting."

Delores gulped air a few times, and then she turned on her heel and headed back to her car. She drove out in a whirl of gravel.

"Well, that went well," Ernie said, laughing.

"Perfectly," Portia said.

"What are you both talking about?" Lilly asked.

"We knew you'd deflate her balloon," Portia said. "And you did."

"Portia and I are tied up in the politics of the Players," Ernie said. "We're both on the board. But you have a clarity of spirit that's refreshing."

"Help me understand this. The goal was to not have the Goosebush Players perform here in the summer?" Lilly asked.

"The goal was to have the Goosebush Players, Delores in particular, be grateful community members rather than performance bullies," Portia says. "Mission accomplished."

Lilly laughed. "What a day," she said. "I'm exhausted."

"Solved the murder yet?" Portia asked.

"No, and not trying to," Lilly said.

"Please. Don't give me that. My grandson Chase has been telling me Tyler stories. If I'd only known the half of them when he was alive I would have killed him myself. Laughing at poor Mary Mancini like that. I'm sorry that Chase ever hung out with him. I'm glad he didn't get him into trouble, not that he didn't try."

"What do you mean?" Lilly asked.

"Tyler had Chase send a few texts to people. They said things like 'I know what you did' and 'I saw you yesterday at four.' He told Chase they were writing prompts and that Chase should report back the conversations he had with people, playing his part. Poor Chase. Too trusting, always thinking the best of people. He thought they were practical jokes until someone called him and gave him an earful about harassment."

"What happened then?" Lilly asked.

"Chase blocked the numbers and deleted the texts," Portia said. "I wish he hadn't done that, of course. But it makes me wonder. How many other people did Tyler involve in his little schemes?"

CHAPTER 18

The next morning, Lilly drove down Shipyard Lane slowly. There really wasn't another way to do it, since the oyster shell–covered path had potholes that would swallow a muffler if taken at a speed higher than 5 mph. She drove past Ernie's new house and saw a flurry of activity taking place. The two-parked-cars-per-house rule wasn't being enforced right now, what with two of the three houses undergoing renovations.

She pulled up to the end of the lane and pulled into the empty space next to the old Dane house; also known as the new O'Connor house. Lilly noted that the scaffolding was still set up around the house and there were several workers outside scraping down paint.

"Hello, Lilly, what brings you here?" Warwick came down the side stairs of the porch and walked over to her. He leaned down and gave her a kiss on the cheek, which she returned.

"I came over to check on the stair project. I didn't

expect to see you here," Lilly said. "I would have brought you some cookies."

"I stopped by to talk to these folks. Nicole is covering my classes this morning."

"I didn't know you were going to have the house painted," Lilly said.

"Neither did we," Warwick said. He smiled and shook his head. "The roof had to be done. The upper windows had been replaced with terrible vinyl ones that weren't standing up to the ocean breezes, so we decided to replace those while the scaffolding was in place. Then—bing bang boom— next thing you know the house is getting painted and more windows are being replaced. We're still within our budget, money-wise, but time-wise we're pushing it."

"What color are you painting it?"

"Sort of a dark yellow with green and black trim, and cranberry red doors. Tamara picked the colors."

"Sounds pretty," Lilly said. For years the three houses had to all be painted white with black trim by covenant, but then the rules changed and each homeowner could use whatever color they wanted to. They were still restricted on additions to the house, however.

"Yeah, I hope Harmon Dane doesn't haunt us," Warwick said. "He kept it white all those years."

"He won't haunt you," Lilly said. "He'd be so grateful that you and Tamara are supporting the bird sanctuary the way you are."

"Please, our pleasure. Come on over and take a look. The stair project is coming along well."

The stair project went beyond building a staircase to give Shipyard Lane residents access to the beach. Harmon Dane had left a substantial amount of money to maintain a bird sanctuary under the staircase. Lilly walked over with Warwick to take a look. The egress path to the stairs, used only by the residents of the three houses, had been moved further on the property line. A fence had been put up, complete with birdhouses on the top of each post. The staircase itself came out several feet from the retaining wall, and then went down to the beach.

"It looks good," Lilly said. "The stairs are more imposing than I thought they would be, though."

"You let Dawn go all in on the design, and she did," Warwick said. "I like them. This way, if the grandkids come over and run down the stairs, they won't be right over the nesting areas. Of course, it helped that Harmon owned the beach, so we didn't have to ask permission."

"It also helped that this isn't a good swimming beach. Too many rocks," Lilly said. She took out her phone and snapped several pictures. "A good place for a sanctuary, actually. Speaking of which. I've finally got the paperwork for the sanctuary, and for the Dane estate's contribution for upkeep. I'll email it to you when I get home. Look it over and sign it for me, would you? Unless you have questions, of course. I'm going to update the site with these pictures."

"I'm sure they're fine. I'll get them back to you today or tomorrow. This is going to be a great place to live," Warwick said, taking a deep breath and looking out at the water. "And a great place to entertain. I'm hoping that Tamara isn't having second thoughts, though."

"Second thoughts? What do you mean?"

"She had the kids come over this weekend and take what they want to."

"She told me," Lilly said. "How did it go?"

"There's a lot of furniture left over. We have room in the new house, but we're trying to pare down. Anyway, she's going through memories and is a bit melancholy. I saw her packing her mother's china this morning, wiping away tears. There's a lot of that going around these days."

"What do you mean?" Lilly asked.

"Nicole. She told me she talked to you," Warwick said.

"Yes, I saw her yesterday."

"She came by my office after school and spilled her guts. There were lots of tears."

"Not your favorite thing," Lilly said.

"No, definitely not. Also, as Nicole and I have a professional relationship, I can't exactly give her a big hug and tell her it's going to be all right."

"Of course you can't," Lilly said. "Though your hugs have gotten me through some terrible times."

"You've got lifetime access to them," Warwick said. "But we're family."

Indeed they were. When Tamara lost her husband at such a young age, Lilly never thought she'd see her friend as happy again. But then Tamara started showing the new high school coach houses, and Lilly saw a spark come back. Tamara fought it for a while. She had three little girls. He was ten years younger than she was. Her excuses piled up, but Warwick held on. Thankfully.

"Should I reach out to Nicole?" Lilly said. "I hate to overstep, but she's new in town."

"That would be great," Warwick said. "She's been going full speed since she got here, but what with the 10K being done and winter coming, she's not as busy."

"And she's lonely."

"And she feels like an idiot for letting Tyler take advantage of her. Her words, not mine," Warwick said.

"There should be a club of people Tyler took advantage of," Lilly said. "I hate to speak ill of the dead, but he really was a piece of work. Portia told me about how he used her grandson to harass people." Lilly told Warwick about the texts.

He shook his head. "You know that the neural pathways for kids don't totally connect until they're twenty-five, right? Bad decision-making is one of the problems with the delay. How old is Chase? Twenty?"

"Twenty-one? Something like that," Lilly said.

"Bad decision-making times. Did he tell Bash?"

"I told Portia to have them connect."

"Then you told Bash to expect the call," Warwick said.

"You know me too well," Lilly said. "I'm not saying that Bash isn't up to the job, but finding Tyler's phone has to be a top priority."

"Higher than finding out who killed him?"

"No and yes. Tyler's phone has information that could hurt people. Is hurting people."

"Like those posts about Mary Mancini."

"Exactly. Now, someone may be accidentally posting. Or they may be taking advantage of the treasure trove of content they found. But whatever it is, Tyler can keep on hurting people, even now."

* * *

"Tamara, are you here?" Lilly called out.

"Back here in the den," Tamara said.

Lilly walked through the maze of furniture and boxes that were cluttering the first floor.

"What happened here?" Lilly said. "Isn't the house going on the market this week?"

"We're staging it," Tamara said. "Which means that all of this needs to go into storage so that the house looks light, bright, and breezy. It's easier to sell that way."

Lilly looked at the pictures leaning up against one of the dressers. "Does that mean taking the personality out of the house?" Lilly asked.

Tamara smiled. "People need to be able to picture themselves living in the house. While I love our artwork, not everyone would. The movers are going to pack this and store it. Besides, I'd hate for anything to happen to it."

Lilly looked around and sighed. "Well, this does it. I'm never moving. Can you imagine me trying to depersonalize my house?"

Tamara laughed. "No, I can't. I can see your house turning into some sort of museum, or a place where scholars go to study."

Lilly nodded. "Both good ideas. I really need to think about all of that, I suppose. I'd hate to leave a mess behind."

"We've both got years in front of us, my friend. But I agree. That's why I'm trying to downsize now, make sure the girls and Ty have what they want as far as furniture and other belongings go. I see too many people in my line of work with a house full of things that no one wants."

"I feel it necessary to remind you that you're actually moving into a bigger house," Lilly said.

Tamara's phone buzzed and she looked down at the text.

"If we ever move into the house," Tamara said. "Warwick said that there's a problem with the chimney flues. I'm going to tell him to text Ernie for some advice."

"He could also talk to Mary Mancini. She has some expertise in home restoration."

"Really? How do you know that?" Tamara asked. Her fingers stopped flying over phone, and she poked the *send* button with a flourish.

"She came by yesterday," Lilly said. "She was helping Roddy order things for his garden—"

"And you were teaching her about what they mean."

Lilly laughed. "Anyway, we had lunch over at my house. We started talking about making the back porch into a room that I could use all year round, and she had some great ideas."

"That would be fabulous," Tamara said. "I like your dining room and all, but I really love sitting out there, looking at your backyard."

"I know, the view feeds my soul. I am going to ask Mary to help me make it happen."

"That will give Mary a boost of confidence. Poor thing. Ray reached out to me last night. He talked to me about what Mary's been through. He said you'd helped her open up."

"I'm not sure I helped that much. She wanted to tell her story," Lilly said. "It's hard to believe she's the same age as your Rose, isn't it?"

"Yes and no," Tamara said. "A bad marriage can age a woman. But I still remember Mary and Rose as girls, bustling around the kitchen making cookies, giggling and gossiping. Seems like yesterday." Tamara cleared her throat and took a deep breath.

"Are you sorry that you've decided to move?" Lilly said.

"No, not really. I'm going to miss the memories of this house, but I look forward to making new ones. And the new house has a lot more room and those fabulous views. I'm guessing the kids will visit us more often, especially in the summer. It will all be fine." Her phone buzzed again. She looked down at her screen. "The movers are ten minutes away."

"I'll move my car and leave you to it. Let me know if you need anything, Tamara. Once you're done staging, you're welcome to come over to my clutter and have some tea."

"I'll definitely take you up on that," Tamara said, smiling.

Lilly drove over to the Triple B and parked. The fact that it was a Wednesday morning made both of those things infinitely easier. She entered the store through the garden center. She fussed with the mums and put a few aside.

"Lilly, I didn't see you come in," Ernie said.

"I snuck in the side door," Lilly said. "I parked out back. I wanted to get some mums for the house on Saturday."

"Mums? For a haunted house?" Ernie said.

"Yes, for a haunted house," Lilly said. "How could I not have flowers as part of the decorations? Besides, I want to see these used."

Ernie laughed. "You're right, of course. I've got

more shipments coming in tomorrow, so take what you want."

"*Take what you want* is never a good thing to say to me, Ernie. You know better than that. Delia would roll her eyes if she heard you making the suggestion."

"Where is Delia?" Ernie asked. "This isn't her teaching day, is it?"

"No, that's tomorrow. She went back over to Cole's house. He's been showing her his family tree."

"And she finds that interesting . . . why?" Ernie asked. "I can barely stand hearing him tell me a story about a dinner party he went to."

"Apparently Cole's research skills impressed her. She's also trying to learn more about his family, on both sides."

"Is there another side besides the descendant of the *Mayflower* side?" Ernie asked.

"There's always another side," Lilly said. She picked up another pot of mums. "Tell you what: Let's use the mums to help decorate all around town. No, not the raffle idea. We can put signs in them to let people know about the different locations on the Halloween stroll."

"We were going to use sticks with cardboard signs," Ernie said.

"Think how much nicer they'll look in a pot of mums. And then they can be a thank-you gift to the folks who are donating their time."

"Great idea, as always," Ernie said. He took out an index card and started making notes.

"Is Mary working today? I'd love to continue the conversation about my back porch."

"She and I had a long talk this morning. We're going to put her experience to better use and get her off the cash register." Ernie went over and grabbed a flatbed carriage and started loading it up with the mums Lilly was selecting.

"I'm glad she talked to you," Lilly said.

"I am too. She's got what my grandmother used to call moxie. People come in and stare at her and she stares right back and asks if she can help them. It's really lousy, you know? No matter what she does, she's going to be living under a cloud because of Tyler's death."

"And she's going to be walking on eggshells, waiting for the next story to drop," Lilly said. "Not just Mary. Tyler was juggling a lot of people's secrets." She handed Ernie a large purple mum.

"Yeah, whoever has his phone has a lot of power," Ernie said. He walked over and got a second cart. "Let's start dividing these up. Which ones do you want for your house? I'll keep the rest and deliver them down to the school where all the preparations are being done."

"As long as you let me pay for them," Lilly said. "Don't look at me like that, Ernie. You've been donating a ton of time and a fortune to this festival."

"It may have started out as a donation, but I'm getting plenty of return on the investment, let me tell you," Ernie said. "The Alden Park voting alone is keeping us hopping. At least half the people who come in for the festival bag end up buying something. I know this has been a lot of work, but it's also been a lot of fun."

"How is the marble voting going?" Lilly asked.

"Only Delia and I know," Ernie said, laughing. "Did you notice when you voted you couldn't see how many marbles were already in the jar?"

"I did," Lilly said. "I thought it was a way to help people remember which entry they voted for, since there were different colors on each one in addition to the number."

"There were also pictures," Ernie said. "Different people have different ways of remembering things. Anyway, we decided not to let people know how many marbles were in each jar. We didn't want it to persuade people to vote one way or another."

"That also helps it not become a popularity contest," Lilly said. "Smart. Not knowing makes it more fun."

"And it avoids hurt feelings. Because everyone tried, even though some don't have an ounce of talent for this sort of thing, bless their hearts."

"Ernie!" Lilly laughed.

"Don't 'Ernie' me! You know some folks have it and some folks don't."

Lilly stopped futzing with the plants and looked at Ernie. "Some folks have it and some folks don't," she said.

"You're thinking, I can tell. You're staring into space. What are you thinking?" he asked.

"Whoever has Tyler's phone. Maybe they don't have the stomach for any of this."

"What do you mean?"

"The second Mary story dropped after the issue with the tablet."

"Right."

"Maybe whoever has the phone thought they must have done something to post the story."

"They turned it on to check and accidentally posted another one?"

Lilly nodded.

"Then why don't they get rid of the phone?" Ernie asked.

"Because they don't want someone else to find it," Lilly said. "We need to get them to turn the phone back on."

Ernie walked Lilly out to the front of the store.

"There you are," Mary said. "Someone's been trying to reach you. You left your phone out here."

"Mary, thank goodness you're here. I'd forget my head if it weren't attached to my body." He picked up his phone and scrolled through the messages. "Tamara *is* trying to get hold of me, isn't she? Let me give her a call. Mary, here's what Lilly is buying. I made a note of the numbers and the codes for each plant. Give her a twenty-five percent discount on the sale. Lilly, don't start. I don't want to hear it. I'll be right back out."

"He's impossible," Lilly said. "Ignore what he said about the discount. The plants were already on sale."

"He's the boss," Mary said. "I have to do what he says." She spent the next few minutes plugging numbers into the tablet that served as a cash register, and then she gave Lilly her total. Lilly handed Mary her debit card.

"That's amazing, that you can use a computer tablet like that," Lilly said.

"It's a new system," Mary said. "It ties more directly into the inventory, so we can track how much of what has been sold. Ernie has me inputting other information into the computer so we can see what affects what."

"What other sorts of things?"

"What the weather is like. Whether or not there's something else going on around town. A rough estimate of how many people come in and don't buy. What the front display looks like and when it gets changed. If we posted a sales code online. That sort of thing."

"Interesting," Lilly said. "I'd imagine some of that information is already being tracked."

"It is, but not as personally. Like today, for example. It could look like there was a run on mums. But I'm going to log in and write a note explaining that you bought a lot of them. That will help us when we're ordering next fall."

Lilly nodded and smiled. She liked that Mary was using the "we" when she talked.

"Mary, I'd love to have you come back over to the house and help me think through the back-porch renovation."

Mary smiled. "I was thinking about it last night. I'd love to talk about it. Maybe get a look at the basement, so we know what we're dealing with."

"Of course," Lilly said. "I'll make sure Delia's around so that she can show you everything. Why don't we plan to have dinner afterwards?"

"That would be great, thanks."

"Perfect. Here's my phone number. Text me yours and I'll coordinate with Delia. What's so funny?"

"You, wanting me to text you. My parents are not texting people."

"I like talking to some people, but texting can be so efficient for this sort of thing. I'd like to think I—"

"You are not going to believe the call I just got," Ernie said, interrupting Lilly's conversation. Since Ernie never interrupted, Lilly knew she had to listen. Besides, Ernie's coloring was higher than normal and sweat was breaking out on his forehead.

"What's wrong?" Lilly asked.

"That was Tamara. Remember when I told you there was interest in my house? Someone put in an offer."

"That's great news, congratulations," Mary said.

"It is great news. And it's a great offer. More than I hoped, which will help a lot with the renovations. But there's a contingency."

"What sort of contingency?" Lilly asked.

"I need to be out of the house by November fifteenth."

"That's less than three weeks away," Lilly said.

"I know. But unless I agree to that date, they are going to go with another house. They want to be all moved in by Thanksgiving." Ernie took a handkerchief out of his pocket and mopped his brow. "I can be out of the house, but my new one won't be ready. Not by then. Maybe not even by Christmas."

"Well, then, you'll have to put your things in storage and move in with Delia and me for a while," Lilly said.

"I couldn't ask you to—"

"You're not asking me to do anything," Lilly said. "There's more than enough room in the house. And you can be on-site to help Delia plan Thanksgiving dinner. Unless you'd rather go somewhere else?"

Ernie smiled, leaned over, and gave Lilly a hug. "No, there's nowhere else I'd rather be," he said. "Let me call Tamara back and then I'll help you load the mums into your car."

CHAPTER 19

Lilly pulled the Jeep into the driveway and stopped before she pulled into the garage. She lifted up the hatch and started loading mums onto the lip of the retaining wall. Lilly liked that people couldn't easily get into her backyard from the driveway, since the further down it went, the lower the driveway was. But unloading plants? That was always a challenge. For larger orders of mulch and the like she had a truck deliver it all and use their elevator to get it to backyard height. But for days like today, Lilly got a workout by lifting things up to shoulder height.

"What's all this?" Delia said. She walked down the back-porch stairs and over to Lilly.

"I bought some mums. We're going to use them for decorations," Lilly said.

Delia looked at the dozens of plants that were lining the ledge. She smiled, nodded, and picked up a couple of pots. "In the greenhouse or out here?"

"Out here. We'll use them this weekend," Lilly said. She smiled. She knew that she would be fine living on her own, but she was so grateful that she didn't have to. Delia was the perfect housemate.

"Lilly, I've had an idea," Delia said. "I wanted to run it by you before I hit *send*."

"All right," Lilly said. "That's the last of the plants. Let me put the car in the garage and then we can talk."

"Keep the car where it is; we're going to need it. Go on in through the kitchen. I'm heating up some soup."

Lilly did as she was told. She washed her hands and hung her coat up in the front hall closet. By the time she got back to the kitchen Delia was there, stirring the soup.

"I've been thinking too," Lilly said. "But you go first."

"No, you go," Delia said. "I want to see if we've been having the same thoughts."

"I have no doubt that your thoughts are much more complicated," Lilly said. "I wonder if whoever has the phone is nervous about the information on it. Did you notice that the second time the phone was turned on was after the tablet posted that story?"

"Not right afterwards, but yes, I noticed the timing," Delia said. "Since that got them to turn on the phone, I've been wondering if another post would get them to turn it on again. Maybe this time for longer so we can track it."

"What are you planning?" Lilly asked. She took two glasses out of the cabinet and filled them with water. She also put spoons and napkins on the table and sat down. Delia walked over with two bowls of soup.

"Chowder," Delia said. "I have oyster crackers to go with it."

"When did you make this?" Lilly asked.

"I didn't. I bought a quart at the fish market. We're having scrod for dinner, by the way. Anyway, I thought it was worth trying the soup." Delia dipped her spoon in and tasted it. "That's pretty good. I wonder what that spice is."

"I'm glad you like it," Lilly said. "Now back to your plan."

"I was finally able to get the passwords to Tyler's email account," Delia said.

"How did you do that?"

"His boss helped," Delia said. "Turns out he wasn't as careful about password security as you would have thought he'd be. She sent me the one he sent here. He used the same password for all of his email accounts."

"So you can reset his social media passwords?"

"I don't have to," Delia said. "I looked in the drafts of his email, and he had them all in there in an email he'd written to himself, but never sent."

"I wonder if his phone has more security?" Lilly asked.

"Probably. That could be part of the problem. Maybe the locked screen shows apps that can be accessed, but keeps the screen locked. Whoever has the phone—"

"Keeps hitting buttons," Lilly said.

"That's what I'm thinking, Lilly. Anyway, I talked to Bash about my idea. He honestly doesn't think much of it."

"What's your idea?"

"I think I should post from the *Goosebush News* site. The one I run. I'll tell people that we're close to getting access to Tyler's videos, since they were stored in the cloud. That people should tune in today at four PM, because I'll post the last pictures he took live."

"Which might unmask his killer. What would make the person believe you're able to do that?" Lilly asked.

"I'm going to repost from Tyler's accounts. To show whoever has his phone that I can get control of it."

Lilly put her spoon down and looked at Delia. "Doesn't that seem dangerous? Are you putting yourself in harm's way?"

"I doubt it. No one will know it's really me doing the posting."

"Why four o'clock?"

"To give the news time to spread around town. I want to be near where Tyler died so we can try to pinpoint the location of the phone. I'm hoping that whoever has it will turn it on for a while."

"And Bash doesn't like this idea?"

"He thinks it's a long shot and probably needs a warrant. He's working on that. But if we do it, as private citizens, there isn't as much red tape."

"Delia, that sounds reckless," Lilly said.

"Maybe, but how else are we going to find his phone unless we get someone to turn it on for a while and try to figure out what's happening? Bash can honestly say he doesn't know why the phone got turned on."

Lilly sighed. She didn't like the idea, but maybe it would work. "How close will you be able to get to the phone?"

"Pretty close," Delia said. "Scottie gave me all the tracking information, so I put the apps on my phone and on my tablet. Bash has the same information. But it's been quiet. That's why I think we need to bait whoever has the phone."

"When do you plan to post the story?"

"As soon as we're done with lunch," Delia said. "We may be sitting in the car for a while, so we need to get ready."

"Where are we going to be waiting?" Lilly asked.

"Close to where he died is the best place, I think," Delia said. "That's where the phone has been the last two times. If it's moved, hopefully it will be on long enough for us to move too. And Bash to get there. What do you think?"

Lilly thought of Mary, Nicole, and Chase, all waiting for the next story to drop, all holding their breath and looking over their shoulders.

"Sounds like a plan."

Delia parked on a side street, a couple of streets over from where Tyler had been found. They'd debated parking closer, but decided that it was better to be out of sight, but within driving distance. They'd been sitting in the car for forty minutes already. Lilly was filling the time by working on a crossword puzzle.

Delia had pulled out a notebook and was making notes while verifying information on her phone. She'd set up her tablet in the front seat to track the phone if it pinged.

"What happens if there's no more power?" Lilly said. "The phone may be dead."

"I doubt Tyler would have gone out with a less-than-charged phone," Delia said. "And it's been off most of the time." Delia had explained this several times already, but Lilly was getting bored.

"What are you working on?"

"I'm taking some notes from Cole's family tree. The Howland family tree."

"He's really invested in his ancestry, isn't he?" Lilly asked.

"He is. But like most people, it's about more than a bloodline. It's about belonging."

"Seemed like he had a difficult relationship with his father," Lilly said.

Delia nodded and made a few more notes. "His father was mostly absent from his life. His mother left him when Cole was a baby. Cole blamed her for him not being around. It sounds really complicated."

"Many family relationships are," Lilly said. "Like the captain and his daughter. Misunderstandings, secrets. They pile up over time."

"They sure do," Delia said. "Cole also values one side of his family over the other, which isn't good. But I think I've convinced him into looking at his mother's side of the family. I showed him a couple of sites he could use to get started."

"How did he do the research on his father's side?" Lilly asked.

"His father left him a family tree and Cole used old-school methods. He does some research online, but he says he doesn't trust all the records."

"Has he ever done one of those DNA tests?" Lilly asked.

"He says he doesn't trust them. Doesn't like the idea of DNA banks."

Lilly looked over at her friend, bent over her notebook making notes and sketches only she would understand. "Delia, who do you think did this?" Lilly said.

Delia sighed. "Cole," she said. "I hate to say it, but I think he had the most to lose. Or he thought he did."

"Tyler may not have known who the bodies were, or been able to guess," Lilly said.

Delia looked over at Lilly and shook her head. "He was following the same information I was," she said. "One of the research fellows I was working with was let go this afternoon. A friend gave me a heads-up that the information she gave me may have been compromised."

"Compromised?"

"She left things out of the documents she was sharing with me. Another student did a comparison and found the discrepancies. Apparently, she was sharing information with Tyler. She included the DNA results from the skeletons in what she shared."

"But did he make all the connections you'd made?" Lilly asked.

"He had the same information I had. He was checking the Historical Society records, but he also spent a ton of time at the library."

"Far be it for me to speak ill of the dead, but I can only imagine what Tyler was concocting for a story. Still, he needed more proof before he went after Cole."

"What would happen if he stole Cole's DNA?" Delia asked.

"Stole it? How?"

"Got a piece of gum that Cole tossed. Or took one of his used coffee cups."

"Like in the movies? That may work for police officers, but for civilians?" Lilly wondered. "Don't you spit in a tube for those tests?"

"Lilly, do you really think Tyler didn't have ways

to get things like gum tested? I'm sure he knew shortcuts, or could find them."

Lilly put the cap back on her pen and turned to Delia. "What would be the point of the story? To humiliate Cole?"

"Cole told me more about what he did before he retired. Actually, he's not really retired. He still has a few clients. Really, really wealthy clients. He helps them move money around. I'm not sure what that means, exactly, but the way Cole said it made me think it was not for public consumption."

"More secrets," Lilly said.

"Depending on what the secrets are, maybe secrets worth killing to protect? I don't know. I've enjoyed talking to Cole these past couple of days. I've seen a side of him—but to answer your initial question, I think it was Cole. You?"

"I'm not sure," Lilly said. "I have another theory that—"

At that moment a beeping sound came up from the tablet. Delia quickly picked it up and expanded the picture.

"It's near where Tyler died," Delia said. "It looks like it's in Cole's house."

"Let's go," Lilly said.

"Where now?" Lilly said.

"The beep hasn't moved. Like I said, the tracking system is only accurate to within a few yards."

"It looks like it's in Cole's backyard. Let's park on the path."

The drove slowly on the path, not turning on lights and coasting to a stop. Delia turned the car off and turned to Lilly.

"What now" she said.

"What indeed? Should we pay Cole another visit?"

"And see if he's on the phone? Sure, that could work. In the meantime . . ." Delia scrolled through her keypad and looked at her contacts. "Maybe I should call Tyler's phone?"

"Wait until we're inside," Lilly said. "If the phone rings, Cole may turn it off."

Lilly and Delia walked around to Cole's front door. He answered the door, looking more disheveled than normal.

"Delia. Lilly. Should I have been expecting you?"

"No, sorry Cole, we thought we'd stop by. I was telling Lilly about your family research methods, and I couldn't explain them well enough. I was hoping you could show her how you set up—"

"I'm rather busy right now. Maybe tomorrow?" Cole said.

"We were hoping to get started tonight," Delia said. "On her family tree. I want to model it after the work you've done, with the stories."

Lilly saw Delia punch a button, probably to dial Tyler's phone. She didn't hear anything, nor did Cole respond. Lilly looked down on the tablet and saw that the red dot had started to move.

"Sorry to disturb you, Cole. We'll check back to-morrow," Lilly said. She gently elbowed Delia in the ribs and tilted her head toward the door.

Delia and Lilly walked back to the street. Cole still stood in the doorway, staring at them both.

"What was that about?" Delia asked.

"The red dot moved. Call Tyler's number again."

Delia did as she was told. The dot continued to move.

"It's going by the marsh, see that?" Delia said. "Let's go."

Delia took off in a run toward the marsh. Lilly did her best to keep up, but it was hopeless. The stitch in her side slowed her down, and the ache in her knees discouraged her from trying again. Lilly looked down at the red dot. It disappeared.

Lilly kept moving in the direction that Delia had run. She kept looking down at the tablet, but the red dot didn't reappear. She kept moving, looking for Delia, but she'd lost her.

Lilly got to the end of the path and went to her right, toward the marsh. She hurried, but stopped when she heard a noise coming from across the street. She peered into the woods, but didn't see anything. Nevertheless, she took her phone out of her pocket and held it up. She hit the button to record a video and did a sweep of the woods. She turned around and saw someone hurrying across the street.

"Lilly, come here! I need you!" Delia yelled.

Lilly turned around and ran in the direction of Delia's voice.

"Lilly!"

"Coming! Where are you?"

"By the water," Delia called out.

Lilly continued walk quickly/jog toward down the road. She came to the intersection that led people to the point. One road split into four, and then all four roads met again to go over the bridge to the beach.

Lilly stopped, looked over to her right, then her left. "Delia!" she called.

"Here!" Delia called. Lilly looked to her right

and saw Delia waving. She ran across the street to the edge of the marsh.

Delia was chest-high in water, wading out toward some marsh grasses. Lilly shivered watching her.

"Delia, what are you doing? It's freezing out here," Lilly said.

"I saw him throw something," Delia said.

"Who?" Lilly asked. "Get out of there!"

"I think it landed over here." Delia pointed to the marsh grass and kept moving forward.

"Is everything all right?" Cole said, running up behind Lilly.

"Cole, could you go get some blankets? We're going to need to warm her up," Lilly said. Cole ran back to his house, and Lilly turned back to Delia.

"Delia, get out of there," Lilly said. "It's dangerous for you to be in the water like that. Nothing is worth it."

"Not even this?" Delia said. She lifted something over her head and started walking back toward Lilly.

"For heaven's sake," Lilly said. She hit a speed dial on her phone. "Hello, Bash. I need you to come down to the bay loop. You're on your way? Delia may have found Tyler's phone. Bring an ambulance with you. She's coming out of the water now."

CHAPTER 20

Delia had started to shiver the minute she got out of the water. Lilly took off her coat and put it around Delia's body. She held the young woman close and started to rub both her arms. They stayed like that for what seemed like hours, but was a much shorter time. Maybe a minute or two. Cole drove up and parked sideways on the side of the road. He opened the car door and grabbed a large gray wool blanket. He draped it around Lilly and Delia.

"Should I call the police?" he asked.

"I already did," Lilly said.

"What on earth was she doing?" he asked.

"We've been trying to track Tyler's phone. We planted a story." Lilly started to shiver as well and Cole ran back to his car. He riffled through the trunk and found a beach towel. He put it around Lilly's shoulders.

"The story about showing the face of his killer?"

Lilly nodded.

"How would that help you find the phone?" The sound of sirens suddenly came closer and Cole stood up to wave the cars down.

"Lilly, you need to go to the hospital," Bash said.

"No I don't," Lilly said. "I'll be fine after a long, hot shower. So will Delia, more than likely, but she's a tiny little thing. Better safe than sorry; good that she's getting checked out. Maybe you could give me a ride back to my car."

"I am not going to give you a ride back to your car," Bash said.

"Did Delia give you the phone?" Lilly asked.

"She did, after a bit of a fight. I can't believe you both," he said.

"Delia said she told you the idea."

"She did. I said we needed to make sure we were crossing t's and dotting i's before we take that step. Besides, there were other leads we were following so we could make the case."

"Following?"

"I had officers following Nicole Shaw," Bash said.

"Bash!"

"And Chase Asher. And someone else was keeping an eye on Mary Mancini."

"Fritz Stewart wasn't on your list?" Lilly asked.

"Fritz? No. Why?"

"Not sure yet. I've got to get into some warm clothes and get to the hospital to sit with Delia," Lilly said.

"You're half right," Bash said. "I'm calling Ernie and asking him to go and check on Delia." Bash took Lilly by the hand and led her to his car.

"Cole, would you make sure Lilly's car is locked up? We'll send someone by later to pick it up," Bash said.

"Of course," Cole said. He'd been standing there with his wet blanket and towel. "Is Delia going to be all right?"

"I'd imagine so," Bash said. "Thanks to you and Lilly."

"Could you call Roddy and ask him to come get me?" Lilly asked Bash.

"No need for that. I'm taking you home," Bash said.

"But you need to check the phone for prints," Lilly said.

"It's already on its way to the lab," Bash said. "Now, let's get you home."

Lilly was wrong. A nice, hot shower and dry clothes made her feel better, but she was still cold. She went downstairs and heard voices coming from the living room. Warwick was adding a log to a fire and Roddy was pouring a cup of tea.

"What on earth did you both do?" Roddy said. He put the teapot down and walked over to Lilly. He opened his arms and she stepped into them. She rested her head on his chest and took the hug gratefully. After a few seconds she stepped back.

"We decided to try and find the phone," Lilly said. "Delia set a trap." Luna tried to jump on the arm of Lilly's chair, but she fell far short. Lilly reached over and picked her up, putting the kitten on her lap.

"Bash said he had a computer set up down at the station with the app to track the phone, but then there was a fire over on the other side of town on top of school letting out, and they missed the phone being turned on. He didn't sound happy about that," Warwick said. "He told me to tell you he'd be back."

"It got the person to turn the phone on," Lilly said. "We thought it was in Cole's house. It looked that way, at least. But then Delia tried to call Tyler's phone and the red dot moved."

"The red dot being the phone," Warwick said.

"Yes, but Cole didn't. Delia must have seen something or someone. She started to run. Oh Delia—how is she? Does anyone know?" Lilly took the cup of tea from Roddy and sipped it. He'd added milk and sugar, which was not her normal way of drinking tea, but it was oddly comforting.

"She's on her way home," Warwick said. "Ernie's got her. They wanted to keep her overnight, but once her body warmed up she insisted she leave. How long was she in the water? Why was she in the water?"

"How long? Not long," Lilly said. "Of course, it's cold out, so any amount of time is dangerous. But it's not freezing. Some people still swim this time of year. They're a little off, but who am I to judge? Now, where was I? Oh, the why? She must have seen Fritz throw the phone into the water and gone in after it."

"Fritz?" Warwick said. "Fritz Stewart?"

"Yes, it's the only thing that makes sense, don't you see?"

"No, I don't," Roddy said. "Drink some more tea and explain it."

"You know that each time the phone went on they traced it to Cole's house, right?"

"Right."

"But Bash searched for it and didn't find it. Delia and I went to Cole's house yesterday. Sure enough, the windows in his mudroom and kitchen looked out to the path. The other windows on that side of the house were blocked. Anyway, Cole said a couple of things that made more sense when the red dot started to move.

"Yesterday he said that he spent as little time in the kitchen as possible. He also said that the morning of the murder he and Fritz had taken a walk, and that Fritz had made some coffee."

"Fritz could have been in the kitchen and seen Tyler," Warwick said.

"Exactly. Who knows what happened? But somehow Fritz ended up with Tyler's phone."

"But he only turned it on when he was at Cole's house?" Roddy said. "Was he trying to set Cole up?"

"I really don't know. I don't know if Bash will be able to prove that Fritz did anything. I hope that the phone Delia found is Tyler's, and that Bash is able to find enough evidence on it to answer some of the questions. At least we know that people like Nicole and Mary can sleep a little sounder tonight."

CHAPTER 21

Lilly was walking around her garden, moving pots around. She had several large, heavy decorative pots that she'd use for invasive plants like mint or ivy, or for decorative seasonal plants. She'd winter the plants in the greenhouse, but she used the pots all year long. Later on she and Delia would plant mums in all of them, an homage to the fall. The mums would be moved into the greenhouse before the first frost. During the holidays Lilly used the pots for more decorative purposes that included branches, greenery, and lights.

She stood back and looked at her handiwork. Not bad, not bad at all. She walked over and took three of the mums she'd bought yesterday and rested them in the pots. She went back for more and looked up at the plaintive face peering through the back door.

"Do you want to try this again?" Lilly asked. Luna tilted her head and opened her mouth. Lilly assumed she'd meowed, but she couldn't hear it through the door. Lilly walked up the stairs and opened the door a crack. She grabbed the kitten before she escaped.

"Listen, little missy, you wandering around back here is not an option," Lilly said. "The last thing we need is for you to jump down on the driveway and try to escape. You are an indoor cat from now on, with occasional outdoor privileges. But only if you wear your harness and you're on a leash. Should we try this again?"

Luna tried to twist out of Lilly's hands, but she gave up and meowed again. Lilly held her body close with one hand while she searched in her pocket for the leash. She found it and snapped it back on the harness. She made sure she was holding it when she put Luna down on the ground gently.

Luna ran forward, dropped to the ground, and started rolling around.

"The harness is staying on," Lilly said. "Let's try walking again. Come on, follow me."

Lilly walked forward gently. Luna stayed put. But after being gently dragged, she realized that she could explore and she ran forward.

"Now, Luna, there are parts of the garden that I don't want you to visit," Lilly said. "Some of these plants will make you sick. But I'll tell you what. Next spring we'll have a Luna section of the garden. We'll plant some grasses, maybe even some catnip. And you can come out on the patio with us, as long as you're on your leash. Don't meow at me. I don't want you to get lost. And there are things out there that are dangerous for a little girl like you."

Luna walked back toward Lilly, sat down, and meowed.

"I'm glad you agree," Lilly said. "Let me show you around the garden. Do you see those statues? Those remind me of some of my favorite people who ever lived. We put most of their ashes out in the ocean, but I kept a few and buried them here in the garden. I hope that doesn't seem odd to you. I talk to them on occasion as well."

Luna walked along the paths with Lilly. She occasionally wandered into one of the flower beds, but Lilly gently yanked her back.

Lilly deluded herself that Luna was learning. Today's goal was to get her used to the harness. The results of the experiment were mixed at best, but Lilly had patience.

Lilly brought Luna back to the patio area. She looped the end of the leash under one of the legs of the chairs. That wouldn't work long-term, but for now Luna couldn't move the furniture, try as she might.

"Lilly, I told you I'd help with the mums," Delia said. She walked down the back door steps. She was holding a cup of coffee in her hands, and sipped it slowly.

"I know you did," Lilly said. "I thought I'd let you sleep in a bit."

"I do appreciate that," Delia said. "I can't believe how tired I was last night."

"We had a full day," Lilly said. "The added bonus of a trip to the hospital put it over the top."

"I was fine—am fine," Delia said.

"Nevertheless, you might not have been. Hyperthermia is no joke."

"I knew you were right behind me," Delia said.

"Though I will admit I didn't think the water was that deep." She shivered slightly and wrapped both hands around the mug.

"I still can't imagine what possessed you—"

"I saw Fritz toss the phone. And I saw where it landed. It looked like it was on top of some marsh grass, but the water was lapping. I didn't want to lose the phone. Not after all that."

"You're sure you saw Fritz," Lilly said.

"Pretty sure," Delia said. "But he did have a base-ball cap on, so I couldn't see his face. Once he threw the phone, I paid attention to that." Delia sat on the chair that Luna was attached to, and reached her hand to the kitten. Luna ran over for some head rubs. "Any news from Bash?"

"He confirmed it was Tyler's phone. They're working on accessing it now, but he had several lay-ers of encryption. And he said that there may be us-able prints. That's all he'd say."

Delia sighed. "We may never know what hap-pened. Not unless Fritz confesses."

Lilly nodded. "You're right, of course."

"He'll want to tell the story to the right person," Delia said. "It would be nice to get this all wrapped up before the Halloween stroll this weekend."

Lilly sniffed the air. "Do you smell smoke?"

Delia nodded her head and got up and looked around. "It's coming from the garden door," she said. She held her hand against the door and turned to Lilly. "It *is* the garden door."

Delia jumped back as a trickle of water started to flow beneath the door. "What the—?"

Lilly took her phone out of her pocket and called Roddy.

"Are you burning down the door?" Lilly asked.

"Good morning to you, Lilly," he said. "I was rather hoping I was going to be able to surprise you."

"Surprise me?"

"I was talking to one of the workers in my house, and he thought that he might be able to cut through the iron bars close to the granite slab. He has a fairly amazing saw that is allowing him to get close to the ground. Anyway, he's working on it, but as the iron heats up the door begins to smolder, so we've had to add cooling time to the project."

"Is that what that racket is?" Lilly said. She'd been hearing sawing and hammering coming from over the garden wall all morning, but she knew that Roddy was trying to finish up work before the weekend.

"Some of it. Sorry about the noise. It's a bit of a madhouse over here."

"No worries. Just don't burn down the door. We'll have a hose ready to go on our side, just in case."

Lilly walked over to the garden hose and rolled it out. She turned it on and misted the door itself. It had survived for a century and a half, but would it survive this?

Lilly and Delia stared at the door for a few minutes, but then they got back to work in the garden.

"Let's use the rest of the mums in the front of the house, for decoration," Lilly said.

"Do you mind if I put them in the coffin planter?" Delia said. "My first thought was a poison garden, but we'd have to explain that all day. And given everything, I thought we shouldn't cast aspersions on your gardens. I thought we could put a fake skeleton in it, but plants would be more fitting for the display, don't you think?"

Lilly shook her head and smiled. "I can't believe I'm saying this, but why don't we make a skeleton coming out of plant materials? We can put the mums around the coffin, like funeral plants."

Delia smiled at Lilly. She took her notebook out and started sketching.

"Or we could do a creepy plant design," Delia said. "Do you mind if I use things from the garden?"

"Use whatever you need to," Lilly said. "I leave this project to you." Lilly's phone buzzed in her pocket. "Good morning, Bash."

"Thanks for coming down, Lilly," Bash said, standing up from his desk until Lilly got seated. She declined his offer of coffee, and turned to him.

"Thank you for calling me," Lilly replied. "I was going to call you later this afternoon to check in."

"I'm surprised you waited," Bash said, smiling. "Here's the deal: We have a situation and I need your help."

"Anything, you know that."

"Fritz won't leave his house," Bash said. "He answered a few questions last night, but I wanted to make sure we got the evidence lined up before we brought him in for questioning."

"Did you do that? Get the evidence lined up?"

"We got into Tyler's phone," Bash said. "It's going to be quite the process to go through it. But we looked at the last few images he took. One was a video of Fritz yelling at him from Cole's backyard.

Another was a picture of Fritz climbing down the retaining wall. A third was of Fritz coming at Tyler with a branch in his hand."

Lilly took a deep breath. "What does Fritz say?" she asked Bash.

"He isn't answering his phone. I sent an officer down to bring him in and he isn't answering his door. I'm not sure—hold on, this might be an update."

"Hello, Steph. Really. Are you sure? Ask Cole to keep him talking. I'll be right there. I'm bringing Lilly Jayne with me."

Bash stood up. "Fritz is threatening to burn down his house. Let's go."

Lilly and Bash pulled up as the fire engine arrived. Bash had called and asked them to arrive without sirens, which they did. They pulled up on the front lawn and Bash went over to talk to them. Another officer joined them.

"Steph's worried he might have blown out his pilot light," Bash said. "If he did and the house is filling up with gas, it's a tinderbox. We're going to try and get in the front door, but I don't want to startle him. Can you keep him talking?" Lilly nodded and walked to the back of the house.

Cole was standing in the middle of Fritz's backyard. "Look, Fritz, Lilly's here," he called out. "She'll know what to do."

Cole walked over to Lilly. "He's lost his mind," he said. "He's threatening to blow up his house and stay inside while he did it. Maybe you can talk to him."

Lilly walked to the spot where Cole had been standing. She looked up and saw Fritz leaning on one of the window jambs on the second floor, his face framed by the open window. She saw a flicker of light and realized that it was from some sort of lighter that Fritz was holding in his hand. He'd create a flame, and the wind would blow it out.

"Fritz, what are you doing?" Lilly said.

"All we have is our reputation," Fritz said. "The one we earn in life and the one we create for after we're gone. It's all ruined, ruined."

"Fritz, you've lived here a long time and know a lot of people who care about you. They'll listen to your story. Your reputation doesn't have to be ruined."

"You don't understand," he said.

"Of course I do," Lilly said. "Tyler Crane was not a good man. He found out secrets and held them over people's heads like it was some sort of game. Did he do that to you, Fritz?"

"Ruined, ruined," Lilly heard him say as he flicked the lighter.

"You know, he made Mary Mancini's life miserable, the poor thing. They had an argument that morning. Out on the path. Did you see that, Fritz? Did you see them argue?"

"He hit her and she fell down," Fritz said. "I went out to help her, but she'd gone."

"Then what happened?" Lilly asked.

Fritz shook his head, so Lilly continued. "Fritz, you're a good man. I'll bet that seeing Mary hurt made you angry. So you went down to talk to Tyler. What did he say? Did he make fun of you?"

"He always made fun of me," Fritz says. "Everyone always does. Cole does, don't you, Cole? I don't mind. I'm easy to make fun of. A bumbling old man with nothing but papers to show for a life. I try to be useful, I really do."

"You are useful," Lilly said.

"And to keep the peace. No more fighting. Fighting isn't good. People die if they don't get along. Like my wife. If we hadn't been arguing that day in the car I would have seen that truck. But we were arguing, so I missed it. We were always arguing. What a waste. I lost her and my beautiful boy. Fighting. What a waste."

"That's a sad story, Fritz," Lilly said. "I'd never heard it before. That must have been why you moved back to Goosebush all those years ago."

"Back home with my mother," Fritz said. "She only liked happy stories, my mother did. Only happy stories."

"Which is why you like happy stories," Lilly said. She began to wonder where Bash was. Fritz was flicking the lighter more often and had slumped back into the house. "Did you tell Tyler your happy stories?"

"I did, but he twisted them," Fritz said. "He started yelling at me, telling me that I didn't share everything with him. He said he'd tell people that I killed my family unless I—" Fritz choked down a scream and started to weep. The lighter kept flicking on and off.

"Told him other stories," Lilly said gently. She said it again, louder. "Fritz, that's how he operated. He pushed people around. He pushed you too far that morning, didn't he?"

"I didn't mean to—I didn't mean to do it," Fritz sobbed. "I pushed him down. He fell, and then he started to laugh at me. So I hit him again. I didn't mean to—"

"Of course you didn't mean to," Lilly said.

Bash came around the corner and waved at Lilly.

"Fritz, let's talk more about this, but not shouting at each other. Bash is going to come in and bring you downstairs. We'll go down to the station and explain all of this to him."

"He won't understand—" Fritz shouted. He moved back into the house.

"Of course he will," Lilly yelled up at him. "Bash is one of the best people I know. Tell you what—Cole can come with us as well."

"Cole doesn't care what happens to me—"

Lilly looked over at Cole. He had a stricken look on his face. "Cole is your friend," Lilly said. "Of course he cares."

"But it's my fault that—"

"Enough of that," Lilly said. "Come downstairs, Fritz. Let's clear the air and get back to the happy stories."

Cole walked over and stood next to Lilly.

"Come on, Fritz. We'll get this entire misunderstanding cleared up, I promise," Cole said.

They both watched Bash reach through the window and take the lighter from Fritz. He helped him stand up and they disappeared from the window.

"Poor old Fritz," Cole said. "I can't believe he could have—"

"Of course you can," Lilly said. "We're all capable of all sorts of behavior. Tyler didn't just trade in secrets. He traded in people's desire to keep those secrets. Tell me, Cole, is Fritz your friend?"

"Of course he is," Cole said.

"Then act like it," Lilly said. "Stand with him now. Get him a good lawyer. Come down to the station with him. Be a good friend, or try to be." Lilly gave Cole a long stare and then she turned and walked back to the front of the house.

CHAPTER 22

"Sorry I'm late," Lilly said to Delia as she walked into the kitchen. "You didn't have to wait for me." She sat down at the table and leaned back in her chair. She closed her eyes.

"I wanted to wait for you," Delia said. "Are you all right? You've been gone for hours."

Lilly looked at her watch. Five o'clock. She closed her eyes again and took a deep breath.

"Fritz threatened to kill himself," Lilly said.

"What? Oh no," Delia said. "Did you stop him?"

"No, actually Cole did. He kept beating the door and calling until Fritz told him to stop it. Cole kept him talking and called the police in to help."

"And you went in to help as well," Delia said. She put a glass of water and a plate down in front of her.

Lilly got up and washed her hands. She paused at the kitchen sink, letting the warm water flow over her hands. They still felt dirty.

She sat back down at the table and broke a piece of the sandwich off, putting it in her mouth. She chewed and swallowed. "I'm not sure how much I helped."

"What do you mean?" Delia asked.

"We were so determined to find that phone, you know? I was feeling so self-righteous about stopping Tyler's legacy from hurting more people. But in doing that, Fritz became collateral damage. The poor man. He's a wreck."

"Lilly, if he's the one who killed Tyler—"

"I don't think he meant to do it," Lilly said. "I'm not even sure what he did is what killed Tyler."

"What do you mean?" Delia put two mugs of tea on the table and sat down.

"I talked to Bash about what the medical examiner found. Tyler has a contusion on the back of his head. He also had a blow on the side of his head, with wood chips in it. The contusion on the back caused the brain bleed that killed him."

"Did Fritz push Tyler down?"

"No, it looks like Tyler slipped on the leaves and fell. The leaves that Cole had been spreading on the path so we wouldn't be able to use it."

"Did he tell you that?"

"I got him to admit it," Lilly said. "No one can say for certain, but there's an argument to be made that the fall itself probably killed Tyler. At least that's the argument Fritz's lawyer is making. Cole hired her for Fritz."

"Is Bash going to arrest Fritz?" Delia asked.

"Not today. Not without more evidence. He's going to talk to the DA tomorrow."

"That sounds like a good result then," Delia said. "Why are you so upset?"

Lilly shook her head. "It's easier when justice

prevails, you know? But breaking Fritz Stewart? Is that justice?"

"That's not for you or I to say," Delia said. "It sounds like Cole is looking out for Fritz and you are too. Let that be enough for now."

Lilly took a sip of tea. "I need to go up and take a nap," she said.

"A nap is a good idea. But we need to be down at the Star by seven o'clock for the festival committee party."

"I don't feel like going to a party," Lilly said.

"But you have to go, to make sure that the Fritz story gets told the way you want it to," Delia said. "Besides, it won't be a party without you there."

Lilly and Delia walked into the Star restaurant as PJ Frank was winding up his remarks to the crowd.

"Anyway, I'd like to offer my thanks to all of you on behalf of Jessie and me. When we started the Goosebush brewery, it was more of an experiment in taking our hobby up a notch. But thanks to the support of so many of you—especially Stan Freeland, who always makes sure we're on tap—Jessie is able to quit his job and make this a full-time gig."

"Just as long as you don't close the lumberyard," someone said.

PJ laughed. "Nope, that's not going to happen. I'm proud that I'll be part of two businesses located right here in Goosebush."

The crowd cheered and Stan took the microphone from PJ.

"I'd like to thank PJ and Jessie for contributing the beer samples tonight. And the Cupcake Castle for their contributions. We're proud to fill in with some sandwiches and our homemade chips. Listen, six months ago this Fall Festival wasn't a germ of an idea. But in those six months, look what we've all been able to pull off. This weekend's Halloween stroll is going to be a great way for folks to get around town and have a good time. I hear there's going to be a fabulous haunted house on Washington Street, and I know I'm looking forward to that. The important thing is that we're having fun. But after what happened last weekend, let's make sure we're not having fun at the expense of anyone else. How does that sound?"

Another cheer went up in the room. Stan raised his hand again to get people to quiet down.

"Before we start eating and drinking, Ernie Johnson wanted me to let you all know that the voting for Alden Park sketches goes through tomorrow night at eight o'clock. The winner will be announced on Saturday morning. So, folks, thanks again for all of your hard work on this year's festival. Eat, drink, and be kind to each other."

Lilly looked around the room and saw Tamara sitting down at one of the tables holding her grandson Alan. She made her way over. Mary Mancini was sitting with her, along with Tamara's daughter Rose.

"Mind if I join you?" Lilly said. When Alan saw Lilly he started to clap and reached his chubby arms out to her. She took him in her arms and sat down at the chair. Alan gave her a sloppy hug and rested his head on her shoulder.

"That child loves you," Tamara said.

"We all love our Auntie Lil." Rose patted Lilly's arm and gave her a smile. "I heard you had a tough day, Auntie Lil. You okay?"

"Better having seen you, Rose," Lilly said. "And

this little darling. What a love bug he is." Alan settled into her lap and started banging silverware on
the table. Rose took it from him and replaced it
with cloth toys that made less noise. Lilly kissed the
top of his head.

"I still can't believe you've got a kid," Mary said to
Rose. "I remember in Girl Scouts you failed the
babysitting badge."

"That's because I didn't want to change a diaper.
But when you've got your own, you really don't have
a choice."

Alan looked at Mary and smiled. She waved at
him and he laughed.

"Auntie Lil, did I hear that you're dressing up
like a witch on Saturday?" Rose said.

"That's the plan," Lilly said.

"You have to do better than that," Rose said. "You
should dress up with irony. You're not a witch, not
even ironically."

Lilly sighed. "Do you have an idea of what I
should wear?"

"I do," Rose said. "I've got a master plan."

CHAPTER 23

Lilly went out to her garden to cut a few more branches for Delia. The front of the house was fully decorated—they'd started at five o'clock in the morning. The branches were going to be put in place to help hold up the giant spiderweb. She laid the branches on the retaining wall for Delia.

"You need to finish getting ready!" Lilly shouted after Delia as she grabbed the branches and ran down the driveway.

"I'll be ready. We have a half hour yet."

Lilly shook her head. Ernie and Warwick had spent the morning helping them get set up. The setup included a series of large frames that held curtains in place. Once the haunted house was open the frames would be moves to create paths for people to walk down. Lilly had to admit, the yard looked transformed. She wasn't sure it was scary, but the decorations were fun.

"Knock, knock. Aren't you dressed yet?" Ernie asked. He walked through the open garden gate from Roddy's house.

"I am all dressed," Lilly said. "You'll need to guess who I am." Lilly put the flowered hat on her head and put a map of England in her dress pocket.

Ernie shook his head. "I have no idea," he said.

"Delia's costume may help. Who are you?"

Ernie was dressed in an Edwardian suit. "My doctor's bag is in Roddy's yard. Come over to his house; his outfit will give you a clue."

Lilly walked through the garden gate, being careful not to trip on the stubs of iron that stuck up from the granite. Since they'd opened the gate on Thursday it hadn't been shut. Lilly supposed at some point one or the other of them would want some privacy, but right now they were enjoying the easy egress.

Lilly stopped and smiled. Roddy was dressed in a large cloak and a deerstalker hat. "Watson, I presume," Lilly said to Ernie.

"Got it in one," Ernie said, smiling.

"Lilly, come over here and meet my family," Roddy said. She'd never seen him smile so broadly as when he said *family*.

"This is my daughter, Emma. My son-in-law, David. And my granddaughter, Lucy."

"It is a real pleasure to meet all of you," Lilly said.

"Guess who they are," Ernie said, gesturing to Roddy's family. They were all dressed in tight red and black uniforms.

"The Incredibles," Lilly said.

"How did you know that?" Ernie asked.

"Ernie doesn't give me much credit for popular culture references," Lilly said to Emma and David. "For good reason. But that movie is one of Delia's favorites, so I've seen it a number of times."

"It's really nice to meet you, Ms. Jayne," Emma said, smiling.

"Lilly, please. Lovely to meet you, Emma. Has your father been showing you his plans for the garden back here?"

"He has," she said. "They're incredible. I can't wait for it all to come together."

"He'll have two gardens to show off next spring," Ernie said. "Your dad won the contest to design Alden Park."

"Oh, Roddy, how wonderful! I'm so glad. Yours really was the best," Lilly said.

"That's great, Roddy," David said. "Congratulations. It was a great design."

"You knew about that?" Emma asked her husband.

"Yeah, well, your dad called me and asked for some advice about a fountain, so I knew a little about the plans." David turned to Lilly. "I do industrial design, so we talked about what it would take to pull it off."

"I was grateful for the help," Roddy said. "I was going to ask Ernie, but he had to recuse himself since he was overseeing the contest."

"Lilly, where are you?"

"Over here, Tamara," Lilly called out.

Warwick and Tamara walked through the garden gate into Roddy's yard. Tamara was dressed in a plaid skirt, knee socks, and a camel-colored sweater set. Warwick's red-letter sweater overpowered his tan trousers and white button-down shirt. They both wore penny loafers.

"Who are you supposed to be?" Ernie asked.

"Nancy Drew and Joe Hardy," Warwick said.

"Rose had wanted us to come dressed as Nick and Nora Charles, but I didn't want to wear white tie and tails all day."

"And the satin dress was cold," Tamara said.

"The outfits are fabulous," Emma said.

"Thank you. Rose gave us some book covers to tape on our costumes, but we forgot them in our hurry."

"Your hurry?" Ernie asked. "Is everything all right?"

"I guess so," Tamara said.

"It's terrific," Warwick said, taking Tamara's hand and holding it to his lips for a kiss. "Tamara had a broker's open house yesterday morning."

"It went well?" Lilly said.

"Really well," Tamara said. "One of the brokers asked to bring her clients by yesterday afternoon, and of course I agreed."

"Of course," Ernie said.

"They made an offer this morning. Ten percent over asking," Tamara said.

Ernie whistled. "Are you going to take the offer, or see if you can get more?"

"We talked it over. We're going to take the offer," Warwick said. "The cash will help us with the repairs on the new house."

"Better a bird in the hand," Tamara said. "Only trouble is, they want to close by Thanksgiving. I'm not sure the new house will be ready by then. I know the kitchen won't be."

"Then you'll have to join Ernie, Delia, and me. Stay with us, if you need to," Lilly said.

"That's so nice of you, Lilly, but we can stay in a hotel," Tamara said.

"We'll talk about it later," Lilly said. They both knew Lilly was not going to let them stay in a hotel.

"You know, Rose suggested that Roddy and I dress as Holmes and Watson," Ernie said. "She had a theme for her costume suggestions. I still can't figure out who you are, though, Lilly."

"Maybe seeing Delia will help," Lilly said. Delia put her head through the gate and gestured to Lilly. "Be right back," she said, running over to help Delia on with her jacket. They both came into Roddy's yard and posed.

Delia had on a bowler hat, a monocle, and a large mustache that was waxed into enormous curls. A yellow vest was stretched over her stuffed belly and the striped pants she wore hit the top of her spats.

"You're Hercule Poirot!" Emma said.

"Yay, someone guessed," Delia said, smiling. "I love your Incredibles costumes! It's nice to meet you, by the way. I'm Delia." Another round of introductions got everyone up to speed.

"Okay, I'll admit it, I'm stumped," Ernie said. "Even with all the clues. Who are you supposed to be, Lilly?"

"Miss Marple," Lilly said, pulling out the map of England and tapping it on his arm.

"But you look like you always look, except with a flowered hat," he said.

"Exactly," Lilly said. She smiled and everyone laughed. "Now, we should probably go out front. Our public awaits."

Gardening Tips

I owe a debt of gratitude to the folks who have shared gardening tips with me. They include Caroline Lentz, George Stockbridge, Carol Stockbridge, Susan Able, Della Williamson, Nancy Luebke, and Sue Hieber:

- Lilly and Roddy started talking about choosing plants for his garden. Lilly is, no doubt, thinking about companion gardening. Often one plant supports another by being nearby. Flowers and vegetables can be potent combinations. There's lots of information available online.
- Trouble with deer, squirrels or rabbits? Try dusting your plants with cayenne pepper.
- Compost! Shredded paper, vegetable scraps, coffee grounds, crushed eggshells. Organic material that is not meat or dairy can be composted. Not only is it good for your garden, it's good for the environment.
- Save all your coffee grounds, then when you break up your garden soil come spring, mix the grounds in. Worms love coffee grounds because they make it easier for them to travel. The more worms you get, the more aeration your plants get and all the worm poo is fertilizer. Freeze your grounds all year until you can use them in your garden.
- Use your chopped-up leaves from your fall cleanup as a natural mulch and plant protector in the winter (again, saving on landfill use).

- Watering and mulching newly planted shrubs
  and plants is the most important thing you
  can do within the first few weeks to help get
  them established.
- If plants consistently die in one area of your
  yard, test your soil to see if there may be a
  fungal disease and talk to your local garden
  center about soil treatment before replanting.
- Create a haven for bees and butterflies by
  using plants to attract them. Monarch butterflies feed exclusively on milkweed; and nectar-
  filled, colorful butterfly bushes attract both
  butterflies and bees. You can also provide pro-
  tective places for them, such as wooden
  houses specifically made to give them shelter.
- Don't restrict yourself to planned gardens
  and what you think you should grow. Plant
  things that make you happy so that maintain-
  ing your garden is a joy rather than a chore.

Acknowledgments

Writing is a solo act, but getting published takes a community. I am, as always, so grateful to my wonderful community.

Thank you to John Scognamiglio, Michele Addo, Larissa Ackerman, Janice Rossi Schaus, and the team at Kensington. The Garden Squad has flourished in your good hands.

Thank you to my agent, John Talbot, for helping me navigate the twists and turns of this journey.

I blog with five amazing women, the Wicked Authors (www.WickedAuthors.com): Barbara Ross, Sherry Harris, Edith Maxwell, Liz Mugavero, and Jessie Crockett are friends, mentors, cheerleaders, and wonderful writers. I would not be on this journey without them and wouldn't want to be.

Huge thank you to Jennifer McKee for helping me keep @JHAuthors running.

I am grateful for my blogmates at Killer Characters (KillerCharacters.com) for letting my characters speak on the 20th of each month.

I have wonderful friends who double as a cheering squad. A special thank-you to Jason Allen-Forrest, my first reader. And to Scott Forrest-Allen, who always is there for title help. Courtney O'Connor, thank you for your friendship. Thank you to Deb Brown, John Montgomery, Paul Weatherbee, Scott Sinclair, Megan Keeliher, Tracy Stewart, Stephanie Troisi, and all my other friends who cheer me on.

Thank you to Grace Topping and the members of the Wicked Cozy group for title help.

The mystery community is wonderful. I'm a proud member of Mystery Writers of America and Novelists Inc.

A very special thank-you to Sisters in Crime, particularly the New England Chapter. If I hadn't joined that organization, I don't think you'd be holding this book in your hand.

And finally, a huge thank-you to my wonderful readers. I love meeting you at events and conferences or hearing from you on social media. Please stay in touch with @JHAuthors and make sure to say hello. Thank you for your reading support, it means the world.

Connect with Us

Visit us online at
KensingtonBooks.com
to read more from your favorite authors, see books
by series, view reading group guides, and more.

for sneak peeks, chances to win books and prize packs,
and to share your thoughts with other readers.

facebook.com/kensingtonpublishing
twitter.com/kensingtonbooks

Tell us what you think!

To share your thoughts, submit a review,
or sign up for our eNewsletters, please visit:
KensingtonBooks.com/TellUs.

Grab These Cozy Mysteries
from
Kensington Books

Forget Me Knot Mary Marks	978-0-7582-9205-6	$7.99US/$8.99CAN
Death of a Chocoholic Lee Hollis	978-0-7582-9449-4	$7.99US/$8.99CAN
Green Living Can Be Deadly Staci McLaughlin	978-0-7582-7502-8	$7.99US/$8.99CAN
Death of an Irish Diva Mollie Cox Bryan	978-0-7582-6633-0	$7.99US/$8.99CAN
Board Stiff Annelise Ryan	978-0-7582-7276-8	$7.99US/$8.99CAN
A Biscuit, A Casket Liz Mugavero	978-0-7582-8480-8	$7.99US/$8.99CAN
Boiled Over Barbara Ross	978-0-7582-8687-1	$7.99US/$8.99CAN
Scene of the Climb Kate Dyer-Seeley	978-0-7582-9531-6	$7.99US/$8.99CAN
Deadly Decor Karen Rose Smith	978-0-7582-8486-0	$7.99US/$8.99CAN
To Kill a Matzo Ball Delia Rosen	978-0-7582-8201-9	$7.99US/$8.99CAN

Available Wherever Books Are Sold!

All available as e-books, too!

Visit our website at **www.kensingtonbooks.com**